PACK OF HER OWN

Visit us at www.boldstrokesbooks.com

PACK OF HER OWN

by
Elena Abbott

2023

PACK OF HER OWN

ISBN 13: 978-1-63679-370-2

This Trade Paperback Original Is Published By
Bold Strokes Books, Inc.
P.O. Box 249
Valley Falls, NY 12185

First Edition: March 2023

CREDITS
EDITORS: JENNY HARMON AND CINDY CRESAP
PRODUCTION DESIGN: STACIA SEAMAN
COVER DESIGN BY TAMMY SEIDICK

To my beautiful Goddess who has always believed in me.
And to Alisha and Steph, without whom this book wouldn't exist.

CHAPTER ONE

Natalie

Running my hands through the thick fur of the husky mix was usually enough to make me forget the woes of the world. Today it wasn't working.

"Oh, Lucy," I said with a sigh, rubbing my fingers against the husky's abdomen as her leg twitched happily. "I'm sorry, girl, it's been a rough month."

That was putting it mildly. Couch surfing wasn't great for getting proper amounts of sleep, and most of my days I did little more than sleepwalk my way around the clinic. Lucy grunted under my hands, and I realized I'd stopped petting her. With a huff, I continued, giving the big girl a wry smile.

"Yeah, yeah. I'm on the job." I worked around the thick cast on her front leg. I set her leg apart from the others, waiting on the boss lady. "Rory will be in here soon and we'll take care of that leg of yours."

As if summoned by my words, the door opened and Dr. Lorelai Gale walked in, all smiles as she held up the tools she was going to need. "Found them! Let's get started."

I nodded, still running my hands through the thick fur as my mind wandered. Rory was the one good thing, the one constant, in my life. If it wasn't for her, things would only be worse.

"Nat? Hey, Nat, you okay?"

"Huh?" My eyes snapped up, meeting her worried glance. "Oh, sorry, Rory."

"You okay?"

"Oh, yeah, I'm fine. Just tired."

She looked at me sympathetically. "The couch not treating you well?"

"I've dealt with worse."

"Natalie—"

"I really don't want to talk about it."

"All right. Later then. Let's get Lucy settled up."

A few hours later, I started turning off the clinic lights. Most days at the clinic I ended the day with a sense of fulfillment for helping all the little animals. Dogs, cats, and even the more interesting animals we saw occasionally. All of them filled my world with joy. Or used too. These days not so much. Not since everything happened with Misty.

"Hey, you okay?"

Rory leaned against the wall, watching me with those big blue eyes. We'd met a little over a year ago right after she took over the clinic from the old veterinarian. She was looking for help and took pity on a twenty-two-year-old college student who only ever wanted to help animals and gave me a job. We'd been close ever since.

"No, no, I'm not." I hung my head. I could feel the dam in my mind cracking.

"Is this about she-who-should-not-be-named?"

"What else would it be?"

"She really did a number on you, didn't she?"

I shrugged. I didn't want to talk about it. I pushed those thoughts and feelings away desperately. I couldn't let them take me over, not now. Especially not in front of my boss.

"It's fine," I mumbled. "I'm just…I'm not over it yet. It gets rough sometimes."

"Losing someone after eight years together can do that." She smiled and opened her arms in an invitation.

I stepped into her embrace and tried to stop the tears from flowing. "I don't know what to do now. Where to go." I held her tight. "I can't keep crashing on your couch forever."

"No, I guess not. But you're welcome as long as you need."

We parted as I gave her a small smile. "Thanks, boss. I needed that."

She clapped me on the shoulder. "Let's go home. We'll get takeout and make a night of it."

I nodded and followed her to the back of the building and out to her car. A peaceful night was exactly what I needed. And maybe, just maybe, I could spend the night getting drunk.

That would be a good way to end what was quickly becoming the worst chapter of my life.

❖

Rory drove us back to her condo apartment, a gorgeous two-bedroom that must've cost at least her firstborn child. We parked in the underground lot and took the stairs to the lobby to grab the mail. A single, thin envelope had been forwarded to her address for me and we went upstairs before I was willing to open it.

"Motherfuckers!" The single piece of paper fluttered to the ground in four pieces.

"What's wrong?" Rory's hand was a feather touch on my shoulder.

I shrugged it off, storming around the living room. "They can't do this! Not now!"

"What?"

"My student loans! They won't pay for my next semester, so they didn't admit me!"

Rory's face went white. "But you can appeal, can't you? What happened? Why were they denied?"

I stomped a foot on the floor, the bit of a tantrum making me feel a little better for only a second. "No! Because the mail system sucks and my deadline for appealing was three days ago!"

She was smart enough not to stop me from pacing around the room, but it was clear she wanted to. "Oh, honey, I'm so sorry."

Her words popped the balloon of rage that was growing in my head. Its deflation left me with nothing but weariness and shivering with a sudden cold.

"It's fine," I said, my mind spiraling. Of course, this was happening to me now. Every time something was going good for me, life tore it all down. I shook my head. My grades were good, I attended classes, extracurriculars, and had a good relationship with my professors.

I sank down onto the couch, face in my hands as I tried to push back the tears. They didn't want me anymore. No matter what I did, who I was. They didn't want me. Just like Misty. Just like everyone else.

"Nat, hey. It will be okay."

Shoulders shaking, I felt her arm wrap around me, but I couldn't even lift my head. I said nothing. It was only a matter of time before she left too. Or told me to leave. I mean, why would she want me around? All I was doing was mooching off her, eating her food, and squatting on her couch. I needed to find somewhere else to be soon. I had to go before she made me.

"Natalie, hey, you're shaking really bad."

Tomorrow. Tomorrow I'd leave and find a new place to stay. And a new job. I wasn't going to get my dream of being a vet anymore, but maybe I could do some physical labor to save up the money and find a new home. Or a ticket somewhere else. Start over in another city, another town. Start life all over again.

"I need you to talk to me, girl." Rory pulled my hands away and I stared up into her face. "I know where your mind is going and it's not true, you hear me?" Her hands cupped my face and wouldn't let me look away. "You are not a burden. You are welcome here in my home. Understand?"

I shivered again but managed a nod with a snuffle. "Yes, ma'am."

"I don't know if I believe you. Try that again."

"Yes, ma'am," I repeated, a little louder this time. The focus on her words, her face, helped push the bad thoughts away. For now.

"Better." She sat on the couch beside me, her arm wrapping around my shoulders once more to ease the shaking. "It's okay. It'll be okay. I'll keep you on at the clinic and we can try to get you into school again next semester. Or we can fight harder if you want to."

I sighed. "I don't know what to do right now. I don't want to think about it."

"All right. We can talk about it later." She put a finger to her lips, like she was thinking about something.

"What now?"

"What do you mean?"

"I know that look."

"I still don't know what you mean."

I gave her a sideways glance. "You have something up your sleeve."

She chuckled and held up her hands. "Guilty as charged."

"So, what is it?"

"Okay, look, I've been considering this for a couple of days now. I know after tonight it might seem like something bad, but hear me out before you get angry, okay?"

I nodded, folding my arms against my chest as I prepared to parse her words for any underlying meanings. An old habit. Not a healthy one.

"Okay. So, my family has a cabin out at Grey Lake."

"Yeah, I remember. You spent last Christmas out there."

"I did. I lived out there before I came here and took over the clinic. But the place is quiet, a half hour out from a tiny village called Terabend. I was thinking..." She drifted off.

"Thinking?" I prodded her.

"Look, you need a vacation. You need to get away and recharge your batteries. And it would get you away from..." She glanced away. "Away from anything that reminds you of Misty."

I stared at her, unable to find words.

"It's in the middle of the woods with a nice clearing around it. It's not easy to get to from the road if you don't know the way, and there's a small beach a short hike from the cabin. The lake is refreshing, and the beach is usually pretty clean. It's a great place to relax and just forget about the world for a while." She smiled. "Which is something I think you need right now."

I opened my mouth to argue but she cut me off. "I'm serious, Nat, you need to take a break. Misty kicked you out a few months ago, and between school and the clinic you haven't had a chance to decompress. To work through it all. You know, to feel better and maybe feel you can move on."

"Move on?" I whispered. "Is it that easy?"

"It's never easy." I looked up at her. I could hear experience weighing down her words. "It'll take time. Effort. But it is doable."

"So, you want to get rid of me for a while?" It was hard not to let my mind slip down the rabbit hole again. She was not sending me away because she didn't want me around anymore. If she didn't, then she wouldn't have even brought up the cabin. "Are you sure about this?"

"You need to get away for a while, Nat. I want to help you."

"Why?"

She laughed. "Because we're friends, you idiot. And you're a damned good vet assistant. I want you to stay at the clinic with me."

I took a deep breath. "Are you sure?"

"Of course, honey. I wouldn't have brought it up if I wasn't."

"How long?"

"However long you need. Figure a month would work."

I turned the idea over and over in my mind. Could I make this work? Would it be okay? I'd never lived alone, not really. First my parents, then I lived with Misty, and now Rory. What would it be like? How long would it take to figure out if I could? What was it like to be alone like that?

Maybe it's what I needed. Some time alone might be enough. Enough to move past Misty, enough to find myself.

"I mean, you don't have to—"

"Okay."

"What?"

"Okay. I'll do it. Tell me where this place is."

Her smile lit up her small apartment. "Oh, you will not regret this. I'll call someone and make sure they clean the place up and make it ready to be lived in for you." She jumped off the couch and headed for the kitchen. "You're going to love it. And when you get back, we'll figure out what to do about school, all right?"

I fought the urge to laugh at her excitement. "Yeah. Yeah. Sounds good. Maybe it's just what I need."

Chapter Two

Wren

The trees around me blurred as my paws smacked the dirt in a sprint that pushed even my wolf's supernatural stamina to the limit. It was moments like this I felt like maybe if I could just run fast enough, the past would be left in the dust and never catch up. But life didn't work like that.

My wolf reveled in the freedom that I most often held back from her. Yes, we shared a body, in a way, but our minds were separate. If she had her way, we'd be shifted and running around the woods all the time. Sadly, that simply wasn't a reality I could live with, and I had to pull her awareness back a little every once in a while, just to make sure she understood who was in charge.

But she was antsy today, as we ran the border of our territory. I couldn't read her mind, but I could feel her anxiety. I sighed inwardly, sure that I knew the reason. She was lonely. We had no pack to run with, no mate to hunt with, no pups to play with. We were alone here, and I didn't see that likely to change any time soon. Especially if I had anything to say about it.

I didn't want a pack. I didn't want a mate. I didn't want anyone to think that I was above them, better than them, just because of the circumstances of my nature. Because I was an Alpha, of all things.

We slowed down and came to a stop at the edge of the trees, looking out on a large cabin settled in a small clearing with a gravel road that led to the highway. Home sweet home.

The wind shifted suddenly, and a familiar scent wafted through the air. I pulled my wolf back and loped easily across the wild grass until we reached the front porch. A woman sat in one of the rocking chairs there, sipping at a mug of something that smelled like old pennies. She was short with long, dark hair that was pulled back from her face in a loose ponytail. She watched me quietly through purple-tinted glasses and raised the mug as if in greeting.

I shifted back to human form, ignoring the way my best friend didn't bother to look away. She was my doctor, after all; she'd seen it before.

"That better not be one of my mugs," I said lightly, reaching for the pile of clothes I had neatly folded on the porch step. "The last one you used for that stuff I had to throw away. I couldn't get it to not taste like blood."

Yoshimaru Hikaru—Dr. Maru to the good people of the town of Terabend—gave me a wide smile, showing off teeth far sharper and pointed than those found in most people's mouths. "Don't worry, Wren, I brought this one from home."

I finished dressing with a tank top, tying my flannel shirt around my waist, then joined her on the porch in a second rocking chair.

"So, to what do I owe the visit? Or do you make house calls now?"

She smiled at that. "You know very well that I do when necessary." Her look turned serious as she added, "You don't need any help, do you?"

I shook my head. "All clear in the woods. No strange smells, nothing unknown to us trying to sneak into the county."

Greyland County, stretching from the west side of Grey Lake to the foothills that preceded the Rocky Mountains, was my land, in werewolf sense. I didn't own it, but I'd held it, protected it, by myself for the past five years, though really that was with permission and at the request of the other supernatural folks who lived in the area. The sanctuary that Vadi, the guardian of Greyland, had envisioned, was no longer threatened by wayward werewolves slipping into the area and causing a ruckus. It was my job to track them down and make sure they didn't cause trouble for the humans who we lived amongst and yet still hid from.

"That's good." Hikaru took another sip of her drink. Now that I was back in human form, the smell was much less pungent. I still turned away, rubbing my nose to try to dispel the scent as much as I could. I knew it was better than her taking it straight from the vein, like most vampires, but that didn't make it any more appealing.

I rubbed my forehead in irritation. I forgot that when dealing with a centuries-old vampire, sometimes getting them to talk was like pulling teeth. "So, you came around to...what? Assault my nostrils with your blood?"

She shook her head. "Well, I had to borrow your kettle to warm it up."

I blanched. "My kettle? Please tell me you didn't put the blood inside it?"

She looked at me over her purple lenses, red eyes sparkling with amusement. "I'm pulling your leg," she said with a chuckle. "I came over because you haven't been by in a while. I worried something was going on."

"What do you mean? I've been at the diner every day." I did own the place, after all.

"And you hole yourself up in your office when you're there," Hikaru said, "and you disappear when you're not there. Your people are getting worried about you."

I shook my head. "They aren't my people. You know I don't want that kind of life."

"You know you don't have a choice who gets close to you sometimes, right? You've made friends around here. People like you. That makes them worry about you."

"I never asked them to do that."

"Come on, Wren. You feel the same way about them. You get so antsy when someone doesn't show up for work. It's like you want to know where your people are at all times."

I frowned at her. "That's only because I want to make sure they're safe. The last thing I need is my past coming back to hurt innocent humans."

"And what about hurting you?"

I shrugged. "That...doesn't matter as much."

She shook her head. "Wren, it's been five years since you left your old pack. When are you going to let people in?"

"I let you in."

"Technically, I'm also your landlord."

I let out a long sigh. "You know it's not easy for me. Not with everything the Cardinals did." I shuddered with the memory. "I mean, you didn't see the way they treated me after my Alpha nature surfaced. Or even before that, with their archaic focus on what wolves they considered to be dominant or submissive. It was disgusting. I never want a life like that again."

"As Alpha, you would get to decide what your pack would be like. You don't have to do it like your old Alpha did."

"What if I just don't want a pack?"

She shook her head. "You can't run from your nature forever."

"Hikaru," I said, rubbing my palms over my face. This was a conversation we'd had before. "I will never have a pack because I refuse to promise a fucking teenager to a man three times her age just because he's considered a fucking dominant!"

"I told you, it doesn't have to be like that within your own pack." She put her hand on my knee and I had to stop myself from pulling away from the comforting touch. "Your pack can be a sanctuary for wolves who don't want to live like that either. Show the Alphas who are stuck in the past how a pack can exist in the modern world."

"I'm not the kind of wolf who's going to change the world."

She drained her mug and stood. "You might not have much of a choice."

"I don't even know how to be a damned Alpha!"

"That, dear, you can learn."

"Not if there's no one to teach me."

"What about the Alpha over in Silva?" she asked.

I glanced up at her. Silva was a town on the other side of the lake, in another county. I'd only met the Alpha there once, Kendra, but she had seemed nice enough at the time. Maybe talking to her might be an option.

"See?" she said. "You can't even tell me I'm wrong."

"I hate you sometimes."

"You only hate that I'm right."

Lacking a worthy response, I stuck my tongue out at her.

She shook her head. "Such a child."

"I'm twenty-five."

"Still a child to me." She held out a hand as if to help me up.

"Everyone is still a child to you." I slapped her hand away lightly and hefted myself out of the chair. "So, did you only come all this way to give me a hard time for being antisocial?"

She looked almost sheepish as she said, "I was worried about you."

I started to say something scathing but stopped. Hikaru didn't deserve that kind of response. I let out a soft groan and glanced away.

"My wolf is anxious," I admitted uneasily.

"It has been a while since anyone from your old pack came by. They used to cause trouble every few months."

"I keep hoping it's because they've finally given up on whatever they were up to, but I don't think I believe it. I know my wolf doesn't."

"Make sure you listen to her—she knows what she's talking about."

I shook my head. "You always seem to know an awful lot about wolf shifters for not being one. Why is that?"

She smirked. "Maybe someday I'll tell you."

I started to say something more but was interrupted by my phone. I pulled it from my pocket and checked the caller ID.

"It's Rory," I said, surprised. I hadn't talked to her in the better part of a year, having missed her when she was in town at Christmas. When no response came, I looked up and saw Hikaru already across the gravel drive and climbing into her SUV. I glared in her direction but gave a small wave before turning and heading back into my house. I answered the phone on the third ring.

"Hey, Rory, what's up?"

CHAPTER THREE

Natalie

The road to the cabin was much more well-worn than I'd expected. The heavy pickup truck handled the gravel road, but the deep grooves made the trip rocky. Rory had let me borrow the clinic's pickup, which had a canopy on the back promoting her business. It was like driving an advertisement everywhere I went.

After only ten minutes on the rough road, I got my first glance of the cabin. It was sitting on a hill with a small clearing around it, set away from the trees. It was idyllic, like something out of a storybook. For the first time since Rory mentioned the idea the other day, this sounded like it might work out.

The road ended beside the cabin, and I pulled the truck up and parked it. The woods were beautiful. The front door opened into a simple, large living area that looked out onto a dining area that had a table just big enough for a small family. The inside was as picturesque as the outside. A small island with stools separated the kitchen. Stove, fridge, everything in the kitchen was shiny and looked gorgeous, and a quick search of the cupboards revealed plenty of food and everything needed to cook it.

"Well, she said it'd be well-stocked."

The words echoed in the empty room, and I shivered. An enormous place for little old me. I had to push down the bad thoughts again before they could take root. I didn't want to spiral down to those depths, not today. It was the first day of getting to know myself. I only needed to figure out where the hell to start.

A short hallway led to two bedrooms and a bathroom that was probably half the size of the apartment I'd shared with Misty. The bathtub was big enough to do some interesting things in, and unfortunately the first thought that came to me was one I didn't want. Misty and I had always dreamed of having a tub like that.

"Damn it," I snarled with a shake of my head. I was here to move past her, not think about her.

Unpacking into the bigger of the two bedrooms, I pulled out my phone and typed out a quick message to Rory. The signal didn't get any higher than three bars, but at least it was something. She replied almost immediately, saying to make myself at home. I looked around the bedroom and smiled. I was lucky to have her as a friend. And honestly, I knew she was well-off, but looking at this damned cabin, she was far more well-off than I'd thought.

As she had suggested, I made myself at home. I lay on the bed, reveling in the quiet. No traffic, no other people, not even the hum of the light pollution from the middle of the city. As the sun set, the darkness became almost oppressive, and I moved around the cabin to turn on the lights. As I did, a heavy rumble broke the silence. I rose to look out the window.

Outside, a rough-looking Jeep pulled up the gravel road behind the clinic truck. Rory didn't drive a Jeep. Did anyone else know I was here? Rory's parents? I backed away toward the kitchen, heart pounding far more than it should've been. A moment later there was a knock on the door.

I itched to call Rory and demand who else might be here. Another knock came, a little harder this time. I took a deep breath then approached the door.

"Who is it?"

"Ms. Donovan? My name is Wren. Rory called me and let me know you were coming down for the month and asked me to make sure you were settling in."

I breathed with relief and cracked the door open a little. On the porch stood a woman probably not much older than I was. She was wearing well-worn blue jeans and a red flannel button-down that fit loosely over her upper body. Her silver hair was short and spiked up in a style that desperately made me want to touch it.

Whoa, where the hell did that come from?

"H-hi," I said. When my mouth opened again, no words came out. She gave me a smile that stole my shallow breaths.

"Ms. Donovan." She offered a hand. "Nice to meet you. I own

the diner down in Terabend, the Tooth and Claw." In her other hand she lifted a paper bag with a small grease stain on the bottom. "I thought you might be hungry."

The smell wafting off the bag made my mouth water, but I resisted the urge to throw the door wide open.

"Oh." I had no idea Rory had told anyone that I was coming down. I mean, sure, someone was probably taking care of the cabin, with it being spotless and everything, but still. Did she think I couldn't take care of myself? "Well, um, thank you, Ms. Wren? Is that right?"

She smiled. "Just Wren. Wren Carne."

I took the offered food. "I appreciate it, but you can let Rory know I can take care of myself."

She raised a hand and started playing with her hair with a sheepish grin. "I think I'll let you take care of that. I've known her a while and know how involved she likes to be."

I turned away from the door, but something made me stop. "How long have you known Rory?"

"A few years now. She used to help out when I first bought the diner."

"And she told you I was going to be here?"

"Yeah, staying for a month. She wanted me to keep an eye on you in case you, I don't know, didn't like the solitude, I guess?"

I mumbled something about overbearing friends and gave her a small smile. "Well, thanks for the food anyway. It's appreciated."

She gave a smile and a wave. "You need anything, just call the diner, okay?"

I nodded, but her back was already to me as she headed to the Jeep. I should've just closed the damned door, but I caught sight of her backside in those jeans and I watched the beautiful thing sway in time with her steps and I couldn't look away even if I wanted to. Which I didn't.

Damn it, Rory.

She had this idea that she was something of a matchmaker. She'd done it before, with other friends and coworkers. I hated the idea that she was doing it to me, but who knew? Maybe this time it might actually work.

❖

I sat back in the chair with a soft burp, staring at the remnants of the meal. Moist roast beef on garlic bread with melted cheese and steak fries with garlic and parmesan, and my Goddess, I was in heaven after eating it all. I let out a little laugh. I'd never have eaten something like this around Misty. A "feast of carbs" is what she'd call any meal that wasn't made up of at least three-quarters healthy shit, and the rest low-carb crap that tasted like dirt.

I froze. And then wondered when I'd started being able to think things like that. I would never have complained to Misty about what she'd make or tell me to eat. It's not like I could cook anything that didn't come frozen in a box with directions on the side. The one time I tried to do an actual recipe from scratch, I burned the meat so badly it caught fire in the oven, and kind of ruined our Thanksgiving with a visit from the fire department.

But if she'd seen me eating something like this, maybe she would've cut me loose ages ago.

"Nope!" I shook my head and started cleaning up the dishes. "We are not thinking about that. We are not thinking about her."

I repeated myself a few times as I stood and gathered the dishes. Cleaning up after dinner was a habit for me, one I enjoyed, because it was something I could do without really thinking about it. I left the table as spotless as I found it and left the dishes to dry on the rack beside the sink. Then I turned and realized I was still all alone, but now the outside world was darker and even more quiet than before.

Idly, I flipped through the collection of loose teas Rory had stored in a cupboard and picked a something-with-peppermint before starting the kettle. A few minutes later, I sat at the table, waiting for the tea to cool enough to drink.

That's when I heard the howl. Staring out into the darkness on the other side of the window, the long, lonely sound drifted on the wind. Shivers ran down my spine when there was another howl, louder this time. Both sounded like the same animal, and even with a third howl, there was still no reply.

"Poor wolf." The words slipped out before I could think about them. Many people had problems with wild animals, even if they normally liked domestic ones. Not me. Once upon a time, I'd wanted to have an animal sanctuary, to be a caretaker for all the wondrous creatures of the world that so many didn't seem to understand. A pipe dream, all but forgotten since I was old enough to know what real life was like. Being a vet was the reality. But what were the odds that someday I'd get to see an actual wolf in the wild?

With that thought, I headed for the door with my tea. The front porch hugged one side of the cabin with a railing high enough that I could lean on it comfortably and wide enough to accommodate the mug. As I looked closer at the railing in the light from the cabin, I noticed dark rings along it. Clearly, I wasn't the only one who liked to stand out here listening to the wolves at night.

A part of me couldn't believe what I was hearing. There was nothing in the city like this. The moment the next howl started, I closed my eyes, enraptured by the lonely song. Sounds of other animals drifted on the wind, owls hooting and smaller creatures running through the underbrush. I longed to walk through those trees and wind my way through the forest with nothing but the sporadic moonlight as my guide. But I was smart enough not to try. Not yet at least. I would not make my first trip into the trees at night in the dark with a wolf howling. Of course, the mere mention of the idea of going at all would've sent Misty into a tizzy.

How much of myself had I given up so I could be with her? I'd lost everyone I'd been close to, people I considered friends, family. I'd left it all behind for her. Cliché, yes, but I truly thought she'd loved me. And maybe she did in her own way. As much as she could manage.

Again, I shook my head, trying to push those thoughts out of my head. It was better not to think about her at all.

The wolf howled one more time and I resisted the urge to howl back. I took a deep breath and coughed, unused to the fresh air of the countryside, and took my melancholy ass back inside. I washed the mug, dried it, and put away the dishes like a good little houseguest, then called it a night.

CHAPTER FOUR

Wren

Most days the sounds of the kitchen were relaxing. It helped me focus when doing the ordering and making sure we had enough for the diner to keep running. It was difficult to get a supplier to ship out all this way more than once a week, so I had to make sure I didn't miss a damned thing. And yet, as I belted out a yawn wide enough to make my jaw kink, all that noise only made me wish I could disappear out into the forest again.

The trees were calling me home, like they had last night as the moon waxed toward full. But I had a job to do, a business to run, and couldn't just go out for a run whenever I wanted. Besides, if the humans in town had too many sightings of an overly large, silvery wolf out in the woods, they might start a hunt that would get people killed.

I wasn't willing to live through that again.

The memories came at me, unbidden. Sleepless nights spent keeping one eye open for whoever was after me this time. It wasn't human hunters, either. My own pack turned on me the moment I came into my nature as an Alpha. I could remember the fear in Ronan's eyes when I confronted him. He knew that if I challenged him for leadership, he might not win.

But that wasn't me. I didn't want a pack, and I didn't want to lead. I just wanted my freedom, and being an Alpha was going to give me that.

Now the urge to go out for a run came back with a vengeance and I groaned, rubbing my hands over my eyes. Instead of just thinking about the forest and running through the trees, my wolf seemed to have a particular destination in mind. Her senses turned to a nice cabin in the woods, the smell of the lake strong in the air, and the gorgeous redhead who was staying in said cabin.

I shook my head. This was ridiculous. I didn't even know if she'd be interested in anything, and I was not going to force myself on the poor girl. From what Rory had told me, she had enough to deal with. Hell, if it wasn't for Rory, I wouldn't even know she was a lesbian, or at least into girls. She wouldn't be the first person I'd been with since coming to Terabend all those years ago, but there was something different about her and I didn't want to just dine and dash.

"Hey, boss." Meg, my front-end server, poked her head into the office. "I need to head to the washroom. Can you watch the front for me?"

"Of course." She ran off and I headed out the double doors to the front of the diner.

Booths nestled against three walls with stand-alone tables in the middle of the open floor. The long bar that blocked the drink machines and coffee makers from the patrons had stools running along it, and one end held the cash register. I grabbed a plate from under the heat lamps and took it out to the table in the corner, where a woman I knew was seated.

"Not being adventurous today, Rias?" I asked the deputy as I placed her plate of pasta and garlic toast in front of her.

Rias smiled up at me, her cheeks dimpling as her violet eyes shone with humor. "What can I say? I know what I like."

We talked for a few more minutes. She was definitely one of my favorite humans, and I had the pleasure of interacting with her on a regular basis. Before long, though, I bid her a good meal and stepped away. The door opened as I returned to my place behind the counter. I looked up to see Natalie Donovan, wearing tight jeans and a pink short-sleeved blouse, step through the door. She was taller than average, had long copper hair, and pale white skin, like someone who hadn't lived a life in the sun. She was an absolute vision. I could feel the beast inside of me perking up and licking her chops at the beautiful lady in front of me. Thick thighs, wide hips, a booty you could eat off, and a look in her eyes that promised…

I shook my head and quelled the wolf. I tried to manage a

placid smile as she sat at the counter, her eyes taking in the entire diner and everyone in it.

"Hi, Natalie. Finally got bored of the empty cabin?"

She looked surprised at the use of her name but covered it up quickly. She smiled like it hadn't happened. "Yeah, was going stir crazy a little. I remembered you mentioned the diner and got hungry, so here I am."

I grinned. "I take it you liked the dinner I brought?"

Her eyes rolled back in her head as if remembering the meal. "Oh, Goddess, yes. Honestly, I hadn't had a meal like that in a long time. Mi—" She cut herself off with a shake of her head and picked up a menu from beside a napkin dispenser.

I didn't pry, despite how much I wanted to. Or more accurately, how much my wolf wanted to. She wanted to know everything about her. She wanted to rub herself against her and mark her with our scent. She wanted to claim her. I took a deep breath and tried to push down the beast once more, and noted a peculiar scent. A delicious scent, enticing, and complex. And it was coming from Natalie.

It was something I should've noticed last night, but I'd been upwind, and she'd closed the door too quickly. Her scent was different from what I was used to. It was like there was something special about it, about her.

Realization hit me a second before she glanced up, her warm brown eyes locking onto mine.

"So, what's good around here?" she asked with a slight smile.

"I can recommend most things on the menu," I replied. "I used to make most of it myself when I first opened the place. The recipes haven't changed, even if the cooks have."

She chuckled. "Had to learn to delegate, didn't you?"

"Not a simple thing."

"How long have you lived here?"

"Little over five years now."

"Is that when you met Rory?"

I nodded. "Yeah, she was one of the first people to come in here. She even worked the register for me a few times." I smiled. "I take care of the cabin for her and her family now that she's moved to the city. We still hang out every now and then."

"And before you came here? What did you do?"

I bit my lip as my wolf howled her loneliness inside my head. "You're going to have to take me out on a date to get that information." I stubbornly ignored the memories that tried to push to the surface with my flirting.

She pulled the menu in front of her face, but not fast enough to hide the blush that showed. A bell rang behind us and another plate appeared under the heat lamps. I took a moment to deliver it, then offered coffee refills around the tables before returning to Natalie. A moment later, Meg popped out of the back and took her place, but when she saw me and Natalie she stayed on the other side, giving us the side-eye as I waited for Natalie to place her order.

I watched her eyes flick from the burger section to the salads as if she were at war with herself. I leaned over, pulling the menu down so it was flat on the counter. "Did you want me to pick something for you?"

She hesitated. "I have a hard time deciding sometimes."

"I get it. There's a lot of options, and sometimes you need to decide between something new and something you know you like."

"Yeah. It's...kind of like that." She let out a long breath. "My girlfriend—ex, actually, used to order for me all the time." She hesitated again. "She had this strict idea of—" She shook her head. "No. I think I just need a moment. Maybe a soda to drink?"

I got her a drink and slid it over to her before I turned away to give her space. I needed to get the supply ordering done soon, but I didn't want to leave her. I motioned Meg over. "You take good care of her, you hear?" I whispered. "Anything she wants, on the house."

"Really? Is there something—"

I shook my head. "Just take care of her, okay?"

"Yeah, boss. You got it."

Reluctantly, I returned to the office and pulled out the stack of supply forms. I plunked my ass down in the chair so I could get back out to the dining room before Natalie finished her lunch and left. Or, from the way my wolf roiled under my skin, before the beast dragged her out into the woods and made her our mate.

You know, whatever came first.

CHAPTER FIVE

Natalie

I watched Wren disappear into the back with equal parts relief and discomfort. I let out a little sigh from behind my menu. It was bad enough thinking about her and the meal she'd brought last night. Or about how damned good she looked today, her ass in tight jeans and the flannel shirt open enough to reveal the dark tank top hiding her lean body. Now that I'd gotten to talk to her...

Oh man, I was in so much trouble.

And what the hell was I doing, baring my soul to her? I'd almost slipped about Misty, about all of it. Wren was being so nice to me right now and I didn't need to destroy this friendship before it even began.

The server, Meg, she said her name was, came by with a refill for my pop and took my order. I'd finally settled on a cheeseburger and fries, something simple enough, but also something I wouldn't even consider ordering around Misty. As she walked away, I let out a little sigh, hoping my meal wouldn't be ready too quickly. The longer before I went back to the cabin, the better. I was about to tear down the walls or something for a change of scenery.

And if I got to spend more time around Wren, well, that was just a bonus.

I pulled out my phone. The middle of nowhere had little chance of a signal, but in town that changed. My finger hovered over my social media feeds, the temptation to check them stronger than I would've liked. So why the hesitation? It was like the mere idea of it made me feel ill. To see how far the friends I'd lost because of Misty had come since I last saw them. My friend Gwen, from the gym, or a handful of other people. I didn't want to tempt myself in trying to reconnect. Not yet anyway. I wasn't ready for that kind of rejection.

I set the phone aside. Despite going stir crazy, it was nice to disappear. To get away from everything. And yet there was still so damned much that reminded me of Misty. And if not her, something else. Someone else.

Okay. We weren't going there. I was on vacation. That all didn't need to come up.

I took my time eating my meal and refused to even pick up the phone again until I finished eating. Wren popped back out of the double doors as I was munching down on the last of the fries, and her smile sent a shiver down my spine all the way to my feet.

"Still here?"

"Had to savor this meal. Too good to eat without tasting it."

The way she licked her lips when I said *tasting* made me wonder exactly what was going on in that head of hers.

"I'm glad you liked it."

"I did. I really did. And that sandwich you dropped off last night. It was absolutely phenomenal. I was looking for it on the menu but didn't see it."

Maybe I was focusing on her too hard, but I could swear her face turned a little red. "It's not on the menu," she said as one hand played with the spikes of her silvery hair. "The fries were the same we have here, obviously, but my brisket grilled cheese is something I make for myself. I thought it might be a pleasant surprise."

"It really was. And even better when I realized I wouldn't have to try and cook something from all that food in the fridge."

She raised an eyebrow. "What do you mean?"

The interest in her voice told me I'd said too much. I didn't want to admit to her I couldn't cook. I didn't want to come clean to her about anything. I'd said too much earlier when I almost spilled the beans about Misty and our relationship and how dependent on her I was. Because that was attractive, someone who had so little experience taking care of themselves.

But I couldn't just not answer Wren.

"Um…I can't cook."

"What?"

"I can't cook," I repeated. "Like at all."

"You can't cook? Like what, you can't put things together or—"

I shook my head. "No, like can't cook at all." I shrank into myself a little under her scrutiny. "It's not like I haven't tried, you know. If it's not something that comes in a box that I can heat in the oven, it just doesn't work out."

Her skepticism was just like everyone else's. No one ever believed me, especially if they knew how to cook or bake or whatever. They never believed that if I tried to do much of anything, it never worked out. Burnt or undercooked meat. Shredded or liquified vegetables. Even trying to do something as simple as cooking eggs had resulted in a grease fire that Misty never let me live down.

"My ex tried to teach me. We ended up calling the fire department too many times and had to stop."

Wren's eyes bored into mine and I found myself unable to look away. Any moment now she was going to tell me what she really thought. I mean, this—flirting?—had been fun and all, but now she knew how inept I was, how stupid. Between last night and today she had somehow managed to get past the walls I'd hoped were strong and impenetrable after Misty. Now I knew I had to build them stronger. If she slipped in that easily…well, I was not ready for something new, not if I couldn't protect my heart.

Then she laughed. Not a small chuckle but a full-throated guffaw that had the rest of the patrons glancing at her like she'd gone mad.

"What?" I demanded, feeling the embarrassment warming my cheeks.

She took her time to stop laughing. "You looked so serious when you said that!"

"I was serious!"

"I know! That makes it even funnier!"

I opened my mouth but faltered. She was laughing at me. Of course she was. Why wouldn't she? Just like everyone else. I got up from the stool and slammed a twenty on the table before heading out the door and leaving Wren laughing behind me.

I was halfway to the car when a something touched my shoulder. I turned so fast that Wren reached out to stop me before I overspun. I stared into her eyes once more.

"Look, I'm sorry I laughed at you," Wren blurted, with her warm hands still on my arms. "I meant nothing by it. You just looked like it upset you so much I didn't stop to think. I'm so sorry."

I shook my head, trying to put some steel in my voice. "I don't care. You don't know a thing about me."

"So, let's change that."

"What?"

"Let's change it. I can come over tonight and cook you something, maybe even show you a few tricks if you'd like. You get a good meal, and we get to know each other a little better." She gave me a big smile. "And we can decide how to take down Rory one of these days."

I couldn't help the little laugh that popped out of my mouth as my brain kept telling my mouth to decline, no matter what else she might say. But when my mouth opened, the only thing that came out was, "Okay."

Her smile made me feel things I hadn't felt in months. "Perfect. I'll see you around seven tonight?"

"Okay."

She turned to head into the diner again before stopping. "You have anything to do around the cabin?"

I shook my head.

"You should check out the trail in the forest. It's not too far, easy to follow, and mostly safe during the day. It's...it's really nice out there. Peaceful." She eyed me up and down. "I think you could use the peace."

She went back inside before I could reply, but I couldn't shake the feeling that there was so much more to her words than I could hear. Or maybe she'd been in the same place I was before and gotten out of it unscathed. I could only hope.

CHAPTER SIX

Wren

I watched Natalie's truck pull out, while leaning on the counter with my arms crossed over my chest. The girl was precious. I was already going over in my head what I had stocked the cabin with and wondering what I should make her. Simple would be good, but not too simple or she might question my cooking chops. I smiled with the thought. Ms. I-Can't-Cook would have nothing to complain about.

A small elbow got me in the side, and I flinched, turning to glare at Meg, who had sidled up beside me.

"Well, look who's all smiles today," she said. "What'd you do, ask her out on a date?"

I froze. "N-no." I wanted it to be true. It wasn't a date, only a nice evening between grown adults. "It's not a date. I'm going to the cabin tonight to make her dinner. You know, so she doesn't starve or something."

She gave me a sly wink and I resisted the urge to throttle her.

"It's not like that."

She grinned. "Sure it isn't," she said and winked again.

"It's not!"

This time she turned to look me straight in the eyes. "If you're being honest and it's really not like that, then what the hell are you doing?"

"What?"

"That girl"—she flung her hand out in the direction of the parking lot—"is totally into you, even if you don't see it. So don't you dare go breaking her apart because you refuse to admit that this is a date."

Getting admonished by one of my employees was not the most comfortable thing in the world. I didn't want to hurt Natalie, and I knew what my reputation was like. I didn't want to treat her like my past trysts. I couldn't exactly get attached to someone like her, after all. She had no idea who I was. *What* I was. It wouldn't be fair to her to start something that I couldn't finish.

Every so often, when someone who caught my fancy came through town for a day or two, I would lay on the charm. I'm a woman, I have needs. And so far, every single time, I had never seen the person again after a night or two of amazing connection. It was how I had to live my life, and I'd made peace with that years ago when I became confident enough to do even that much. Now, thanks to Rory, that approach to companionship was crashing down around me.

It made sense in some ways. Rory never liked my unattached enjoyment of life. She thought I needed to settle down. But hey, even she didn't know what I really was. She had never met my wolf. Only a few around here had. And that's the way I had to keep it.

I hung my head, feeling chagrined. "I won't, I promise."

"Good!" Meg said, slapping my arm lightly. "Now I'm going on my break. You okay to cover the front?"

I jerked a thumb over my shoulder. "Yeah, go sit and get something to eat. I'll cover you."

"Thanks, boss." She disappeared into the back, and I made a round with the coffee pot, filling mugs for the regulars that came around in the early afternoons. The diner's clientele was steady, mostly either townsfolk tired of cooking at home or passers-through who needed a rest and a meal. Today was a slow day, which I would not complain about with my mind clearly not on the job.

My back was to the door when it opened, and a scent hit my nostrils. I turned slowly and watched the three newcomers as they came in the door. The leader was a tall man, his salt-and-pepper hair gelled up into a small fauxhawk. His T-shirt was loud, covered by a brown leather vest with a fringe over the chest. The young man flanking him was dressed similarly, with a leather jacket over torn jeans and a dark tank top. The woman seemed reluctant, and as they walked in, I could see her hesitate, like she wasn't confident, or didn't want to be here. She was wearing torn jeans, too, but hers looked like they were torn from being lived in, not for esthetics. Her gray eyes caught my gaze and she looked almost shocked for a second before the man beside her nudged her.

My wolf growled inside as the scent of the leader triggered memories for both of us. Jason Reid, brother to the enforcer from my old pack, Craig Reid. The man I'd been promised to when I was just a teenager, before I became an Alpha.

The younger man made a scene moving to a booth against the front window as the woman followed meekly. I shot a glance at my regulars. One older couple kept their heads down and ate as quickly as they could without looking like they were. The others were openly glaring at the newcomers, and I worried for them. If something went down, would I reveal myself to help them? This town was my home. I couldn't do nothing.

Then Jason leaned over the bar and his eyes focused on me.

I crossed my arms, letting my wolf speak through me a little as a low growl uttered from my throat.

"You're on my land," I hissed, low enough that only he would hear me. "Show more respect."

He cracked a crooked smile. "Oh, this is your territory? That's news to me. A pathetic excuse for a wolf like you can't hold land like this. One who pretends to be an Alpha."

I slammed my hands on the bar on either side of him and leaned in close with a sharp growl. The other two newcomers turned to stare at me. Jason only raised an eyebrow.

"This county is my territory. I don't mind other wolves passing through, but you will do it with respect, or you will get the hell out."

He glared at me and lifted his face to take a long sniff. His smile widened, showing off teeth that looked just a little too big and sharp for a human. "Oh, yeah? And who the hell is going to stop us from doing whatever we want? There's only you around here." He leaned forward and made a show of taking in my scent again. "And, girl, you don't measure up."

"Then let's step out back and we'll see how well I *measure up*." I held his gaze for a long moment before he waved a hand nonchalantly.

"No need, puppy." He straightened up and whistled, sharp and loud. The other two moved in behind him quickly like a pair of enforcers. The male was taller than Jason but lanky to the point of almost looking ill. The girl glared at me like the other two, but there was something in her eyes that made me wonder why she was submitting to them. "A reckoning's coming, little wolf. I'd suggest you learn to play nice if you want to stay alive." He turned around and headed for the door with the other two on his tail.

"Say hi to your brother for me," I snapped. He stopped in the doorway and held the door open with a dramatic flair.

"This ain't over, puppy. Not by a long shot."

I rolled my eyes at the corniness as they left, with only disgruntled customers in their wake. Meg took that moment to reappear from the back and stared at the door.

"Who the hell was that?"

"Some assholes fucking with small-town folk," I said, eyes on the heavy-duty truck the three wolves had gotten into. "Nothing you need to worry about. If they come back, I'll handle them."

She gave me a long look, up and down, as if considering whether I could do what I said. "Are you sure?"

I smiled. "Oh, I'm sure. They won't know what hit them."

CHAPTER SEVEN

Natalie

It was with equal parts relief and trepidation that I returned to the cabin. Absolutely nothing had changed since I left. As much as that wasn't surprising, it was almost disheartening.

Stagnant. It was a feeling I'd had for a while in my life. The last few months had certainly tossed that on its head, but definitely not in a way I would have wanted. I never asked for the upheaval I was going through now. Maybe I should've been happy with life before, and all of it would never have happened.

I shook my head as I parked the truck and cut the engine, letting it settle. I sat in the seat for a long moment, fighting back tears. I had thought Misty loved me. I had thought she was all I had left in the world. A scoff slipped from my lips at that. Misty had made sure she was everything I had left. She took everything else away from me.

I couldn't believe how gullible I'd been.

Fuck, Natalie. It's time to move past this. She dumped you like nothing. It's time to find something new.

Wren is something new.

I froze with my hand on the door lever. I mean yeah, the woman was sexy as all hell, and damned if she wasn't my type in a lot of ways, but I was in no condition to even consider doing anything with her right now. I'd been single for only a few months, and I was out here to find myself, not find another person to shack up with and put my life on hold. Again.

Besides, who was I to know what Wren wanted? Was a relationship something she wanted? Was it what I wanted? Whatever it was about her that kept her in my mind wasn't going to be sated with a single night, I could feel that, but it was too soon to dive into something.

Wasn't it?

Nope. Nope, not thinking of that. As I focused on the idea of keeping those thoughts well away from my consciousness, I went into the cabin and headed for the bedroom. I changed into a pair of worn jeans and a plain black T-shirt. I put my sneakers on, then grabbed my phone and a water bottle and headed out the back door toward the small pathway I'd seen in the trees past the cabin.

Both Rory and Wren had said the forest was beautiful and peaceful during the day, and they weren't lying. Birds were chirping as sunlight filtered through the top branches of the deciduous trees that showed off their beautiful summer green leaves. It was slow going, but I wasn't in a rush. Every step had to be carefully situated to avoid injury, but the restfulness of the forest was weighing down even my logical mind. It wasn't my first time walking in a place like this, but it had been almost a decade since the last time I went hiking with my family.

That memory was the first step on a downward spiral of destruction. No matter what the forest looked like, no matter what I saw or how deep I went, I couldn't escape the thoughts and memories that haunted me. My father, standing in his hiking boots with his heavy walking stick. He always took the lead, picking the pace and expecting the rest of us to keep up or get left behind. Mom always brought up the rear because, hey, kids. Between me and my sister, I was the only one who kept up with Dad on the regular, and he always made me work for it.

Until the day I told him that I wasn't the son he wanted. That I was transgender, that I was a girl. I tried to get him to understand who I was. Hindsight made me realize that a steep incline in dry weather was not the best place to come out of the closet to my dad. I could still feel his hand on my face, his screaming in my ear, and the world spinning around as I tumbled twenty, thirty, forty feet down to where my sister and mom still stood.

Don't touch the little shit! The words echoed in my head, my dad's voice raw and angry as it always was. I kicked at a rock, listening to the solid thunk when it hit a tree. My family had stood there, watching me bleed. *Get up, little shithead! You ever say anything like that shit again and I'll kill you.* His voice was harsh in my mind, and I let the tears begin to fall. I needed to reopen these old wounds and get rid of the poison I had been carrying for years. I didn't know if I could do it by myself.

I stepped over a fallen tree that was clear of branches. My ass plunked down on it when my foot slipped on a patch of moss, and I let out a shuddering gasp. More tears stung my eyes as I sniffled. I had never been good at keeping my emotions hidden. Misty complained I cried too much, that I was a baby. She didn't date babies, she'd yell at me. It only ever made me cry harder.

This was a mistake. Why was I here? Why had I come all the way out to this peaceful place only to corrupt it with my utter bullshit? Misty was right. I was a baby. Crying over something that happened so long ago. It shouldn't be affecting me now. It was ancient history. Nothing could change it, so why bother crying over it.

And yet you can't help feeling it.

I wiped my face with a grumble and climbed to my feet. Enough feeling sorry for myself. Enough remembering the bullshit of my childhood. Enough of Misty, enough of my parents. Letting the past run my life wasn't a luxury I could afford anymore. I needed to take care of myself, no matter what happened next.

And Wren?

I shook my head at the thought of her. Rory asked the woman to look out for me, and that's all she'd been doing. She felt sorry for me not being able to cook. It was the only reason she offered to cook tonight. *She's not the answer.* That's what I had to tell myself to keep moving. I meandered through the trees. The path disappeared behind me, but I didn't care. The forest was going to give me peace if I had to stay out here for the rest of the day. And night. And however long it took to leave all those memories behind and become a new person.

Yeah, if only it were that easy.

❖

The sun was dimming, and I was still surrounded by massive trees with little clue which direction I was heading. Here and there, if I closed my eyes and listened, I could hear the soft sound of waves on a beach. Yet each time I tried to find my way to it, I only found more trees. Washing away the memories of a past that made me what I am today quelled the brief panic that tried to take root. Nothing could hurt me like those memories did. Like what I'd survived.

But I was officially lost. Maybe if I waited until night, I could use the stars or the moon to find my way back to the cabin. I kicked myself for ever leaving the path. What a stupid, rookie mistake. Another mistake in a long line of them.

I pulled out my phone, thinking for a simple moment that I could call someone and reach out for help. And funnily enough the damned thing had a single bar. Forgoing the lure of social media, I opened my contacts and stared at the massive list of names that I barely recognized anymore. That one was one of Misty's friends, this one was someone I'd worked with years ago. I kept scrolling down, hesitating only once over the name Gwen. Then I shook my head and kept going. I hadn't seen her in so long, she probably didn't even remember me.

"Misty," I whispered. My thumb hovered over her name. Why hadn't I deleted it yet? I shook my head and kept scrolling down to Rory's number. The moment I pressed the call button, I lost the single bar again, and the phone came up with *no connection.*

I wound up to slam the phone against the nearest tree, but stopped. No. That wasn't me anymore. I slipped it back into my pocket and knew I had to keep trying. Even if it was for no other reason than to see Wren and get to taste her delicious cooking once more.

The trees around me suddenly shivered like a chilly wind had blown through the forest. I felt nothing, but something prickled on the back of my neck, and I spun around with a gasp. But the forest was still empty save for the trees. And me.

Then the wolf howled. I fought the instinct to turn on my heels and run, but it was close. I backed up a step or two before planting my feet. The sound was far too close for comfort, and I needed to get back to the cabin. The wolf howled again—this time joined by a second one that echoed from the other side of me. They were on both sides.

The panic overwhelmed my rational thoughts, and I turned to

run, when something stepped out from behind a tree. I slammed into something hard and large, falling back on my ass.

"Easy there," a low, soft voice said. "Are you all right, girl?"

I looked up. Standing over me was an older, androgynous-looking person, tall and statuesque. They looked made of marble, or like someone who would escort people around an art gallery. Their simple hiking clothing did not do them justice at all, and when they opened their mouth, it sounded rough, like they didn't speak aloud often.

"Now, what is a little thing like you doing all by yourself out here?"

I didn't want to look them in the eyes. "I was wandering the paths and got lost."

They crouched down to my level. "No fear, young lady. It happens to everyone at one point or another. Where are you headed?"

I hesitated. What other choice did I have? "I'm staying at a cabin that shouldn't be far from here. I was told there's a path there through the forest to the lake."

Their brows furrowed for only a second. "Oh! You're staying at the Gale cabin."

I nodded dumbly.

They smiled. "Why didn't you say so? I can lead you back to the cabin if you need."

I swallowed my pride and my first instinct to refuse the help, and nodded again, unable to allow myself to answer them. They stood and held out a hand and I took it, ignoring Misty's voice in the back of my head telling me how pathetic I was.

"Thank you, um…"

They smiled down at me. "You can call me Vadi."

"Natalie Donovan."

"A pleasure," they said smoothly, and then beckoned for me to follow them. "Come, let's get you home."

"But what about the wolves?"

Their brows furrowed slightly, but only for a second. "You heard them, did you?" I nodded. "Don't worry your head about them, my dear. They know better than to come around these parts."

Vadi turned and started to lead the way through the woods as I puzzled over their last statement. Maybe they meant that the wolves had been scared away from these woods before? I guess that made sense. Still, something about the way Vadi said it made it sound almost ominous.

In no time at all, Vadi led me to the edge of the clearing where I could see the cabin. Joy filled me at the sight of the somewhat familiar surroundings. All I wanted to do was make a cup of tea again and enjoy the view of the woods from the safety of the porch.

"I suppose this is where I leave you, my dear."

I looked up at Vadi's soft smile and suddenly didn't want them to leave. There was something comforting about the older person. "Do you live in Terabend?"

They chuckled. "No, my dear. I live in a cabin not far from here. I suppose you could call us neighbors, in a sense."

"What are you doing all the way out here?"

"I like to travel around the lake from time to time, cleaning up the beaches, and ensuring tourists don't cause trouble."

I laughed. "That's a noble goal."

"Indeed, it may seem so, but I enjoy it." They let out a small sigh as they pushed me out of the tree line and into the clearing. "Thank you for the wonderful company, my dear. It was an absolute pleasure to get to meet you."

"You, too. Thank you for your help."

"Good night, my dear."

I started heading for the cabin as they disappeared back into the swiftly darkening woods. I turned, considering going after them. I blinked, confused. They were gone. Completely gone, like they'd never been there at all.

I shook my head. I must be seeing things. They had to know the woods well if they were walking through them at night. And with the thought of Wren showing up soon, I didn't want to go back out there to make sure. Not tonight.

I all but ran to the cabin and didn't let out a breath of relief until I was safely inside and behind solid, wooden doors.

CHAPTER EIGHT

Wren

I pulled my Jeep up behind the vet clinic truck and put it in park. I took a couple of deep breaths before I had the courage to open the door.

This is not a big thing. She's a nice girl, but nothing we do could possibly last. Spend some time with her, maybe enjoy the company, then she'll go back to the city and life will be simple again.

This woman didn't deserve what I normally did. Hooking up with someone who was passing through or staying for a short time wasn't new to me. Natalie deserved better, at least it felt like that. My wolf felt it too. She wanted more from Natalie than I'd ever thought I could have with anyone. She wanted the woman in such a primal way it almost scared me.

She wanted to mate with Natalie. Despite how taboo it would be to mate with a human. My old pack would have kicked out any wolf who even considered doing anything with a human. I didn't want to think of myself the same as them, but how would it even work to have a human as a mate? Was there any way I could have a life with her? Especially when she didn't even know what I was? It had to be more trouble than it was worth.

The woods called to me, and the full moon above made it difficult not to answer. The moon pulled at my wolf and restlessness ached in my bones. I had two or three hours before I'd have to make the change. I was strong enough to resist my wolf for a while, but not forever.

If it were anyone else, I wouldn't even be considering doing something like this. Having a date with a human on the night of the full moon? Any other wolf would call me crazy. But the words had been out of my mouth at the diner before I could think about what day it was. Even from our interaction this afternoon, I knew the girl was wounded. Canceling on her at the last moment was not something I wanted to do to her.

So, with no time to waste, I headed for the door. Beautiful Natalie opened it a moment after I knocked, relief plastered on her face along with her sweat-soaked copper hair.

"Hey," I said, trying to put some smoothness into my voice.

"Hi."

"You look worn out."

She ran a hand through her hair, grimacing at the sweat that came with it. "Yeah, I, uh, I kind of got lost in the forest and almost didn't make it back in time."

That explained the bare hint of fear that still colored her scent. "Well, if you want me to get started, you can go get a shower and get more comfortable."

She perked up a little. "Yeah? You'd be okay with that?"

I smiled. "Of course. I know my way around the kitchen. It won't be the first meal I've cooked around here."

"Oh, my Goddess, that would be wonderful. Thank you!"

I waved her in the direction of the bathroom and started setting myself up in the kitchen. In no time, I'd dug through the fridge and freezer and found everything I needed. I heard the shower start down the hallway. I smiled. Wolf hearing was handy in most situations, and as I listened to the woman in the shower, I enjoyed putting together what I thought would be a wonderful dinner. But I kept being distracted by the vision of being in that shower with her, the water dripping down our bodies, touching each other, writhing against one another. My wolf was making herself heard. Loudly.

"Stop it, Wren," I hissed at myself and my wolf, then tried to focus on the meal.

Forty-five minutes later, I was dishing out a baked shrimp scampi with a light coleslaw. I hesitated over the second plate, realizing I hadn't asked Natalie if she was allergic to anything, before placing the meal on the table. A second later, the woman in question came into the kitchen, her hair mostly dry and wrapped in a fancy updo that I couldn't figure out how she made. She wore a black swing dress with white polka dots that, true to its name, swung around her thighs as she moved. She paused, staring at the table.

It took a moment for my brain to reboot after she appeared, and I waved my hand over the table. "Dinner's ready." She smiled and took a seat with a plate in front of it, and I moved back toward the counter. "Would you like some wine?"

"Um, sure."

"Red or white?"

She laughed. "I don't even know. I've never had to choose the wine before. What would pair well with this?"

I laughed too. "I have no idea. I'm a simple gal. Beer is usually good enough for me."

"I don't really drink a lot of alcohol," she admitted. She stood up suddenly. "Oh, never mind the wine then. Excuse me, I have to go grab something."

She disappeared back to her bedroom, as I put the wine away and grabbed myself a bottle of beer and her a can of Coke. I poured a couple of glasses of water, too, and finished setting up the table. Natalie returned with a thin, almost sheepish smile on her lips.

She sat down and I followed. "I hope you aren't allergic to anything."

She shook her head "Thankfully not." She glanced at the meal. "I really like shrimp, though. Excellent choice."

"Thank you."

She toyed her fork in the dish for a moment, as if she wasn't sure what to do with the meal. I smiled and started eating, trying not to make her feel uncomfortable. She gave me a smile and took a bite. Her eyes widened in surprise.

"Wow, this is amazing." She all but moaned and the wolf inside me panted in desire. "I don't think I've had this before."

I smiled. "I wanted something a little less heavy than your dinner last night and lunch today, so I went with the shrimp. It might not be the healthiest, but it's a good meal."

She nodded with another forkful in her mouth as she reached for her Coke and pulled the tab. I sat back and enjoyed how enthusiastic she was about the meal. Outside, I was all calm smiles, but inside, my wolf would not settle. She whined and barked and howled to be released, to get to run her muzzle against Natalie until our scent was all over her.

Want! She cried out inside me, but I pushed her back down. The full moon above us made it even more difficult than usual.

"So," I said, breaking the silence, "you work with Rory at her clinic?"

She smiled and swallowed her mouthful before taking a quick sip of Coke. "Yeah, for a while now. I just finished my second year in college to be a vet myself." She gave me a big smile. "What about you? Did you always want to be a diner owner?"

I shook my head, laughing. "It more kind of fell into my lap. I was twenty and had come into a bunch of cash and was looking for someplace to start fresh. I ended up putting a down payment on the diner, opening it back up, and having my first job…ever."

Her eyes were wide as she listened, like she couldn't believe what I was saying. "You just decided to buy a diner?"

I shrugged, my turn to look sheepish. "I could cook, I needed an income, I had some money, so that's what I did."

"Must be nice to have that kind of control over your life." She sounded almost jealous. I looked up, but she refused to meet my eyes.

"It was a long time coming," I said.

She shook her head. "I'm sorry, I didn't mean to come off like a jerk."

"It's okay. I get it." She gave me a wan smile and a companionable silence fell over us as we continued eating. Her scent was growing on me, making both me and my wolf want her even more with every sniff. I had to push my wolf back before she did something I wouldn't be able to explain away.

I said a little prayer to the Mother of Wolves, knowing full well that I was truly getting hooked.

❖

After dinner, we relaxed on the back deck, with our open drinks in hand, and stared out into the night sky. This close to the woods, my wolf should've been going berserk, but she was content to stay curled up near Natalie, listening to her low, somber voice.

"You don't get to see how many stars are out there when you're in the city," she was saying. "If I'm lucky I can make out the North Star, maybe the Big Dipper, or Orion depending on the night, but that's about it." She shook her head sadly. "I used to dream of having a big, open sky like this when I grew up. I wanted a place outside the city, away from all the noise, all the light. But my girlfriend—" She cut herself short again, like she did every time she came close to talking about whomever had hurt her. From the little I'd been able to piece together thus far, I honestly wanted to disembowel the bitch. The breakup was fresh, and it must have been rough. She took a deep breath. "My ex-girlfriend. She wanted to live in the city. She wanted a condo in a high-rise nowhere near the ground."

"Had her head up in the clouds, did she?"

Natalie snorted and I smiled as my wolf stretched out, wanting to get nearer to her and the noises she was making. "I never would have said anything when we were together, but yeah, that sounds like Misty."

"Rough breakup?"

"I don't know. I really don't have anything else to compare it to. She was my first everything. Girlfriend, partner, roommate, all of it."

"Sounds hard," I said. "How long were you together?"

"Since high school, through the years after, and then into college. Seven, no, eight years. At least."

I gave a low whistle. "That's not easy."

"I didn't know anything else. She was…" She trailed off with a distant look in her eyes. "She rescued me." The words were said so quietly I thought I'd imagined them for a moment. I followed her stare out into the trees and finally my wolf decided that she'd had enough. With a pull that sent cramps through my abdomen, she was ready to shift and run.

"Damn it," I muttered. "Down, girl. Give me a minute."

Natalie turned to me as I got up, downing the rest of my second beer. "Are you okay?"

"Oh, yeah, it's just getting late, and I have some things to finish back at the diner." It was an easy enough excuse. "I hate to leave already. It's been a wonderful night."

The smile she gave me flooded my senses with light and

warmth. "You're right, it really has. Thank you so much for dinner. We should do it again."

I smiled. "I'll happily be your cook for a while, as long as you supply splendid company."

"Well, I can't promise splendid, but I'll try."

"I'll take what I can get." With a simple hop over the railing down the few feet to the ground, I headed around the cabin. "I'll see you tomorrow!"

Natalie hollered something that sounded like a farewell as I hurried to my Jeep. I started the vehicle and sped down the road away from the cottage before my beast could force me into a change.

"Hold on," I said, trying to quiet the wolf. "A little longer. We need to get the Jeep out of sight first."

It wasn't hard. I knew the forest better than anyone at this point. I knew where to pull the Jeep off the road to hide it in the trees. I left my clothes on the front seat and let out a long howl as the change took over and the world went black.

Chapter Nine

Natalie

I listened to the growl of Wren's Jeep, trying hard not to fall off the cliff of disappointment that her sudden departure created in my mind. I wanted to believe she had a good reason to leave, I really did. But it had to be because I'd done something wrong. Maybe I talked about Misty too much. I leaned back as the sound of the Jeep faded, fingering the can of Coke, and staring out into the trees.

Even Rory wanted nothing to do with me, shoving me into this cabin and out of her way. She probably asked Wren to look in on me only to make sure I didn't come back early. I'd imposed upon her so much and she must've needed a break. When I got back, I'd have to look for a new place to stay, maybe a new place to work. Get out of her hair. It's not like I hadn't started over before. Never by myself, though.

I blew out a deep breath and choked on it when a wolf howl broke through the night. By the time I caught my breath, a second howl echoed the first, and I hoped maybe the wolf had found a friend. After a third howl, I realized all of them had been the same wolf. It sounded so lonely.

I reached over to collect Wren's beer bottle and took it and my empty can back inside. The cabin seemed lonelier without Wren there. The wolf howled again, and I again resisted the urge to howl back. I wanted the poor thing to know it wasn't all alone out here. Then again, I guess I was alone, too.

Puttering around the cabin didn't make me feel much better, but at least the wolf seemed to have gone quiet. I guess most people would probably fear the wolf and its pack. Interest was at the forefront of my mind. And this wolf, sounding so alone, made me want to go out and find it, to take care of it. Though I didn't know if the animal would see it that way.

Less than an hour after Wren left, I threw in the towel and allowed myself to go to bed. I hoped I'd dream of the sexy diner owner, and yet was terrified that I might.

❖

A sudden crack jolted me from sleep like a bolt of lightning. Disoriented and confused, I floundered in the blankets until I toppled off the bed. Another crack broke the silence of the night but there was no rain pelting on the roof, no lightning illuminating the sky. I was up on my feet when a third crack echoed from the forest, and I pulled on leggings and a shirt before running out the front door.

Bent over the railing, I tried to stare into the trees, willing them to show me whatever was going on out there. There was absolutely nothing to see, even under the light of the full moon, but a fourth crack split the night and I finally realized what they were. Gunshots. Something powerful if it was echoing all this way. A second later, a pained howl cried into the night, and I clapped my hands over my mouth.

No! Not the wolf. Hunters maybe? Someone in town must've gotten scared of a lone wolf hanging around. Damn it, what had Vadi said? Something about the wolves knowing better than to come around here? This poor wolf! I searched around for my shoes, needing to run out there and find the wolf and bring it back. Help it. I needed to do it.

I'd barely gotten the sneakers on when something staggered out of the woods. I froze. A massive, silver-gray wolf tottered out of the trees. It was moving far too slowly. The wolf's eyes swept over the clearing like it was looking for something before it focused on me. Its lips pulled back in a snarl, but it still moved steadily forward. A dark stain poured down one of its front legs and it favored the limb heavily, but still kept moving.

Then it fell, toppling onto its side. I gasped and leapt off the deck and closed the distance between the beast and me. It snarled as I approached, and I raised my hands. I tried to appear nonthreatening.

"Shush, shush," I said, "everything's going to be okay. I'm

going to help you. It'll be okay." Slow, cautious steps forward brought me to the wolf. Its lips peeled back, showing teeth that could easily tear my throat out with one swift move. I crouched next to it with steady hands. "Come on, I can't carry you, but I can help. Come with me. I promise I can help."

It was the damnedest thing. The wolf almost seemed like it could understand me. I helped the animal back to its feet, and together we made slow progress back to the cabin. The steps up to the door were the worst part and I had to push the wolf up the last bit, getting a clear look at the underbelly while I did so.

Okay. Definitely a she.

I left the wolf in the entranceway and ran to the clinic truck. I opened the side storage around the canopy and pulled out everything I thought I might need.

Two years of vet school, less than that of actual practice, and now I'm going to perform surgery on a fucking giant wolf. I shook my head as I ran back to the cabin.

What the hell am I doing?

After that there was no time to hesitate. The wolf had fallen to her side once more and was breathing shallowly. I set everything down beside her and pulled on a pair of gloves. I said a silent apology to Rory about destroying the rug the wolf was on and got to work.

CHAPTER TEN

Wren

The world flashed in and out of focus, skipping time as I tried to shake off the pain. Stupid, Wren. Stupid, stupid, stupid. My front leg felt like it was on fire, but I had to keep moving. Something hit me and I couldn't move properly or think properly. I should've been healing. Why wasn't I healing?

The world went black, and when I could see again, the scene had changed. The trees disappeared and we were staring at a well-lit cabin in the middle of a clearing. Rory's cabin. I stopped, hesitating, but my wolf pushed us forward and Natalie came running down the front porch.

No! We can't involve her. My wolf ignored my growl and kept limping forward as we whined every time our leg moved. I fought it, but between the pain and the moon overhead, I was nothing but a passenger as my wolf moved toward something familiar and desperately desired.

❖

A pitiful sound broke from our muzzle, bringing my mind back into focus. Something was touching our wounded leg and it felt like it was being torn off. I struggled and snapped and growled, but the wolf was still in control, and she was too busy staring up into Natalie's face. Suddenly, something pulled away from the leg and the pain lessened, not entirely, but enough I could think clearly again and start communicating with the wolf.

"Okay," I heard Natalie say. Something metal struck something else, the ringing lasting for only a second. "Okay, I got the bullet out." She faltered for a long moment, and I shared my wolf's view of her sweat-streaked face and frightened eyes. "I'm going to clean the wound. It's going to hurt, but please don't bite me, okay?"

We cried out as she did her job, but my wolf would never hurt this woman. She could do anything she wanted to us, and she would be safe. I never wanted to hurt her.

Pain seared itself into our minds and we both cried out for relief, earning nothing but an affectionate pat from the human above us and a slow, repetitive whispering. "It's okay, it's okay, it's okay."

Desperately, I tried to focus my mind, tried to shift back. Doing it in front of Natalie was not a good idea, but I had little choice now. I couldn't risk the change coming when I couldn't control it, or worse, when I was unconscious. If she was going to see it, I was going to be in a headspace to explain everything. But as I grasped at the threads of my true self, the pain flared, and they evaded my numb willpower. I growled and tried again, but only got the same result. I couldn't pull it together, couldn't shift. Fear wormed its way down deep inside until my wolf growled at me to stop being fussy.

We were both too distracted to notice what Natalie was doing next. It wasn't until we felt the prick of the needle that we realized. *Sedation!* I screamed at the wolf, but there was nothing we could do about it now. I could only hope she used too little, or that our system could beat it. I didn't want to be unconscious right now. There were too many questions and not nearly enough answers.

Even as the thought went through my mind, I could feel everything slowing down. My wolf conked out quickly, not knowing how to fight it at all. I finally got a chance to take the reins and I stared out of my wolf's eyes at Natalie. Her hand stroked our fur softly, and she hummed something under her breath over and over, as our eyelids drooped and the darkness engulfed us.

❖

Minutes or hours, I had no idea how much time passed before I cracked open my eyes to see light again. It was the ceiling lamp in the living room, of course, but beggars can't be choosers. I checked on my wolf, finding the inner beast still sound asleep as if Natalie's tender care had sated her. Then I glanced down.

"Oh fuck!" I was naked—sort of. As I'd lain unconscious on the bloody rug, I'd gone through a partial change. Partial, meaning I still had silver fur covering most of my body, and a tail and wolf ears, but as I leapt to my feet, I stayed upright and brought my hands up to my face. Fingers were in their proper place, but at the end of them were sharp claw-like nails. Immediately, an ache began in my right shoulder, and I put a hand to it, then yelped with pain. It made no sense. Even a partial shift should've healed my shoulder like nothing happened.

My wolf and I shared a body, more or less, but what happened to one could be healed by shifting to the other. I'd come to terms with my wolf a long time ago, being born this way, but this was the first time I'd been injured like this. Not to say I hadn't been shot before, but something was different this time. Something bad. Something I was missing.

I glanced down and saw Natalie curled up on the floor, sound asleep with her head on the hard floor. I searched my memory for anything from a few hours ago. She must've fallen asleep beside us. Was she worried about her patient or just exhausted? Either way, I couldn't just leave her like this.

Oh, this is a bad idea. I went into the bedroom and removed one of the comforters. I brought it back and draped it over her body, careful to avoid touching the blood-stained rug I'd been lying on. A pang from my shoulder reminded me of the reason for the stain and I grimaced. I'd have to repay Rory someday.

I put a hand on the front door, ready to leave, when my wolf decided to wake up and start yapping.

Stay! she howled. *Warm!*

"We can't, buddy," I said under my breath. "We can't let her know what we are. It won't work out, you know that."

But my wolf was as stubborn as I was, and we were both loopy from the sedatives. I swayed on my feet, then shook my head. I couldn't make it back to town like this. And with Natalie still here, I couldn't take the risk. She couldn't see me like this. But I couldn't shift either.

Back to the Jeep, I decided. I headed for the door again when something small caught my eye. A small jar with a mangled piece of shiny metal. My wolf growled, and the sound slipped past my lips as I picked up the jar and sniffed.

Silver. A silver bullet. It had to be the one Natalie pulled out of me.

I held on to the jar and opened the door, barely able to hold on to the anger coming from me and my wolf. Someone was out there with silver bullets. Someone was out there with the intent of taking down werewolves. On my land. It was my job to stop them.

But not tonight.

A chilly breeze drifted in through the open door and I watched Natalie roll over in her sleep. She moaned slightly and I was glad I had covered her.

"I'm sorry, Nat," I whispered. "This wasn't supposed to happen."

I couldn't help but think that Jason and his cronies had something to do with this. I hadn't scented him in the woods, but then I hadn't scented the hunters either. Not until it was too late. I pressed my hand to the wound, grimacing at the pain as I tried to stop the trickle of blood that was still running down my fur.

Silver tainted the blood, tainted everything, making it much slower to heal. If this was only the beginning of whatever was going to happen, I needed to be capable by then, before they hurt someone from town.

I left the cabin, closing the door tight behind me, and stumbled down the stairs in the direction of the forest. Twenty minutes later, maybe a little more, and I finally found my way back to my Jeep. I opened the back with my good arm and let down the rear seats, pulling out the spare sleeping bag and pillow I kept in there. Curling up in a way that didn't hurt, I closed my eyes and willed myself to sleep.

My last thought was the image of Natalie curled up on the floor. She'd been so brave, taking care of a wild animal like that. There was no way she could have known it was me, but she ran out to us anyway. That took a kind of strength I wasn't sure she knew she had.

Want! my wolf howled.

"Me too, buddy," I said quietly. "Me too."

CHAPTER ELEVEN

Natalie

Surrounded by massive tree trunks, I ran through the darkness. Even with the moon overhead, barely any of its light filtered through the canopy, and I found myself all but blind. I ran with something behind me, hunting me. I felt its breath on the back of my neck—I could feel it in my bones. I could taste the thrill of the chase as my legs burned and lungs labored. I was the prey and there was a part of me that was loving it.

My foot hit an exposed root and I went down. I rolled and came back up in a smooth maneuver that wasn't very much like me. But the pain caught up with me, and it wasn't long before my run became something of a limping waddle. The predator was catching up to me. I needed to move, but the pain was too much, and I stumbled again, hitting the ground on my knees.

Movement echoed in the trees on either side of me. I fought down the wave of panic, desperately trying to get to my feet, but my legs refused to listen. Out of the trees to the left a massive silver-gray wolf erupted from the shadows. Its paws struck the forest floor and the ground trembled beneath the beast. I focused on letting the fear flow through me and out, instead of letting it control my actions. I was not weak. I could handle this.

Then another sound came from behind me, and I spun to stare at a tall, silver-haired woman who crouched in almost a mirror image of the wolf on the other side of me.

"Wren!" Her name dropped from my lips before I could stop it. My heart pounded at her savage grin, and I took in the feral green eyes that seemed to want to devour me.

"Natalie." My name emerged from her lips like a sensuous

moan, and I gasped in response. She wore the same flannel and loose jeans she'd been wearing at supper. She looked the picture of comfortable and wild all at the same time.

Movement behind me made me turn again, and I saw the wolf backpedal a step or two. Its eyes looked on in interest. If it felt threatened by us, it didn't show.

My eyes were drawn back to Wren, who stared at me with naked desire. And it didn't scare me. It didn't make me want to run. I wanted those hands of hers all over me. I wanted her lips on mine, our skin touching. I wanted to know what she tasted like.

I took a single step toward her, and it was like an open invitation. She lunged forward and wrapped her arms around my neck. Her lips locked upon mine. It started out awkward but became easier as I learned her lips, her taste. I closed my eyes and took her deeper into me. I tested the waters with my tongue, and she opened for me with a gasp and a moan, and I felt myself falling into her.

We parted, the kiss lingering between us, and I exhaled slowly. Her grin pulled her lips back, showing teeth that looked almost as impressive as the wolf's, as she took my wrists and held them high above my head. She pushed me back until we hit one of the tall trees, the bark biting into my back as she held my wrists in place with a single hand. She reached up under my shirt with her other hand, and I gasped and moaned as she explored me. I struggled instinctively but gained no ground against the powerful woman.

She pushed her thigh between my legs, hard, and I writhed as panic and need warred within my chest. Even in my dreams, the fear of rejection reared its ugly head.

"Please!" I gasped when I could catch my breath.

"Please what?" she growled.

"Take me!" I screamed into the darkness as she ground her thigh upward.

The panic bubbled up, but I couldn't stop her as she released my hands and tore my shirt away with a single tearing yank. She released my wrists, then her hands were on my chest, and she ran her fingers over my nipples, pushing me toward the edge of my climax already, but it wasn't enough. I wanted more. Needed more.

I reached under her shirt and pulled it off before she could argue. I began to shadow her movements. I focused on her budding nipples and took one in my mouth while I used my hand on the other. I sucked and licked and clenched my teeth around her nipple. I ran my tongue roughly over my captive. She played with one of my nipples and I moaned loudly as she traveled south with her other hand.

"No!" I cried. The panic overwhelmed everything I was feeling and I twisted my hips away from her hand and her thigh. "Please, no!" I wanted to be perfect for her, even in my dreams. But I wasn't.

She faltered and I wanted to wipe off the hurt and confused look on her face. I couldn't, not yet. But there was more than one way to enjoy ourselves.

"As you wish." The growl in her voice was less of a warning and more an outlet for frustration—one I couldn't blame her for. But I didn't want to stop entirely. She pressed her lips to mine again in a kiss that threatened to overwhelm me. I probed at her mouth with my tongue until she let me in. She gnashed her teeth at my lower lip and took it in a sudden bite and pulled until I gasped in equal parts pain and pleasure.

We parted and she darted forward to mouth one of my nipples and I made no move to stop her.

"Wren!" I moaned. I held her head to me like it was a life preserver—the only thing keeping me from drowning in her. She pulled back and spun us so her back was to the tree, and then put pressure on my shoulders.

"Kneel." The command was hardly out of her mouth before I fell to my knees in front of her. I ignored the rough forest floor under my legs as I tugged her loose pants down. She tangled her hands in my hair and pulled me forward. She spread her legs and I lunged the rest of the way as she growled. "Take it all."

I slid my hands up her ass and hips and anchored myself to her as I licked at the warm depths of her core. I tasted her like someone trying wine. I took small sips and tested her reactions until I knew how she would respond—and what would make her come undone. I pulled back a little and ran my tongue up her inner thigh while I played with her hidden clit, buried near the top of her lips.

"Natalie!" She gripped my hair tighter and sent shocks down to my core. "By the Mother, don't you dare stop!"

I clenched her ass tight and I felt my nails break her skin, while

I thrust my tongue into her, going as deep as I could. I sucked away at the hood that tried to conceal her swollen clit from me and raked my teeth over it to make her shiver and shake. I pushed my finger next to my tongue inside her and she bucked and rolled her hips, but she held me steadily between her legs as I lapped up everything that came out of her as fast as I could.

I held in a laugh as I heard her yip and growl like a dog as I worked her into a frenzy. Wedged between me and the tree, there was nowhere for her to escape to, and she twisted and moaned as I could feel her climax coming. I turned up the heat and pushed harder and faster with a second finger alongside the first and she let out a strangled moan that turned into a human howl that echoed through the dark trees. A gush of fluid followed the trail of my tongue, and I lapped it up with slow, lazy strokes as I took her all in.

I smiled up at her. I knew that she could see herself on my face, and I let her pull me hard to my feet and take my lips into her once more. She didn't seem fazed that she could taste herself, and she devoured me anyway.

A howl split the air and I tottered on wobbly legs as the wolf who'd been forgotten made its displeasure of being left out known. I smiled at the furry beast, hoping to make friends with it. Suddenly, the darkness in the trees loomed and everything started to disappear.

"Wren?" I screamed. I toppled to the ground as she reached out her hands for me, her eyes full of concern. "Wren!" The trees closest to us disappeared. Then the wolf. "Please!" The moment the word left my mouth, the entire world went dark.

CHAPTER TWELVE

Natalie

I clawed my way out of darkness and pulled the heavy comforter off my face to let in the bright sunlight. I cringed at the light, then groaned and pushed harder at the blanket, far too hot under the heavy weight, and felt the softness of the mattress beneath me. The adrenaline from the dream slowly faded, leaving me more tired than I would have expected. Maybe if I'd gotten a good night's sleep, I would've been more aware, but it took a good five minutes before realizing I hadn't gotten myself into bed last night.

I shot straight up. I was breathing hard as I tried to remember exactly what had happened the night before. I had woken up to gunshots. And then the injured wolf came to me and I helped it—I pulled out the bullet. Then that dream—

"The wolf!" I yelped as I threw aside the blanket and dashed out of the bedroom in nothing but my panties.

The rug at the front door still had the blood stain on it, but the wolf was nowhere to be found. I was about to run out the door when a sound in the kitchen drew my attention. Then I smelled the mouthwatering aroma of bacon and eggs.

Then I realized I was standing in the living room almost completely naked as Wren turned away from the stove. Her eyes fell on me, and she froze, a frying pan in her hand.

"Um…good morning?" She recovered enough to gently put the pan down.

"Fuck!" I screamed and ran into the bedroom, slamming the door behind me. "What the hell? What the fuck? Oh, my Goddess!" I desperately dug around in the closet and was tossing clothes onto the bed when there came a soft knock on the door.

"Natalie? Are you okay?"

Damn it! Why did she sound so caring? She was the one who was in the cabin without telling me. She did leave last night, didn't she? I was pretty sure she did.

"What are you doing here?" I yelled back through the door, not up to opening it yet.

"I wanted to apologize for leaving so abruptly last night." Her voice filtered through the door. "When I got here this morning the front door was wide open, and you were asleep on the rug with the blood, and I panicked."

"What do you mean?"

She let out a heavy sigh. "I thought it was yours, so I picked you up and made sure you weren't hurt. When I realized it wasn't your blood, I put you in your bed."

"And my clothes?" I felt the heat creep up my face even though she couldn't see me.

"They were covered in blood! I didn't think you wanted them on the sheets."

Well, didn't she just have a damned answer for everything? The problem was I couldn't fault her for any of her actions. She knew this area better than I did. If I wasn't hurt, then what was the point of calling the police, especially if she could get the story about the bloody rug when I woke up? Hell, I was probably lucky she hadn't woken me up earlier to demand answers.

After a couple of calming breaths, I pulled on a simple black T-shirt and pair of cargo pants. Dressed now, I opened the door and stepped out into the hallway, forcing her back. I gave her a glare but softened it enough to show I wasn't entirely angry with her.

"Thank you." I didn't want to look her in the eye while I said it, but I did catch the smile that bloomed across her face. A flash of that same smile surrounded by darkened trees rocked me and I stumbled into her, clutching her shoulders as I shook my head to clear it. She winced under my weight, and I pulled back quickly.

"Are you okay?"

I took a moment before nodding. "I think so." I proceeded to brush imaginary dust off her shoulders where I'd grabbed her. "Sorry."

"Don't worry about it." She took my hand in one of hers and

pulled me back to the living room with her. "Breakfast is ready, and you can tell me what happened after I left last night."

I joined her at the island as she slowly dished out the eggs and bacon onto two plates. She was favoring one of her arms this morning.

"What happened to your arm?"

She fidgeted under my scrutiny. "Pulled my shoulder last night at the diner," she said, focusing on her plating. "Stupid, really. The box was heavier than it looked." She shrugged. "I'll be fine in a couple of days."

I leaned back in my chair, relaxing a little. Normally, having someone in my living space who I didn't know well would have me on edge enough to cause anxiety attacks. Wren was different. She moved like she owned the world, always in balance, always knowing what she was doing and where she was going. Her presence didn't make me anxious—it calmed me. As I watched her, it was hard to believe anything possibly managing to damage that lean body of hers, even if it was something stupid.

"So?" she said softly, settling her breakfast beside mine on the kitchen island. "Are you going to tell me about the rug?"

I glanced over my shoulder at the blood-stained rug and cursed. I'd have to replace that for Rory. I didn't want to stick her with the bill to clean or replace it.

"I woke up in the middle of the night," I began, telling her everything that had happened the night before, as we enjoyed the culinary queen's breakfast. I faltered a little, talking about the wolf. It had been the biggest one I'd ever seen, not that I had a lot of experience working with wild animals. I thought again of working with a wildlife sanctuary or something, but that required a school degree. And if my life kept going the way it was now, I wasn't going to get that degree anytime soon.

"Wow, that must've scared the shit out of you," she said when I'd finished. I felt I could only give a shrug.

"I was scared at first, but when I got the wolf back in the house, I was too focused on helping her to be scared." I looked back at the rug again. "I thought I'd locked the door behind us, but if she got out, then I must not have. I hope she's okay out there."

Wren nodded. "I'd say maybe ask someone in town, but if there were hunters out there at night looking for a wolf, then someone has probably declared it a nuisance, and they want it gone. I worry what will happen if they go back out there tonight."

"I hope she goes to a new area maybe. But probably not, huh? I just don't want her to get hurt again. She was a beautiful creature."

A sparkle gleamed in Wren's eyes as she smiled. "You know, that's kind of adorable."

"What?"

"How much you loved that wolf last night."

"I did not! I was scared out of my mind!"

She laughed. "You just admitted that you weren't."

"I—" My words failed me in the moment, and I smacked her lightly on the shoulder. She winced again and guilt flooded my mind. "Oh, Goddess, I'm so sorry. I forgot."

She held up a hand. "It's okay. If I couldn't take something like that, I'd have to return my butch card."

A surprised laugh slipped out of my mouth, and she joined it with her own. I stared at the smile on her lips, wondering how things felt so damned easy with her around. So comfortable. Even Rory rarely had me this at ease.

"Wren—" I began as a phone started to ring.

"Sorry," she said, pulling out her phone. "It's the diner, I should take this."

I nodded and she pulled herself off the chair and wandered into the hallway. I finished off the last forkfuls of my breakfast before Wren's voice rose in anger and worry.

"What do you mean she's not picking up?"

There was no way I could hear the other side of the conversation, but something was clearly wrong.

"No. Stay at the diner. I'll deal with this. Keep calling her until she picks up or you hear from me. Understood?"

Again, an answer came, but Wren hung up the phone and stormed back into the kitchen.

"I'm sorry, Natalie, but I need to go." She headed for the door, slipping her shoes on with practiced ease.

I leapt off my stool. "What's going on?"

She shook her head. "Just business with the diner."

"That sounded like some pretty sketchy business."

"I'm sorry I have to run again."

I waved a hand. "It's fine. I'll just come with you." The words surprised the hell out of me the moment they were spoken, but I wasn't going to take them back. I didn't want her to go. I didn't want to be alone.

"No," she said shortly, reaching for the door.

"Why not? It's just diner business, nothing secretive or anything, right?"

She let out a low grumble. "Look, I can't talk about it right now, but I need to go."

"Are you—" I began but she was already out the door and climbing into her Jeep. I didn't remember seeing her move between the two points. As I tried to puzzle out this new side of Wren, the Jeep kicked up gravel as it spun around and took off down the rough road.

Before I could think about what a bad idea it was, I grabbed my wallet and keys and slipped my shoes on. I locked up and headed out after her.

CHAPTER THIRTEEN

Wren

The Jeep barreled down the highway as I flattened the accelerator to the floor. As confident as I was that no cop in the county would bother with a speeding ticket if I offered them a few free meals from the diner, it didn't even really matter. One of my people might be in danger, and damned if I was going to sit back on my ass and drive the speed limit.

I knew I was overreacting. It might very well be that Meg just slept in and her phone died or something. I *knew* that, but I couldn't get the thought of her being in danger out of my head. First Jason and his buddies in the diner yesterday, then the hunters with silver last night. I wasn't willing to take the chance that someone I cared for was in danger.

When I got to the diner, I could see one of the cooks, Leslie, fretting behind the bar. I parked the Jeep and took a moment to breathe, knowing if I went in there showing the anger that I was feeling, it would only make things harder for everyone. When I felt calm enough, I walked into the diner, throwing the door open with more force than I meant to.

Thankfully, nothing broke, but I did get a few curious glances from the early patrons.

I went to the bar where Leslie was wringing her hands. "What happened?"

She took a breath before starting. "My brother and I stopped at Meg's to pick her up, like we usually do, but there was no answer." She glanced away sheepishly. "I figured she was just sleeping in or had talked to you about having the day off or something and forgot to tell me. It wouldn't be the first time. But no one else can reach her either."

"You've been taking care of the front since then?"

She nodded. "We tried calling her, but her phone goes straight to voice mail. We figured we'd see someone come in this morning to cover for her, but when no one showed up..."

"You called me," I finished. "Okay. We can deal with this. Did you see her when you left last night?"

"I dropped her off at home. She got in fine." She shook her head. "I should've waited longer this morning or something. Maybe she was just—"

I waved a hand and cut her off. "Don't do that to yourself, Leslie. Whatever is going on it's not your fault." From the feeling welling up in my gut, I was certain it was my fault, but I didn't want to tell them that. "Call Alisha and see if she can come in, otherwise you can keep covering the front until I get back." I kept my voice calm but firm, like the slightly distant boss I tried to pretend to be. Honestly, I probably cared about my people a little too much, but I couldn't help that. I refused to have a pack, but that didn't mean these people weren't important to me. They were *my* people, after all. "I'm sure she's fine. She probably slept in, and her phone is dead or something, you know? I'll head out and check in with her."

Leslie hesitated. "It's not like Meg to miss a shift. She never misses a shift."

I tried to make my shrug seem nonchalant. "There's a first time for everything."

She frowned and I reached across the bar to put my hand on her shoulder.

"Don't worry. I'm sure she's fine." Yeah, and maybe if I told myself that enough, I'd start to believe it. My wolf howled inside my head, her uneasiness making it hard for me to think clearly. She was certain something was up, and I was inclined to take Hikaru's advice and believe her.

I turned to leave—only to see a very conspicuous truck pull into the parking lot beside my Jeep. I couldn't help the growl that burst from my throat as I stomped outside when Natalie climbed out of the truck.

"What the hell are you doing here?" I was barely able to keep my wolf in check. Agitated that one of our people was missing, the wolf instantly wanted to keep Natalie nearby. But if Jason or one of his people had possibly hurt Meg, I didn't want Natalie to be involved. I couldn't risk letting her get hurt.

"I'm sorry. I didn't realize you owned the parking lot!"

"It's my diner! Of course I own the parking lot."

She faltered. "Oh, right. Well, fuck, I just wanted to come and help. You left so quickly, and you didn't tell me what was happening!"

I held a hand to my head, fighting the headache that was starting to build. "I don't have time for this!"

"That's fine," she said, heading for the Jeep. "You can tell me on the way."

"No!" She froze when my voice came out lower than normal. "No, you are not coming with me!"

She stood with her hands on her hips, and I restrained myself from wringing her skinny little neck. "Why the hell not?"

"Because it's none of your business!"

"I know that! But that doesn't mean I can't help out a g—" She cut herself off quickly. "A friend!"

It was my turn to falter. Years of learning that to get through life you couldn't count on anyone else made it hard to accept help. My wolf—the traitor—clearly had no problem with Natalie tagging along, but I knew I couldn't put her in any sort of danger. I hoped I was overreacting, that Meg was fine, but I couldn't take that risk. If Jason hadn't shown up yesterday, it wouldn't be a problem, but I wasn't an idiot. He and his older brother had made my life hell for years when I was in their pack. The last thing I wanted to do was put Natalie on their radar—if she wasn't already after last night.

Three deep breaths later and I had pushed the wolf down enough that I could think clearly again. "Listen. I appreciate that, I really do. I'm not used to people putting themselves out to help me and you're an amazing person for doing so, but I don't want you to get involved with this."

"Wren," she said, "I know we only met a few days ago and I don't mean to pry into your life or anything, but..." She drifted off, looking away until I couldn't see her eyes. Her voice softened, forcing me to strain to hear it properly. "The way you left the cabin scared me, Wren. I feel this…connection to you. I feel a strong desire to be around you, and I don't want anything to happen to you if this is as bad as you seem to think it is. I want to help. I want to help *you*." She looked up at me with a wide smile that only looked slightly scared. "I mean, who's going to cook amazing food for me if something goes wrong?"

I couldn't stop the laugh that came out at her words, and a cute pink flush lit up her cheeks like I'd made her fucking week. It made my wolf howl with need, and it was hard not to let that out of my mouth. She did not know what she was saying. She couldn't—there was so much she didn't know about me. But here she was, wanting to help.

She shrugged after a moment as her smile faltered. "And I mean honestly, what else is there to do besides hang out in the cabin all day?"

I ran my fingers through my hair. "Fine," I said. Natalie's eyes lit up and she smiled as her feet came off the ground in a happy little jump. "But!" I added, earning a narrowing of her eyes. "You will promise to listen to what I say and do it without argument. I will not send you away or make you do something without good reason, I promise you that." I shook my head. "Truthfully, I'm probably making a mountain out of a molehill, but I worry all the same. I intend to keep you and the rest of my people safe, and to do that, you need to listen to me." I held out my hand to her. "Deal?"

My regard for her shot up a few notches as she paused for a moment, apparently considering the terms, before taking my hand in a hearty shake. "Deal."

❖

"So," Natalie said as I pulled the Jeep through the quiet streets of the town. "We're headed to Meg's house to check on her?"

"If she's not there then I can try to track her down, but honestly I hope she just slept in really deeply or something." But the more I considered that thought, the more I knew it wasn't the case. My wolf was too riled up, like she knew something I didn't, and I wanted to listen to her. I worried that I had no idea what I was getting into, though. Between the wolves yesterday and the hunters last night, this was already proving to be more than the usual trouble with wolves coming after me from my old pack. I shook my head. I should never have trusted Ronan, my old Alpha, and his promise that no one would come after me.

Natalie was quiet for most of the ride, and I appreciated her silence. Distractions get people hurt, and she was aware enough not to let that happen. We were both silent until we reached Meg's house, a small bungalow with only two steps up to the front porch, and siding that looked like it needed to be replaced.

"So, what's the plan?" Natalie asked, and I stopped with my foot halfway out of the Jeep. I wondered what would be safest at this point. The longer she was with me, the greater the risk she'd be in danger because of me. At the same time, I didn't want her to leave my side. Neither did my wolf.

"Um, come with me, okay?"

She nodded and was at my side as we approached the front door.

Please be something simple. Please be something silly.

I knew far too well that wishing for something wouldn't make it come true. I pounded on the front door, shouting Meg's name through it. The second time I nodded to Natalie. "Let's go around to the back door."

"Got it, boss."

I led the way to the side gate to the backyard. Natalie fell in behind me without a complaint, and my wolf howled in happiness at our closeness.

Easy, girl, I know how you feel.

The backyard was all flat lawn with a single concrete step up to the back door. The moment I noticed the door wasn't closed, I threw out an arm and stopped Natalie from moving forward.

"Are you okay?" she whispered.

I nodded. "Stay close, and behind me."

She did as I asked as I moved to the doorway. The back door was hanging by a single hinge, parts of the doorframe cracked and shattered, with debris on the floor. I stared at the mess, clenching my fists and taking deep breaths so I didn't do something to scare Natalie. Was it bad to think that I hated that my wolf was right?

I stepped through the doorway and stopped, immediately

noticing the mess. Meg was a pretty neat girl, always keeping things as tidy as she could, even if she ended up grumbling about lazy coworkers. But the place was a disaster zone.

The kitchen was torn apart, the small table flipped over and drawers pulled out of the cabinets. From the door I could see out into the living room, too, where more destruction lay. I moved slowly into the next room, hearing only Natalie's steps at my back as I looked around. The couch was overturned, television smashed, and debris from what looked like a fight was scattered everywhere. But what my vision focused on was the remnants of the glass coffee table in the middle of the room—and several shards of glass that were coated in blood. I knelt and picked one up, holding it under my nose. I sniffed.

MINE! My wolf howled, and it came out of my mouth as an angry scream.

"Wren?"

I held up the piece of glass. "Someone took her," I growled, "someone *hurt* her!"

She looked from me to the glass to the broken doorframe, and I could smell the wave of fear and insecurity. The growl that had lowered since seeing her came back full force, vibrating in the air between us until she took a step back, then another.

"Is…Is there anything w-we can do?" she asked.

I turned my eyes away from her. "Get in the Jeep." She didn't even argue, just ran past and headed for the front door—unlocking it as she went.

They'd come in the back door, probably early, when Meg was in her room, either asleep or just waking. That's where the trouble started. I moved around the house, following the scents and signs of attack. Besides Meg, Natalie, and myself, I caught the familiar scents of three more people. My wolf growled inside me, and I corrected myself—three wolves. Jason and the other two I'd met the day before at the diner.

"Those sons of bitches! They dared to take one of mine?" I snarled into the empty house. I closed my hand around the bloody glass, feeling it bite into my skin and reveling in the pain. I dropped the glass, letting it shatter on the floor as the cuts on my hand healed. "We need to get her back."

Hunt!

"Oh, yeah," I agreed with my other side. "We're going to hunt. They won't get away with this."

With one last look around the house, I walked out the front door. I pulled open the passenger side door, and Natalie stared at me with wide eyes. "Drive." I growled.

"Are you sure?"

I tried hard not to let her think my rage was directed at her. "Drive," I said again, forcing my voice to be a little softer. "And follow my directions." She stayed motionless in the seat. "Can you do that?"

She paused for a long moment, then nodded. "I can do that." She got out and ran to the other side as I climbed in the Jeep and rolled down the window. I took a long sniff of the air, focusing on Meg's scent. "Pull out, head right."

With only the smallest bit of hesitation, she pulled the Jeep out of park, and we hit the road, following a slowly fading scent trail. I was not going to let them get away with messing with one of my people. They were going to pay.

Hunt!

My feelings echoed my wolf's feelings. Now I just had to figure out what to do with Natalie.

CHAPTER FOURTEEN

Natalie

I watched Wren out of the corner of my eye, waiting for her next barked order. I didn't mind her telling me what to do, especially when I told her I'd do it so she'd take me along. But the way she snarled every word was starting to make me worried. She was angry, I understood that, but that didn't mean she had to take it out on me. It reminded me of when Misty would get mad at something, taking her frustrations out on me and whatever she felt I was doing wrong in that moment.

But Wren wasn't like Misty. Yes, I was seeing a different side of her right now, but I could also understand it. She was scared, worried for her friend, and she even seemed worried about me. I couldn't even understand why she'd worry about me, of all people, but the fact that she did made me feel a kind of warmth in my chest. There was some sort of connection between us, that much I could feel. Maybe that dream had something to do with it.

Wren had the window down, her face halfway out of the Jeep as I turned out of the residential streets and back toward the highway. "Right," she barked when we were still a kilometer or so away. I had no idea how she knew where the hell we were going, but I was going to trust her.

We hit the highway and I sped up, ignoring the sporadic buildings that passed by. In a minute we were outside of Terabend, moving quickly down a tree-lined highway as I listened for the next direction. Wren's face tilted upward. She closed her eyes against the rushing wind and left most of her face still out the window. How she could see or hear or whatever was beyond me.

I turned back to focus on the driving, almost feeling like I was in one of those books I used to read when I was waiting for Misty to come home from work. They were always about some mythological being partnering with a scrappy human sidekick to save their people or the world or something else. And of course, that scrappy human sidekick would just happen to show that powerful being that they weren't so fragile or frail and could keep up with the monsters. Then they'd kiss…

I felt my cheeks heating up at the thought and shook my head a little. *Not the time, Nat. Not the time.*

And besides, I decided, I'd never been able to find one of those novels that featured someone like me. Sure, there were plenty with lesbians, and sometimes creatures of indeterminate genders, but I never saw another person like myself in the primary role as that plucky human sidekick. I grinned inwardly. Maybe I'd have to remedy that someday.

That thought was quickly followed by a sinking feeling in my stomach. "Shit!" I blurted before I could think better of it.

Wren's head snapped around to stare at me. "What?"

I fidgeted sheepishly under her hard gaze, wishing I hadn't said a thing. "I forgot to take my medication this morning."

She let out a rough breath and her eyes softened a little. "Are you going to be okay?"

"Oh, yeah, I can go a day without them. Or a morning, since I take more in the evening." I gave her the side-eye and grinned. "It's when I miss them for an extended period that things get a little hairy."

She raised an eyebrow and I sighed. Of course she didn't get the joke. She didn't know that I was trans. That my pills were a blood pressure medication called spironolactone that blocked testosterone production. Those pills, with the estrogen patches I changed twice a week, helped make me who I was. And as much as I might have yearned to share that information with people openly, I couldn't.

But oh, how I wanted to, I realized a second later. Especially with Wren. How would she react if she knew? We were just starting a friendship—at the very least—and who knows where it might go. Would she run away if I told her?

"Never mind." I shook my head and focused back on driving as she only grunted and stuck her head back out the window.

Another ten minutes passed as we barreled down the highway before Wren's head perked up. "Turn right up here," she said, not even bothering to look at me.

I stared out the windshield, trying to see where I was supposed to turn. There were no roads, no turnouts, nothing to turn onto. I glanced at her, but she was still facing away. I slowed the Jeep, earning a frantic honking from a car behind me, and flipped on the turn signal, pulling off to the shoulder. The jerk passed with an obnoxious honk and a flip of the bird. I ignored them and watched the trees.

In the distance I could make out a large sign on the side of the road, welcoming drivers to the next county over. But in the trees just ahead of us was a break in the forest and a worn tire-trail that pulled off the highway. Looking to Wren for any kind of sign, I slowed and turned between two large trees. The road—if you could call it that—wasn't even gravel. Instead, it was only two deep ruts worn over time in the grass. I grimaced as the Jeep bounced, but thankfully it was high enough not to hit the ground. I'd pity anyone who tried to take a sedan or hatchback down this road.

"Slow down," Wren hissed, her eyes focused on the trees as they surrounded us. I did as she asked, keeping quiet. But I did cast a glance her way. Her head was still out the window and she focused intently on the trees around us. Her focus and intensity made me wonder just what she was seeing and hearing out there. I hoped one day she would tell me what was going on—preferably before I went back to the city. With a shudder, I pushed that thought far, far away. *Focus on today, tomorrow will come later.*

The path through the trees widened briefly, with enough room on one side for a car to park. From the tire tracks on the grass, it was safe to assume some drivers had done just that. In the instant we started passing the turnout, Wren's hand was suddenly on the wheel, turning us toward it. The Jeep bounced wildly as we exited the ruts, and I fought hard not to just slam on the brakes before we were safely out of the road and settled. When the Jeep came to a safe stop, I stared at Wren.

"What the fuck was that?"

She looked at me, her mouth peeled back in a snarl as I challenged her.

I shook my head, keeping her gaze. "No way, you don't get to go all quiet and angry on me. You could have killed us! If you're going to grab the wheel out of fucking nowhere, next time at least warn me!"

She backed off a few inches. "I didn't want you to miss the stop."

"Okay, so words work better than just grabbing the fucking wheel and taking over!"

At least she had the good decency to look chagrined. "I'm sorry."

"Good!" I said with a snarl that could rival hers. "Glad we got that out of the way. Now, what the hell are we doing here?"

"Get out."

My foot was on the ground, my ass still on the seat, when I realized I hadn't even considered arguing with her. *What the hell was that?* We met at the front of the Jeep, but her eyes locked on the trees in front of us.

"If you dragged me all the way out here just to kill me, I want you to know I don't plan on going quietly or easily." I tried to sound confident while I said it, but a part of me was starting to wish I hadn't followed her to the diner this morning. A very small part of me. The rest of me didn't want to leave her alone for a minute.

She turned back to me with a look in her eyes like she was going to devour me. Another flash in my mind of us pressed up against a tree, kissing and fondling, almost kicked my feet out from underneath me.

"She's here," Wren whispered, "and so are the people who took her."

"Shit." I looked around as if I was going to see them through the trees. "What do we do?"

She looked at me for a long minute. "Do you trust me?"

"Yes." The word was out of my mouth before I could even think about it.

"Follow me."

She set off into the trees, moving slowly enough that I could keep up with her. I had the feeling she could probably move faster.

Guilt rolled through me. If we took too long getting there, it'd be my fault for slowing her down. Again, I second-guessed chasing after her.

There was no discernable reason that Wren knew where she was going, but she led the way unerringly, until even I could smell the acrid smoke of wood fire drifting through the trees. She stopped, then crouched down. I followed suit.

"There." She pointed between a couple of trees. I peered through them and saw a small, cleared area of ground that had a simple firepit built with stones ringing the outside. The fire was burning low, probably having not been fed in several hours. Beyond the flames was a body wearing dark clothing. It wasn't moving.

"Is that Meg?"

Wren nodded. She lifted her head and sniffed the air. I had no idea what she might smell over the scent of the fire. "All right, we're downwind, so we should be okay. I need you to listen carefully to what I'm about to say. Can you do that, Natalie?"

I shivered when my name crossed her lips, but I recovered quickly. "Okay."

"Good." She smiled and heat flared in the bottom of my gut. "I'm going to move forward and confront whoever took her. I need you to move straight to Meg, untie her, and get her back to the Jeep as quickly as you can." Wren reached into her pocket and pulled out a small pocketknife, handing it to me as she pointed to the side, and I saw the ruts of the makeshift road. "Follow that trail back, then get in the Jeep and drive back to Terabend. In the GPS you'll find a name, Dr. Maru. Take Meg to the clinic. Dr. Maru will take care of her." She looked me right in the eye, and I could see her green eyes almost shining with gold flecks around the irises. "Can you do that for me, Natalie?"

I opened my mouth, but nothing came out. I wanted to say no, that I wasn't going to leave her out here, but I had to believe that she knew what she was doing and there was a reason for what she was asking me to do.

"Okay," I said. "I can do that."

Strong arms wrapped around me in an awkward crouching hug. I let out a little gasp before leaning into her, nestling into those arms like I belonged there. "You know, I'm glad you talked me into letting

PACK OF HER OWN

you come with me." Her voice was barely a whispered breath, but the words twisted through me until they smothered all the doubt I'd been feeling.

"Okay. Let's do this."

She nodded and burst out of the trees faster than I managed to track. One second, she had me in her arms, the next she was kicking dirt over the fire and challenging anyone in the clearing. I heard a yell and a screech but ignored it, pushing my way into the clearing and running to the limp woman.

"Meg!" I yelped as I lightly slapped her face. I recognized her from the diner the other day, but she looked like shit. Her hair had blood in it, the side of her mouth was swollen, and one eye was so swollen and bruised it was completely shut. Her hands and ankles were bound with rough rope that had rubbed her skin raw, and I hissed in sympathy. I used the knife to cut through her bonds as someone yelled and attacked Wren. Wren blocked a wild blow from her attacker and slammed a fist into the guy's gut, which doubled him over. From there she literally picked him up with both arms and tossed him into the trees with a loud grunt of effort.

I tore my gaze away from her and kept working on Meg. Her good eye opened slightly, sticky from blood and tears.

"W-w-who?"

"Shh, it's okay." I tried to soothe her. "I'm Natalie. I'm here with Wren. We're going to get you out of here."

She looked scared of me until I mentioned Wren's name. She looked past me to the amazing efforts of her savior. It was hard for me not to look too, but I focused on the task Wren had given me. "Is she…"

I shook my head. "She'll be fine. We need to go."

"But—"

"We can't. I promised her I'd get you out of here, and I'm going to do that." I got her to her feet, took her weight on my shoulder, and we hurried down the road. I heard grunting and shouting behind us but didn't look back.

CHAPTER FIFTEEN

Wren

Panting heavily, I held a hand to my wounded shoulder. Stupid, picking the asshole up like that. In the frenzy I wasn't thinking, and now my arm wasn't working properly.

The younger man rushed me again and I stepped aside, kicking him in the knee as his weight came down on it. It buckled and he screamed, loud and long, until I put my other boot into his head. He fell with a soft grunt and didn't get back up.

Seconds passed as I waited for another attack. This punk wasn't alone yesterday, and there were more scents around the campfire. One I knew was Jason, but it was muddled with other scents. The only other scent that was clear belonged to the girl who had been with them yesterday, but her scent was strange. And close.

I heard the Jeep rev, and the tires start to crunch back down the road as it headed for the highway, and I breathed a sigh of relief. Natalie had Meg and they were on their way. Once more, I was glad I had brought Natalie with me. Now I had no reason to hold back.

I lifted the asshole by his neck as his eyes flickered dazedly and focused on my other hand until fur rippled from fingers to elbow, claws elongating at my fingertips. His heart sped up as if he knew what was coming and I laughed. He had taken one of mine. Now he'd pay.

"Stop!"

Someone grabbed my arm. I growled, throwing the man away as I turned. The girl who'd been with him at the diner was beside me, gray eyes wide in fear, but her mouth set in a determined grimace.

"Please! Don't hurt him any more!"

With a shrug of my shoulder, I threw her off and she fell to the ground. She landed beside the fire, her hand almost touching the flames as she scrambled away.

"You came into my county," I snarled, as I took slow steps forward while she backed away in an awkward crabwalk. "You took one of *my* people and you beg—*beg!*—me not to hurt him?"

"We didn't have a choice! You don't know Jason!"

"You always have a choice! Always!"

"You don't know him!" she cried. "He would've killed us! You don't cross the Reid brothers and live!"

I faltered for only a second. The brothers had done enough to scar me in my time with the old pack. I shouldn't have been surprised that they'd done it to others since I was gone.

"Where is Jason?"

She shook her head. "He told us to take her! To bring her out here! Then he just ran off. He had other wolves with him, wolves I hadn't seen before today. They didn't come from the Cardinals with us."

Had they only been using Meg as bait? Was he gauging how I responded to a threat? Whatever was going on here, I wasn't liking it. I sniffed the air again, staring down at the girl.

"What are you?"

She hesitated. "I...I'm a wolf like you!"

I shook my head. "Bullshit. I'm only going to ask you one more time. What are you?"

She shook from head to toe. "I swear. I swear I am a wolf."

Her scent puzzled me. She smelled only barely like any wolf I'd ever met, but maybe she wasn't lying. I let out a huffing growl and turned back to her compatriot. "Stay put," I said to her. She froze in place.

The young man shook his head like he was coming out of a daze. I let the girl watch my arm change back to normal before I confronted him. His eyes widened as he saw me, and I felt his fear drive me to lift him up by his throat again. Anger stirred deep in my heart but couldn't find an outlet. I didn't want to kill the wolf, but an example had to be made. Something had to happen to him.

"It's your lucky day," I said, hefting him high in the air. "I'm going to let you live." I shook him a little to make sure I had his attention. "What is your name?"

"C-Callum Palmer," he choked out.

I nodded and let his feet touch the ground enough that he wasn't going to pass out on me. I took a deep breath and felt the power inside me swirl with intent. The magic that melded my wolf and me together, that made us what we are, drew up and into my voice. As if in a dream, the words came to me without thinking.

"Callum Palmer," I said in a clear, ringing tone. "As Alpha of this territory, I hereby banish you from it and revoke any and all access to it. You will never set foot in my territory again, wolf. And if you do, I shall know, and you will be hunted and made to pay for your transgression." I let him fall to the ground. "So mote it be."

The moment the last syllable left my mouth an unnatural wind exploded into the clearing, blowing the campfire out and leaving nothing but wisps of smoke. The girl on the ground leaned into the wind and let out a keening scream that was lost in the storm. The wind whipped around Callum, forcing him back. He howled in fear and crouched as fur overtook his body. His face started to shift, and his muzzle jutted out as his ears rose to the top of his head. He howled again, this time all wolf, and the wind pulled at him even harder. The storm threw him up into the air and hurled him into the trees where he disappeared from sight.

Both the girl and I stared at the empty space where he'd been. There was one last long drawn-out howl before it faded into silence.

What the fuck?

The girl turned her wide, fearful eyes to me. I did my best to deserve to be looked at like that and tried to keep my composure. *Yup. Totally knew that was going to happen and planned the whole thing. Yessir.*

I mean, I knew my knowledge of how to be an Alpha was severely lacking, but now I could just *do* things like this without knowing about it? That definitely wasn't in the brochure.

I turned back to the girl. "Now, what do I do with you? I mean, since you claim to be a wolf and everything. You're still within my borders, and you took one of mine. That comes with consequences."

"I told you! Jason made us do it! I have no idea where the hell he went!"

"And he'll get what's coming to him when I find him. But for now..." I looked down at her. She needed to be taught a lesson. She needed to be held accountable, but she was in such a sorry state that I couldn't bring myself to do anything rash. Even the power I'd felt when I banished the other wolf had settled down inside me. "What do I do with you?"

"Please!" she said. "Please just let me stay! I can be useful! I can help you!" She wiggled around until she was on her knees in front of me. "Let me join your pack! You're an Alpha, I can help you!"

The moment she said the word *pack* I had to fight not to run away. Pack wasn't a dirty word in the werewolf world. It was supposed to be the way our world ran—wolves in packs and sticking together.

Not for me.

I didn't have a pack. Didn't want a pack. I'd claimed my territory and would fight for it, and for the humans who lived there, but I'd do it by myself. No one else.

"No," I said. "No. No pack. Never again." I shook my head to clear it. "C'mon. You're coming with me anyway, though."

She nodded without argument and stood with her head lowered like she didn't want to look me in the eyes.

"You might not be pack," I told her, "but you can still help fix the damage you've done."

"Yes, Alpha." I cringed at the title, but the words were already in the air. Not something I ever wanted.

I helped her to her feet, taking one last sniff of the air. There was no clear scent of Jason or the others he apparently had with him. I guessed he left these two as sacrifices to see how I reacted. I wasn't about to let him hurt my people ever again, but I couldn't chase him if he went onto another Alpha's lands. Not without seeking permission from that local pack leader. And I wasn't sure if Kendra, the Alpha who controlled the surrounding counties, would okay my hunt in her territory.

"C'mon, girl." I motioned for her to get moving. "Let's get walking."

"Heather," she said quickly. "My name's Heather McKenna."

I hesitated for a second before offering my hand "Wren Carne." She took the hand tentatively, giving a light shake. "Now, let's get out of here."

CHAPTER SIXTEEN

Natalie

I glanced at the speedometer again, took a breath, and eased off the accelerator. Despite the age of the Jeep, Wren had a GPS, and I looked up the doctor's address. As we hit the town outskirts, I was ready to turn in behind the main highway through town and drive directly to the doctor's office.

My mind wandered back to Wren, standing tall and protecting us from whoever had taken Meg. She'd looked larger than life, willing to put herself on the line to save a friend. And I couldn't help but admit she looked damned sexy doing so. I wished she'd been turned toward me, so I could've seen her eyes and her face, as she growled and fought against the kidnappers.

Something hit my shoulder and pushed me out of my thoughts as I glanced at Meg. Her eyes were closed, her breathing strained, and her head was limp against me.

"Hey!" I shouted and pushed the pedal down a little harder. "Hey, hold on. Don't you pass out on me. I don't know what the hell I'm doing!"

Maybe the slight movement of her head was some kind of reply, but I couldn't tell. I stared at the GPS, trying to make sure I followed the damned thing. I turned onto one of the roads that led deeper into the town, then several more turns, before pulling into the parking lot indicated on the system. The strip mall was small and unassuming, with a medical clinic, a pharmacy, and a convenience store with a gas station. The front was all glass windows and doors, but the building itself looked like it'd been built in the sixties.

I parked the Jeep in front of the doors and climbed out as quickly as I could. I had to stop and push Meg back up to sitting in her own seat, then ran around to open her door. By the time I'd levered her out of the Jeep and barely managed to keep her standing, the door to the clinic swung open and a short woman in a lab coat with deep black hair stormed out. Her eyes were hidden behind a pair of slim glasses with purple-tinted lenses, and they were focused on Meg.

"What happened?"

I shook my head. "I don't really know. Wren sent me. Meg's hurt."

Her gaze softened a little as she pulled Meg from my grasp with a surprising amount of ease. "Get the door, I'll get her inside."

I opened my mouth to argue but was rebuked solely by her glare. I let her take Meg and ran forward to open the door for her. Dr. Maru—I assumed—carried Meg in like she weighed no more than a sack of potatoes.

"Is she going to be okay?" I asked as I followed her into the clinic. The waiting room was small, only a handful of chairs lining two of the walls, and a young blond man sat behind the reception counter. He glanced up at us curiously, but evidently knew better than to interrupt whatever was going on. Clearly a lesson I could learn. "I can't tell how badly she was hurt, but she passed out on the way back."

"Let me take care of her and I'll let you know."

I followed her past the reception desk to a long hallway where she kicked open one of the doors. She disappeared into the room, and I peeked in before the door closed. I only caught a glimpse, but it was much nicer than any examination room I'd ever seen in a doctor's office. It looked almost like it was a full-on hospital suite— but that was impossible. Why would it be like that?

I didn't get a chance to even ask. I started to follow the doctor into the room, when suddenly she was standing there, arms empty, holding up her hands. "No. Please wait outside. I will make sure she's okay."

I stared into her eyes through those tinted shades and faltered. She didn't know me from Adam, I couldn't blame her for not letting me in. "I'm not the one who hurt her," I whispered.

Her mouth curled up in a hint of a smile. "I know. But let me help her, then we'll talk, okay?"

I nodded and she closed the door in front of me. With nothing else to do and nowhere to go, I returned to the waiting room, took a seat, and tried to keep my mind occupied with anything besides what had happened to Meg.

Unfortunately, that left me only a couple of options. The past, or Wren. Or what the hell I was doing here. I mean sure, it was great of Rory to let me borrow the cabin, to get away from everything and try to put myself back together. I honestly didn't know if I could ever thank her. But what the hell was I doing out here? Why was I sitting in a waiting room at a clinic with a girl I barely knew, others I didn't know at all, all while hoping the one person I'd met only a couple of days ago arrived soon to take my mind off everything?

Never mind that I left her out in the wilderness with no vehicle to get home. I jolted to my feet at that thought. I needed to get out there and go back to her. I reached for my phone, thinking to call her, or Rory, or something, but the pocket was empty.

Fuck. It was still in the kitchen back at the cabin. I'd been in such a rush to catch up to Wren I must've forgotten the damned thing. *That settles it.* I opened the door but stopped still when a small hand shoved it closed again. Dr. Maru was beside me, staring up at me from a few inches down, but in no way did I feel she was smaller. Her posture, her presence, took care of that.

"No, girl," she said quietly, "she will be fine. She would want you to be safe."

I shook my head. "What are you talking about?"

She glanced over her shoulder at her receptionist. "Call Sheriff Zeke and let him know to head east and look for Wren." He nodded without question and picked up the phone. She turned back to me with a small smile. "Come, my dear. We'll talk."

She led me deeper into the clinic, past the examination room she'd taken Meg into, and to another door. It opened into a large office, the entire back wall of which was lined with massive bookshelves that were full to bursting. A window on one wall let in the sun, but it didn't quite reach the large desk on the other side of the room, where two plush chairs faced one side and a nice leather executive chair was on the other side. She took a seat on the far side and gestured to one of the plush chairs. I glanced around, noting the sofa against the wall under the window, but it didn't look like it got a lot of use.

"So, you must be Natalie. I'm Yoshimaru Hikaru. Call me Dr. Maru." I looked at her, confused, at the sound of my name. "Wren told me about you."

I opened my mouth, with my mind too full of questions to be sure what I was going to say. "Is Meg okay?"

"Yes, Megan will be fine." She gestured to the chair again. "Please, sit. Wren would wring my neck if she thought I treated you as anything but royalty."

I took the offered seat. "What do you mean, royalty?"

She smiled as if she were offering to share in the joke, but it only made me more confused. Her eyes met mine for a long moment and I couldn't decide what unnerved me more—the purple lenses or the eyes behind them.

"Well…you've been around Wren a lot the last day or two, so I assumed something might be going on—"

I shook my head quickly, desperately dismissing the memories of that dream. "No! No! There's nothing going on between us. We're just—I mean—she's been really nice to me, and I didn't know anyone here and…" I drifted off, knowing I was rambling and protesting far too much. I glanced around the room to get an idea of something else to say. "So, what's with the glasses? Why the purple?"

She smiled again. "I have Irlen syndrome," she said, shrugging. "Fluorescent lighting gives me migraines. The glasses help with that."

"I've never heard of that before."

She chuckled. "Not a lot of people have. It's kind of a newer thing and there are a lot of scientists that don't agree or refute it. But hey, the glasses help, and I can still do my job to the best of my ability, so suck on that, stupid science gatekeepers."

Dr. Maru was a puzzle. Looking at her, I'd guess she was maybe in her early thirties at most, but the way she held herself spoke of someone older and more confident. Then she opened her mouth, and said that, and it made me take almost a decade off her age.

"So, you're friends with Wren?"

"It's a small town, you kind of get to know people. I was here when Wren showed up several years ago, wad of cash in hand, and looking to buy the diner."

"She just showed up?"

"Yup. Drove into town in a beat-up old station wagon, ratty clothes, and covered in dirt and grime. I swear the girl had been homeless for a while or something. I offered her a place to stay, just for a while, when she saw the For Sale sign on the old diner." She smiled. "I owned the building, and this girl just pulls out a huge wad of cash and asks to buy it! I didn't know what the hell to do!"

"So, you took the cash?"

She nodded. "Yup. Took what it'd cost me, not a penny more, and helped her find all the right people to get the place up and running again." Her eyes took on an almost faraway look. "It was so nice to see the diner put back together."

"What had happened to it?"

"One of the owners died. His husband didn't want to stay in town, so it closed down and he sold the building to me. It was a few years before Wren showed up." She smiled. "That girl had no idea how to run a business, never mind a diner. But we all chipped in, the whole town, and she was a damned quick learner to boot. Had the place up and running within four months."

I tried to read between the lines, to glean any sort of information about Wren that I could. I didn't want to stop Dr. Maru from talking about the past, but how much of this was Wren okay with me knowing?

I opened my mouth to speak, but it was cut short when she leaned forward, elbows on the desk, steepling her fingers.

"But enough about the past," she said. "What about you? Why are you in Terabend?"

I took an extra minute just to find my breath and steady my nerves. "I'm staying up at the Gale cabin. I work for Rory—Lorelai Gale. She gave me a vacation and let me stay at her cabin."

"Rory must be a good friend," Dr. Maru said. "People would pay good money to rent out a cabin like that one."

I raised an eyebrow. "Really? I've never actually thought about it. I've never even been outside the city before."

"And how are you liking being closer to nature?"

I remembered the injured wolf. "It's not so bad, but I feel there's a lot I don't know."

Her eyes locked onto mine and I could almost feel myself drowning in the purple tint.

"So are you enjoying your vacation? Is it serving your purpose?"

"I'd like to think so," I said, unable to look away. I hesitated, unsure if I should say more before continuing. "I kind of...lost myself. In another person. And when it ended, I didn't know who I was supposed to be. I couldn't be that person anymore, but I didn't know how to be anyone else. It was starting to affect my work, and Rory, well, she told me to come out here and find myself."

She smiled. "And have you?"

I started to shake my head but stopped. "Maybe? I don't think so, not yet anyway. But I hope I'm on my way."

She leaned back and the tension between us snapped like a rope pulled too taut. "I hope so, too," she said, then glanced toward the door. "Come in."

The receptionist didn't look surprised at all as he opened the door, glancing between the two of us. "The sheriff is out looking for Wren. Meg is awake and asking for her." He nodded to me.

Dr. Maru's eyebrows shot up. "Really? She's awake already?" She glanced aside with a quiet word, then got out of the chair. "Thank you." He nodded again and left back down the hallway as I stood.

"Can I see her?"

"For a minute or two. She still needs time to rest, but it should be okay."

Dr. Maru led me to the room across from the one where she'd originally brought Meg. She was lying on a large hospital-style bed with an IV in her arm and an oxygen line around her nose. She glanced at us with bleary eyes and smiled.

"Natalie, right?" Her voice was barely louder than a croak.

"Yeah, that's me."

She glanced behind me at Dr. Maru and gave her a small nod. I don't know what passed between them, but the good doctor gave us some space. I walked up beside the bed, taking Meg's non-casted hand in mine. Her other arm had a cast that ran from thumb to elbow, one of her legs had another one that sat mostly over and around her knee joint, and the number of bandages and Steri-Strips I could see almost made me gag. The poor girl. Why did all this happen to her?

"I wanted…" she said. She seemed to lose her voice as she gulped for more breath. "I wanted to thank you. And Wren. Both." She looked around as if expecting to see her boss.

"She's not back yet, but the sheriff is out looking for her," I said. "And you don't need to thank me. We were just doing the right thing."

She shook her head and grimaced. "No. Wren was. She always does. But you came too, even if you weren't a part of this."

I looked around as if wary about eavesdroppers. "What is this about? Why did those people hurt you? Take you?"

"I don't know. I was getting ready for work this morning and they just kicked in the back door. I was so…panicked, I couldn't do anything!" She stopped and took a deep breath as I rubbed circles into her hand with my thumbs. I wanted to be comforting. "Until the tall one grabbed me. Then I struggled and fought back." Her eyes glazed over a little like she was lost in a memory. "Then the other guy hurt me. And he talked about Wren. About taking her down a peg. Showing her who was boss or something? I don't know."

I hesitated. "Do you think this only happened because you work for Wren?" I didn't want to sound accusatory, or blame her for anything, but that's what this sounded like. Then I remembered what Wren had said before, acting like it'd been her fault the whole time.

"I mean, maybe? It's not like it would stop me from being with her anyway."

At those words, my heart sank. There was only one thing *being with her* could mean. Clearly, I'd been barking up the wrong tree this morning. And last night. And yesterday.

Her eyes caught mine and she looked a little confused. "I love working for Wren. She's a great boss. She always listens when we have a problem and helps us with scheduling if something comes up. I wouldn't be here if it weren't for her."

I nodded along, trying not to let the pang of heartache cross my face.

"And shit," she scoffed, then followed it with a couple of coughs. "I don't know why they took me. It's not like I'm her girlfriend or anything." She gave me a look that made me all too uncomfortable. "I'd say you've got a better chance of that than I do."

I stared at her. "Wait, what?"

"I've seen the way she looks at you, how she acts around you," she said, smiling a tired little smile. "It's not every day she not only goes out of her way to tell us to get you anything you want on the house, but also makes a date to cook you supper."

"I...I mean...that's not...we were just..."

She pulled her hand out of my grasp and waved it tiredly. "Just calling it like I see it. Whatever happened, I'm glad she had you watching her back. And mine." Her eyes slowly started drifting closed. "Thank you, Natalie."

I stood over her, staring at the now-sleeping woman. "You're welcome," I whispered, then turned and ran out the door. I was through the waiting room and out of the clinic before Dr. Maru or anyone else could stop me. I dropped Wren's keys on my way out the door. I didn't want to take them with me. But I couldn't be there right now.

I shouldn't have come out this morning, shouldn't have gone after Wren. What the hell was I doing? Getting involved with someone else right now? I mean, I was supposed to be here to find myself, not shack up with some chick who clearly had a hell of a lot more going on than she wanted to tell me about. Who the hell was she in this hick town to earn one of her workers getting beaten and kidnapped, and then going after them herself without calling the police?

I must be losing touch with reality. That was the only rational answer to all this. I didn't know how to live without Misty, so I was starting to lose it. Fuck it all, this might even still be a dream. Maybe I was still in the cabin, curled up on the floor next to the wounded wolf. Or in bed! Maybe the wolf was a dream too! I didn't know what was real anymore.

"Back to the cabin," I told myself. I remembered the streets that led back to the highway, and right across it was the clinic truck, still parked in the diner lot. I bumbled my way across the road, jumped in the truck, and pulled out as quickly as I could, flooring the accelerator until the truck started to shake from the abuse.

It was time to pack and leave. I couldn't stay here with Wren, but I didn't want to get back to Rory and have her tell me I didn't try hard enough. I shook my head. Enough of this. It was time to get my stuff and get out of here. Whatever came after that, well, I'd figure it out as I went.

And Wren, well, I guess she could have whatever mob life she was a part of. I needed to find me. Somehow.

CHAPTER SEVENTEEN

Wren

I warred with myself about how to get back to town. On the one hand I could move fast, even in human form, and taking the woods would get me back rather quickly. But the problem was Heather, who couldn't move as fast as I could, and the fact that I didn't want to risk being seen either partially shifted and carrying the girl, or leaving her in the dust moving at my top speed even in human form. This meant traveling at a quick walk along the roadside, hoping someone might come along to pick us up.

At least the company wasn't too annoying. Heather kept right on my tail, no grumbling or complaining, which was surprising. She still hadn't said what Jason had promised them, or told them, to get them to take Meg, but it was clear he didn't have Heather's loyalty in the traditional sense. She looked like someone who'd been kicked so many times that she didn't know whether to accept a helping hand or bite it.

If I were a regular werewolf in a regular pack, I would say that she hadn't found her place yet. She wasn't an Alpha, but she didn't seem to stand out as anything else either. Not that most wolf shifters had any special hierarchy embedded in our bones. Other than Alphas, as far as I knew the idea of dominants and submissives was only something that old pack culture pushed on their wolves. But damn if there wasn't still something off about Heather, and the longer I kept her scent in my nostrils, the more I felt certain that she was corrupted somehow.

But that wasn't for me to pry into. Everyone deserved privacy, to live their own lives. That's what was missing from most of pack life. Always being surrounded by other people who all seemed to have a say in your life. All because you were considered pack or family. There were plenty of reasons pack life wasn't for me, and that was one of them.

"Tell me about Jason, about what's going on," I said. My voice filled the silence of the empty highway. "What pack did you come from?"

She shook her head as she moved up next to me. "We were in the Cardinal pack, down south. I don't know a lot. I was really low in standing so no one ever really talked to me." She looked away from me, letting her light brown hair fall over her face. "Callum was a little higher than me, but neither of us were anything special."

"So, he went looking for expendable wolves," I said, not surprised. I'd grown up in the Cardinal pack and knew exactly how a lot of those wolves operated.

"I guess so."

The asphalt rumbled beneath us as a semi roared by, spraying up dirt. Heather cried out and I spun. I pulled her into me and shielded our faces. She clutched hard to me, and I had to resist the urge to shake her off. She trembled a little, eyes shut tight, and I tightened my grip on her. Okay. Maybe I had a soft spot for strays somewhere deep down inside, but that didn't mean she was going to get off lightly with what happened to Meg. I'd make sure of that.

"Tell me what happened at Meg's."

"I didn't want to do it. I stood back for most of it. Jason kicked the door open, and he and Callum went for the girl. He yelled at me to grab her, but I refused. I didn't get involved in this to hurt innocent people, especially not humans."

"Why did you come with him?"

"He promised to help me."

Another car started to pass, then screeched to a halt, throwing up another spray of gravel as it pulled onto the shoulder. Twin bulbs on top of the old model Ford flashed in alternating red and blue as an older man climbed out. His stark blue uniform was pressed and creased in all the right places with a shiny badge pinned to his chest.

"Zeke," I said, giving him a polite nod.

"Wren." His frown deepened when he looked between Heather and me. "Was told you got in a bit of a dustup."

"Nothing I couldn't handle."

His eyes narrowed at Heather. "Clearly." He glanced around then lifted his head, sniffing the air. "Please tell me there's no need for a cleanup crew this time."

I grimaced. "No, not this time."

Heather stepped forward with a low growl. "Back off."

A red glow bled into his eyes as he snarled, showing rows of sharp, shark-like teeth. I threw an arm between them but had to be impressed that she didn't back down from him.

"Mutt," he snapped.

"Corpse-eater," she said with a snarl.

"Enough." I came between them. "Are you going to give us a ride back to town or not?"

One second. Two. Three. Then Zeke backed off a step and nodded to the police car. "Get in the back," he growled. "Doc Maru asked me to pick you up."

He opened the back door, and I pushed Heather in before getting in behind her. Zeke got in and pulled off the shoulder and performed a tight U-turn to head back to Terabend.

"Natalie got there with Meg okay?" I asked him.

"Sounds like it. I got a call to come and pick you up. Said something was going on. Is there anything I need to be made aware of?"

I hesitated. It was my affair, and the ghoul who was the sheriff of our county didn't need to know about it. But if this ended up all too much for me, then someone had to make sure the people of Terabend were going to be okay. Besides, if things got over my head, it was definitely something that would get back to Hikaru—and Zeke.

"Some asshole is trying to make waves. Werewolf business."

He snarled. "If this business affects the people of the town, then it's my business, too, Wren."

"I'll handle it."

"Before or after there's bodies to be taken care of?"

"I'm not asking you to do that."

"You don't get it, do you?" He glanced back over his shoulder to give me the stink eye. "Do you have any idea what I had to do when you showed up here? Half-beaten and starved with wolves on your trail?"

I ignored the shocked look from Heather and focused on the sheriff. "I did what I had to do, and I already apologized more than once. They kicked me out. They came after me even when the Alpha told them not to. I didn't ask for all this bullshit! All I want to do is live my own life!"

"You are an Alpha werewolf," he said. "You will never have your own life."

My fists clenched tight enough that several knuckles popped. And yet I couldn't argue with him. "I'll keep myself out of all of it as long as I damned well can." I knew I sounded like a petulant child, but there was nothing else to say.

"And the people living in town? Or that nice girl staying at the Gale cabin? What about them?" He slammed a hand on the steering wheel. "What kind of collateral damage are you willing to risk just so you can have your own life?"

"I'll never let anyone hurt Natalie."

"And if you're not there? Like you weren't with Meg this morning?"

"Fuck you! You fucking ghoul!"

He gave me a hard look through the mirror. "We are what we are, Wren. One of these days you'll have to come to terms with that."

I sat back, arms crossed, and fell silent. Heather gave me a curious look but was smart enough not to pry. Which I was thankful for, more than she would ever know.

❖

Hikaru was waiting for us as we pulled in beside my Jeep. It looked a little dirty from the crappy road, but it seemed Natalie had made it back without any issues.

"It's about time," she said, taking my hand. "She's resting, and we need to talk."

I turned back to Zeke and Heather. "Stay in the car," I told Heather. "I don't want her to see you."

Heather lowered her eyes, her hands still on the door. "Yes, Alpha."

The title made me twitch and Zeke raised an eyebrow.

"Don't." I warned him before we headed inside. "Hikaru, is she okay?"

Hikaru gave me a hard look. "She is lucky, my friend. But if something like this happens again…"

"I'm going to make sure it doesn't."

She gave a short nod before leading me into her office at the back of the clinic. Zeke followed me, closed the door, and leaned back against it.

"Sit." Hikaru indicated the chairs in front of her desk. I knew better than to argue with her. One of the chairs smelled like Natalie, like she'd just been sitting in it, and I took that one. Even without her in the room, that scent made my wolf perk up and try to run in circles. I felt my senses heighten, and Hikaru's eyes narrowed.

"I never meant for something like this to happen, you both know that." They gave each other a look that I couldn't read, but it didn't make me feel any better. I knew I'd brought this trouble to town. I'd put us all in a situation they wouldn't be in if I weren't here.

"Wren, we are more than aware of that," Hikaru said. Zeke gave a grunt of acknowledgment, which was more than I thought he'd give. "And you do need to understand that we are here to help if it is required."

"Speak for yourself," Zeke said. I glared at the ghoul, knowing too well that if push came to shove, I couldn't fight him and his family. And when they were done with me, no one would ever find even a piece of my body.

She glared at him. "This is our town, our sanctuary, too. You are not alone in this."

I shook my head. "I get that, but this is my problem. I need to settle it."

"It'd be settled if you left the county," Zeke said.

"Ezekiel! Enough!"

"We had no problems here for decades!" The low growl in his voice rumbled around the room. "Then this mutt shows up, and we've had wolves and worse sniffing around like we're an all you can eat buffet!"

I glared at him. "It's not like I've been inviting them to fuck with me!"

"Zeke! If you can't keep a civil tongue in your head, then get out!" He grunted but didn't leave. Hikaru turned back to me. "Listen, Wren, this isn't an attack on you, and I'm not saying you need to leave or anything, okay?"

"Okay, I'm listening."

"We—"

Zeke coughed, and Hikaru shot him another glare. "I am only worried about you. We have worked hard to make this place our sanctuary, a home for those who don't want to deal with the difficulties inherently found in most of the human world. It's why we—I accepted you here with the rest of us. I do not blame you for the trouble that is coming down upon us. It was inevitable at some point anyway."

"It wasn't supposed to happen," I said, unable to keep the shakiness out of my voice. "Ronan promised he would leave me alone if I left. You know I never meant to bring anything down on anyone else. I wanted to be safe here. To just have a life." I hung my head. "I didn't mean for Meg to get hurt just because she works for me."

"Things don't always work out the way we wish them to." She sat forward in her chair, tilting her head until I could see the blood-red irises over her purple glasses.

"We have covered your ass for years," Zeke snarled.

"I am aware of that."

"These are not the first wolves to come here and try to start something."

"None of them attacked a human, though! Whatever is happening now is new."

"Zeke, just say what you need to," Hikaru said.

He looked almost sheepish to be put on the spot like that. "I'm just saying that we never had this much trouble until she showed up!"

"Then why don't you just kick me out?"

Hikaru raised her hands. "No one would do that, and you damned well know it."

"Vadi would," Zeke muttered.

Vadi was the genius loci who basically ran the town. I'd only talked to them a handful of times since they decided I could stay here. I still didn't know exactly what they could do, but they knew about what was happening in their town at all times, and I feared doing something that would bring their wrath down on me.

"Look, I'm sorry," I said, "you know I never meant to bring my problems with me."

"We don't want you to leave, Wren. Neither does Vadi. We just want you to be safe," Hikaru said.

"You all would be safer without me."

"Enough with the self-pity. This isn't all your fault." She glared at Zeke, who opened his mouth to say something, but she cut him off. "But there is something else we need to talk about."

I tilted my head. "What do you mean?"

"Zeke." The name came out as a command. Zeke grunted again and then left the room, his heavy footsteps moving away from the office. She turned back to me. "We need to talk about what you're doing with that young woman."

I stiffened. "Meg? I'm not doing anything with her, she works for me."

"No. Not Meg."

My hands clenched the arms of the chair. "I'm not talking about this with you."

Her grin showed off sharp fangs in the corners of her mouth. "We are talking about this right now. Because you need to hear it and you need to make a decision before it's too late to go back."

I waved a hand. "She's just another fling. Like all the rest have been."

"That's bullshit and you know it. Her scent is all over you. And you involved her in what happened this morning. You know better than to do that with someone who doesn't know about our world."

I shook my head. "I really do not want to talk about this with you. I can't."

"Why not?"

"Because it is none of your business. Natalie and I are grown-ass adults. What happens between us is between us."

"I'm not asking for sordid details. I just need to know if this is going to jeopardize what we've all been trying to build here."

"You know I wouldn't risk us like that. I would never."

"I know you wouldn't mean to."

I slammed a hand on the desk. "I know, I know—she's attached! We're connected. I felt it the night we met but didn't even want to consider it. And she was in my dream, and she pulled a silver bullet out of my shoulder…"

"What?"

"She didn't see anything!"

"How the hell did she pull a bullet out of you without seeing anything?"

I fidgeted. "Well, I mean I was a wolf at the time." I told her the story, about hurrying away from the cabin to shift, then sticking around because I didn't want to be far. How I hadn't gotten a scent from the hunters at all, and that the pain of the bullet was so much that I couldn't really remember much else from the night. "So, I had to fill in the blanks with what I gleaned from Natalie the next morning. You know she's pretty good at what she does. I mean she got that bullet out really well."

Hikaru only stared at me. "Are you fucking kidding me right now?"

"She doesn't know what I am!"

"Are you fucking kidding me?" She leapt to her feet, glasses falling to the desk as blood-red stains ran down from her eyes, over her cheeks, and down her neck. I froze, knowing now exactly what a deer felt like when it could smell the wolves nearby. "Not only did you not bother to tell me that you were shot with a silver bullet by hunters on the night of the full moon, but you let a *human* operate on you for it? Do you have any idea what we'd have to do if she saw you shift?"

I shot to my feet, slamming my hands on the desk. My wolf growled through my mouth, "Don't you dare threaten my fucking *mate!*"

I slapped my hands over my mouth when I realized what I'd just said. My wolf backed off as the heat under my skin cooled. Hikaru slowly regained her human form as I stepped away from her desk and stared out the window.

"Oh, sweet Mother of Wolves," I murmured.

"That about sums it up." I turned back to her as she sat down, slipping her glasses back on. "This is a very dangerous position to be in, Wren. For both you and her."

"Why? What does it even mean?"

"The fact that you have chosen her as your mate?"

I nodded. "But I didn't exactly choose her. I mean my wolf did, and don't get me wrong, I like her enough, but I mean, my mate? I—"

"If your wolf has chosen Natalie, then it will be difficult to change the beast's mind. They tend to get focused on these things."

"Would that…would that explain my dream?"

"What dream?"

"I had a dream of her last night, after I left the house. After she patched up my wolf. I thought it was just…just a dream. Is this… more Alpha stuff?"

Hikaru shook her head. "More a mate thing than an Alpha thing. I wouldn't be surprised if she was having dreams of you too."

I stared at her. "How do you know so much about shifters?"

"I know a little about a lot of things, my dear. Just enough to be dangerous."

"What does it mean, Hikaru?"

"That's not an easy question to answer. Wolves tend to be monogamous, and the shifters often follow this as well. Your wolf has chosen Natalie, and she wouldn't have done so without knowing that you want her, too. You are in sync with your wolf, as you should be. And you both have chosen what you want, even if you don't wish to believe it."

"But it's…it's taboo. I mean, she's human. I can't mate with—"

My words failed when my gut twisted suddenly. Inside my head, my wolf howled in agony, and I crumpled to my knees.

"Wren!" Hikaru shouted and was at my side in a blink. I clutched at my stomach, moaning as she put her hands on my back. "Breathe, Wren, keep breathing."

"What is happening?"

"I don't know, but you need to focus, okay? Breathe and focus."

"I don't…I don't get it!" Closing my eyes, I focused on trying to calm the wolf down. Her howling wasn't helping things. *Mate!* she howled. *Mine!*

Then I realized this wasn't coming from me. It was Natalie. Her panic. Her fear. Her pain.

"Natalie!" I screamed, throwing Hikaru off and heading for the door. "Where is she?"

Hikaru recovered and followed me. "I think she headed back to the diner."

I sped out the door, forgoing the Jeep and running as fast as I could back to the diner. I slammed open the door hard enough to rattle the glass.

"Wren!" Leslie yelped, barely holding on to the coffee carafe. "What the hell?"

"Is Natalie here?"

She shook her head. "Who's that?"

I growled and slammed a hand onto the bar. "The truck that was parked out here this morning, the vet clinic truck. Where did it go?"

Leslie's eyes were wide and staring, but she pulled herself together. "It left an hour ago, maybe a little less. No one came in here."

"Shit!" I turned to walk out.

"Wren! What happened to Meg?" Leslie called out after me.

"I'll tell you later." I didn't give her a chance to argue. I was out the door and sprinting around the side of the building. A quick glance around told me I was alone, and I allowed the wolf inside to take control. With a single long howl, we took off in the direction of the cabin, leaving shreds of clothing behind. All I could do was hope Natalie was all right.

CHAPTER EIGHTEEN

Natalie

It took everything in me not to turn the truck around and head back to Dr. Maru's office to wait for Wren. She was going to be okay. They had someone out there looking for her. I knew I couldn't sit there and wait for her, though. Being around all those people who knew her and knew this town and would sit and look at me like they expected something. I'd only disappoint all of them. Especially Wren.

I pulled onto the gravel road that led to the cabin, and a few minutes later, I parked the pickup. The cabin was familiar now and felt almost comfortable compared to being back in Terabend. There weren't any other people here, just me and the cabin and some peace and solitude. I'd enjoy it for the rest of the day, then pack up my stuff and head back to the city in the morning. If I timed it right, Rory would be at the clinic when I showed up at the condo. I could grab my things and get the hell out of there. Maybe change my name and disappear.

In some ways, it wouldn't be the first time.

The truck was barely parked before I was out and hauling ass into the cabin. I leapt over the bloodstain on the carpet and almost slipped on the hardwood floor. Luckily, I caught myself before I face-planted. The place was still a mess from Wren cooking breakfast and my quick wake-up and departure. I itched to focus purely on packing and getting ready to get the hell out of this place, but I couldn't leave it all a mess. It wasn't fair to Rory.

The rug was probably a lost cause, but I threw it in the bathtub and hosed it down with the showerhead anyway. Letting the heavy thing soak, I returned to the kitchen, cleared the plates, and filled the sink to start washing.

Washing dishes was a cathartic experience. It had been my chore when I was a kid, and one of the few times my parents left me to my own devices. The same thing had happened with Misty—she cooked and I cleaned up afterward. We'd had a dishwasher, but I almost always did it by hand. It was soothing. Pleasing. Something I could do without thinking, without worry.

As I slipped into that comfortable mind space, my breathing evened out and my eyelids got a little heavy. The only thing missing was my earbuds for some music, but I couldn't remember if I'd even packed them.

Wren. What the hell was I going to do? And why the hell couldn't I keep my mind off her? I tried to relax and there she was, the first thing my thoughts went to. I went to sleep, and I dreamed of her and a wolf and the trees. I shivered at the memory, a fork slipping out of my fingers. Even being away from her there was a faint ache in my chest, like my heart missed her. With my mind quiet, my body going through the motions, it was like I could feel her even more strongly. Anger and worry, exactly what I should be feeling about being with her.

The cabin suddenly shook as something hit the back door. It splintered, flying into the cabin to crash into the couch. I whipped around and the steak knife I was washing sliced into my hand as I screamed. A stocky man in a fringed leather jacket and a lazy fauxhawk stomped through the door, a wicked smile on his face.

"Find the mutt!" he shouted as I squeaked. He spun on me, feral eyes freezing me in place. "And anyone else who's here."

His voice shunted me out of my terror, and I threw myself backward out of his reach.

"Fuck off!" I screamed and sprinted around the island to head for the front door.

It burst open, and another large man with wild eyes stormed in with a growl. He ignored my yelp of surprise as he grabbed at me. I ducked under his arms and twisted past him and dashed out the door.

"Idiot!" the other man shouted. "Get her!"

I threw myself down the steps and toward the truck—but realized I hadn't grabbed the keys. I changed directions and headed for the trees. Footsteps behind me got louder and I screamed again, desperate for someone else to hear me. Anyone else.

"Wren!" I cried out. "Please! Wren!"

The words echoed out into the ether, unanswered. I hit the tree line a second later, slowing enough to make sure I didn't trip over jutting roots or slippery undergrowth. The trees slipped by in a blur as I moved as if I were born to run through the forest. I leapt over a fallen log and landed easily on my feet and kept running. I had never felt anything like this before—I felt exhilaration rise through my fear. It was almost like I wasn't being chased by large men who seemed to have something against me.

I froze when the hairs on the back of my neck stood up. I spun around, deaf from the silence of the trees. Not even the wind was blowing. A rustle jolted me back into action and I took off deeper into the forest. Now I could hear the bastard behind me, laughing and shouting things I couldn't make out.

I was done being chased. I ducked under a low-hanging branch, then stopped and spun. The branch was sharp against my fingers, but I held on tight, pulling it until the damned thing was ready to snap. The countdown began in my head as I heard movement coming closer.

Three. The footsteps slowed.

Two. Laughing and growling.

One. I released the branch.

It whipped around and poleaxed my pursuer with a sickening crack. I didn't wait around to see the results. I took off again and I tried to keep my mind on my breathing. With no one behind me, I began to calm down. Keep the mind clear, keep the head up. My father would tell me that every time we went out into the woods.

I shook my head. Never thought I'd want his advice after I ran away, but desperate times called for desperate measures.

In a blink, a man was in front of me. By the time my brain registered what I was seeing, it was too late. Huge arms wrapped around me as I slammed into his chest. With a scream, I pushed against him. It was like trying to push over a tree.

"I got her!" he roared, glaring down at me.

I went limp in his arms, surprising him, then slammed my heel down on his instep. He let out a howl and I slipped out of his grip, spinning around and getting back into the trees. A few seconds later, with the asshole breathing down my neck, I found the pathway back to the cabin and put on a burst of speed.

Wren had to be coming, right? She said she wouldn't let anyone hurt me. But how could she know? She was probably just getting back to town and had enough on her plate with Meg. I needed her. But there was no way she'd know that.

"Please, Wren," I implored her as I hit the clearing and headed for the cabin. "Please, find me. Help me. Oh, Goddess, please."

Then something cracked against my head, and I fell into pure, empty darkness.

❖

"Shit!" My eyes snapped open as something smacked my cheek. "What the fuck?"

The man in the leather jacket stood over me. My cheek throbbed and the asshole smiled and waved his hand in the air like it hurt.

"Wakey, wakey, princess. We need you conscious for this next part."

"What the hell do you want from me?"

He laughed. "From you? Nothing at all." He pulled me off the ground by my shirt, thrusting his face into mine. "No, princess, I'm waiting for your little girlfriend to show up."

I shook my head. "I don't have a girlfriend!"

His nostrils flared. "Her scent is all over you." He took a big sniff of air over me. "More than that diner bitch we dealt with this morning."

I gasped. "You? You took Meg?"

He grunted. "Your girl needs to learn her place in this world. No more running. No more hiding. She's going to learn what it is to be a wolf."

Wolf? What the fuck was this guy on? "What the fuck are you talking about?"

"Poor princess, left in the dark about your precious wolf." He tapped me lightly on the cheek and I flinched. "She hasn't told you a damned thing about all this, has she?"

"Who the hell are you? Why are you doing this?"

He grinned and inclined his head in a mocking bow. "Of course, how rude of me, princess. I never introduced myself." He grabbed my arm and pulled my hand to his lips, placing a kiss there. "Jason Reid. Let's just say that Wren and me? We're old family. Family that she decided to run away from."

"I don't blame her!" I shouted as I tried to push away, and he let go, letting me fall back to the ground. I coughed and labored to fill my lungs with air, when I saw the third man, the one who'd chased me into the forest, walk out of the trees. He was scraping blood off his face, and when his hand lowered, I noticed his nose was badly crooked.

"What the bloody hell happened to you?" Jason demanded.

"She hit me with a branch!" The henchman's voice was almost comically nasal.

Both Jason and his man who'd chased me out of the woods doubled over with laughter. I steeled myself and climbed to my feet as fast as I could. Dizziness overcame me, but I got several feet away before something wrapped around my arm and yanked me back hard. With a scream, I swung at the asshole holding me and smacked Jason in the face. His grip only tightened, and I gasped.

"Big mistake, princess," he snarled. "See, I was going to let you get away with messing up poor Manny's nose like that. I mean, it is bloody hilarious." He shook his head. "But then you hit me. That's going to cost you."

I spat at him and missed his face by scant inches. "Fuck you!"

He smiled, and then twisted my arm until something cracked.

My scream echoed through the clearing. My eyelids got heavier, and I fell to my knees with another shriek as he let go of my arm. Blood dripped from around my elbow, and I cried out again.

"Aww, it's not that bad," Jason said, "it's not like you don't have an extra one!"

I sniffled around the tears and my runny nose as I tried to focus on breathing. I'd had worse, I told myself. I'd survived worse. I survived my father, and my family turning on me. I survived Misty. This was not going to beat me.

"She's going to kick your ass," I said. I hoped there was some sort of menace in my voice. "Wren is going to fucking kill you."

They all laughed. I swung wildly with my good arm but came

nowhere near them. Something smashed into my head. I screamed as I fell onto my side. I tried to drag myself away from them. I tried to push the pain away, to compartmentalize it like I'd done so many times. My vision blurred as pain spread in the back of my head.

I tried and tried to focus on nothing but Wren. I could feel her. In my gut, I could feel her.

She was coming.

I only hoped it would be soon enough.

CHAPTER NINETEEN

Wren

My ground-eating lope through trees and across fields took me unerringly in a single direction.

Wren! Please!

I could hear her voice in my mind and it drove me forward, faster. She was hurt. Scared. She needed me.

And I wasn't there yet.

The growl rumbled from deep in my throat as I pushed harder, faster. Outside of Terabend, the trees thinned and I leaped the fences of another farmer's field before entering the shadows of more trees. My shoulder ached from the still-bloody wound from last night, but I pushed the pain away.

Faster. I needed to go faster. Natalie's scream echoed in my head, and I let out a howling bark into the air.

Then the trees ended and the cabin appeared in the middle of the clearing. Voices reached my ears and unfamiliar smells made my snout twitch as I slowed. Four—no, five—distinct smells. Four wolves. And...

Natalie!

As much as my wolf wanted this fight, I needed to do this a different way. When I reached the cabin I shifted back to human form, panting heavily. Blood ran down my shoulder and I knew I needed to do something about it, but not yet. Not until I knew Natalie was safe. Instead, I let the pain fuel my anger and stormed around the corner. I stopped only a handful of meters away from a horrible scene.

"Get the hell away from her," I roared. Natalie was on the ground, clutching her bloody arm and cringing away from Jason.

Two other shifters I didn't recognize flanked him. All of them turned to me as I spoke. Natalie's eyes widened. I took another step forward. "Natalie, it's okay. I'm here to help."

Her mouth dropped open. "Wren—" She screamed when Jason planted his foot in her side, and she rolled away with a gasp. His eyes never left mine as his lips spread into a sinister smile.

"Mutt! Nice of you to finally join us!"

Another step forward, the grass tickling my bare feet. "Whatever this is between us, keep it between us. You don't bring humans into our world like this!"

"Who gives a shit?" he snarled back. "Humans are expendable! And if you can't defend your lands, then maybe you shouldn't have them."

The others laughed at his words, and I took a quick survey of the area. Three wolves, plus Natalie. There was one missing. It didn't matter, though. I needed to end this here and now.

"Natalie," I said as I caught her eye and held it. "I'm sorry."

"Wren…" she began, but her breath hitched as I pushed my body to start to shift. Her eyes went as wide as dinner plates as fur sprouted up and down my arms and legs, around my chest and belly and upper thighs. The hair on my head grew longer and became mane-like, as my teeth elongated and sharpened to create wolf-like fangs. Razor-sharp claws burst out of my fingertips and silvery fur grew up to my elbows.

Immediately, the blood from my shoulder started to drip into my fur, but I ignored it. I focused on the wolves in front of me. The two with Jason weren't powerful enough to do the partial shift. Instead, they shifted fully into their wolf forms, and both growled at me from the safety of being on the other side of their prisoner.

"This ends now!" I growled and sprang forward. The wolves charged and one leaped over Natalie. He was an idiot. I sidestepped and caught his throat with one hand. I grabbed the scruff of his neck with the other and tore his throat out in one swift yank and tossed his body to the side. My shoulder flared in pain, but I pushed it aside and rolled away from the pounce of the other wolf.

"Kill the mutt!" Jason yelled, drawing a long-bladed knife from behind his back. Sunlight glinted off the metal and I knew all too well what it was coated in.

"Silver?" I growled, "You'd use silver against your own kind?"

He charged and slashed at me with the knife as I dodged the other wolf a second time. Jason was fast, but he was still in human form and was no match for my strength and speed.

"Still afraid of your wolf, Jason?" I taunted him. "C'mon, shift and come at me."

"I don't need to shift to kill you, bitch!" he shouted and lunged quickly. I sidestepped again and pulled his arm past me, which forced him to abandon his position or stab the other wolf. The wolf in question tried to close huge jaws on my leg, but I kicked him away and sent him flying halfway to the tree line.

Thunder cracked through the air, and I threw myself to the ground. A puff of dirt and dust shot out of the earth near my head, and I looked up. A man was perched on top of the cabin, a long rifle in his hands. I snarled and leaped up, moving closer to the cabin to get out of his line of sight.

"This is not how you claim territory! You aren't even an Alpha! How would you keep a pack together?"

"Somebody fucking kill her already!" Jason screamed.

I spun and dashed at him, came up inside his wild swing, and put a fist into his gut. He doubled over and the knife fell from his grip. I caught it by the handle in midair. The shifted wolf returned and lunged toward the easier target on the ground—Natalie.

"No!"

Faster than the shifted asshole, I was there before his teeth could come down on her as she curled into a defensive position. I held the blade but lashed out with my claws and scored a deep gash running from his neck to his rear. He whined and spun to flee when I grabbed him by the tail and heaved him upward and back down into the ground with a sickening crack. He stayed down and stopped moving.

Jason backed away to the tree line, panic and rage written all over his face. I began moving in his direction when his eyes flicked to the cabin's roof. Right. Sniper. I smiled at Jason and brandished his knife.

I rolled out of cover, came up quickly, and sighted on the sniper. He was just bringing the rifle around when I launched the knife. It tumbled end over end until it hit the man square in the chest and sank to the hilt. He sputtered a choking cry and tumbled backward. The rifle skittered along the slanted roof until it fell. I was there to catch it, and forced a quick shift in my front paws to make them a little more human and able to fit on the rifle.

Jason shouted something and started sprinting to the trees. I took a knee and brought the rifle to my shoulder. The scope was barely necessary with my enhanced senses in my partially shifted form, and I snapped it off before taking a deep breath and sighting down the barrel. In a single action, I breathed out and pulled the trigger.

Jason fell with a scream and writhed in the grass barely five feet from the forest and possible safety. I worked the bolt action, ejected the long case, and let the magazine load the next. I sighted down the weapon again and watched him try to drag himself through the grass toward the trees. Another crack split the air before he screamed again, brought to a halt with a finger touching one of the trees. I brought the rifle down over my knee hard and bent the barrel and broke the stock. I sauntered up to the wounded wolf, ready to make him pay for what he'd done.

I kicked Jason in the side then rolled him onto his back as he coughed out blood. Two massive wounds had all but destroyed his upper body, and I could see the skin under his tattered clothes turning a sickly gray.

"Silver bullets?" I snarled. "I can't believe any wolf would fall so far." I kicked him again for good measure, but he only laughed.

"Doesn't matter how it's done. As long as I win!"

"You're not an Alpha! You can't control a territory and you can't bond with a pack." I bent down, grabbed his shirt, and pulled him up slightly. "Where is your brother? Where's Craig? He's the one who sent you, isn't he?"

He spit blood at me, or tried anyway. It came nowhere near touching me. "Fuck you, mutt! This ain't over!"

I let my free hand shift, and the razor-sharp claws slid out of my fingers. I pulled him closer, ignoring the pain in my shoulder, and snarled. "It's over for you." His eyes flew wide as I buried my claws in his throat and ripped out pieces of whatever I could grab before leaving him to bleed out on the grass.

In a second, I was back near the cabin, moving to Natalie's

side. I shifted my hand back to normal, touching her softly on the shoulder. She shied away from me and a terrifying sound slipped out of her.

"Natalie..." I tried to sound soothing, but it was hard to do around teeth like mine. I focused on shifting them back too. It took longer than the hands. My emotions were still running high, and my wolf didn't want to back down, but she knew how much we needed to keep Natalie safe. And scratching the woman with my claws or terrifying her with my teeth was not the way to do that. "Natalie, it's okay. You're safe now."

Her eyes stared wide at me first, then darted around like she was trying to take everything in. Her mouth gaped open as her gaze focused on the bloody wound on my shoulder. It had reopened because of my race to get here, and the fight had made it worse.

"The wolf," she whispered, "the silver wolf."

I nodded, but my gut roiled nervously. "Yeah, that was me. I...I'm sorry."

I reached out to her with a bare but bloody hand. She screamed and threw herself backward with a shout of pain as she slammed her back into the cabin wall.

"I'm not going to hurt you! I promise I won't. Please, Natalie, let me help."

"Get away from me!" she screeched. "You...you...you..." Her voice drifted off and her eyes fluttered shut as consciousness fled her body all at once. I dashed forward and tried to support her before she could get hurt falling the rest of the way to the ground.

"Shit," I said under my breath. Then I heard the sirens in the distance. I picked up Natalie, being careful of her broken arm, and carried her back into the cabin. I pulled off the sheets on the bed and laid her down before I returned to the front porch. Zeke's police cruiser pulled up, along with an ambulance and a large, white unmarked panel van.

"Did we miss the party?" Zeke called as he got out of the car.

"Not by much." I gestured around to the back of the cabin. "Left some dessert for you and your boys, though."

He gave me a grim smile. "How thoughtful."

"You know me. Always thinking of my friends."

He scoffed and rounded up several of his people before heading around the cabin. The ghouls would gather up the bodies scattered around and put them in their refrigerated truck for transport. I was lucky that I'd never had to see their truly demonic visages when they decided to eat, but I'd heard the sounds once.

I'd had nightmares for a week.

Heather stepped out of the car next. She was watching me carefully as she followed them. If she ran, I'd know it. And I'd catch her. She wasn't in any shape to do it.

Out of the ambulance came Hikaru, who hurried up to the cabin. "Where is she? Is she all right?"

I opened my mouth, but nothing came out. Instead, I led her into the bedroom so she could take a look at my wounded human. It took her only a couple of minutes to examine Natalie. Hikaru winced sharply at some of the wounds and paid special attention to her arm.

Then she turned back to me with a small smile. "It's not bad," she began. "The arm will need to be reset and immobilized for a while, but the rest is relatively minor." She put fingers on Natalie's head and gently prodded around her ginger hair. "And I'll maybe run a CT scan for any head injuries. I'm worried about this contusion on her head."

I turned away from Natalie's body, laid out on the bed like that. "This was my fault," I whispered.

"Wren, don't do that to yourself. You couldn't have known this was going to happen."

I shook my head. "I don't care. I shouldn't have befriended her. I made her a target. I put her in a position to get hurt, and now look!" I flung my hand out in her direction. "All because I wanted to be friendly! To cook her some food so the poor thing didn't starve! This is why we don't get involved with humans!"

"Stop! If you want to get all pity party and woe-is-you, you do it later. Right now, I need your help to get her in the ambulance so we can take her back to the clinic. Got it?"

I didn't turn. "Can't you just, you know, give her your blood or something? Doesn't that heal humans?"

Something small but hard hit my shoulder. Hikaru's fist. "Healing the natural way would be best for her, you know that. I don't know what she's going to remember when she awakens, but this is not the right way for her to be introduced into our world. Giving her my blood is one of the last options I would reach for."

"Why?"

"Because if I give her too much she might turn. Do you want that? Taking that decision away from her and making her like me?"

I shook my head. "No. No, I don't. I just want her to be okay."

"Then help me make her okay."

I rubbed my hands over my face, trying to draw in a deep breath. Then I focused on the shift, letting my body return to its human form. "Okay," I whispered, "let's do this."

I helped Hikaru get the gurney and transfer Natalie onto it before putting her in the back of the truck. If anyone had an issue with me being naked, they didn't speak up. Which I was thankful for. Heather came around the corner as we were getting ready to leave, and climbed into the passenger seat with a determined look on her face.

"What are you doing?" I asked.

"Coming with you."

"Why?"

"Because you're my Alpha now."

I raised my eyebrows at her. "No, I'm not. I'm nobody's Alpha."

"You killed the asshole who held my leash. Now it's yours. If you want it."

"I don't! I don't want anyone's leash!"

"And that's exactly why I'm freely giving it." She took in a deep breath like she was trying to cleanse something from her body. "For the first time since I found out I was a wolf, I can give it to who I want to. You gave me that freedom. So, I'm sticking with you."

My hands clenched into fists on the steering wheel hard enough to make indents. Hikaru cleared her throat from the back. "Wren, maybe I should drive."

I didn't bother trying to argue. I slipped into the back to sit beside Natalie as Hikaru took the driver's seat. I ignored everything and everyone as we pulled out and headed back to Terabend. I took Natalie's hand in both of mine, clutched it tightly, and whispered a prayer to the Mother of Wolves that she would be okay.

And maybe, just maybe, she would see me as a woman. Instead of a monster.

CHAPTER TWENTY

Wren

Hikaru had been practicing in Terabend for a long time, and her clinic was probably almost as equipped as any small, regional hospital. It helped to have a small community of supernatural beings like myself in town, able to provide assistance, or to ensure we were the ones to get hurt over the humans. But, clearly, sometimes the humans got hurt too.

Meg was still resting in the smaller recovery room, the one that most of the town knew about. Me? I was sitting in an armchair in the other room, the one in the back that most of the town never saw. An IV was hooked into my arm and a bag of my own blood trickled down the line. It was supposed to help defuse the silver still in my system from the bullet, so that I could heal properly. We'd never had a reason to test the theory until now.

Natalie was still asleep, her broken arm held immobilized in a cast after Hikaru and I had reset the bone. Bandages covered her legs and arms and around her head.

There was no way my wolf was going to let her lie there alone. Hikaru had been nice enough to lend me a pair of scrubs, and let me tell you, I was seriously considering adding a theme to the diner—a hospital theme or something. These things were damned comfy.

My shoulder too had been repatched and rebandaged since shifting had destroyed the old bandage. Never mind it had been covered in blood from the fight in the woods. Looking back, I felt a sense of loss for ruining Natalie's work from the night before.

I shook my head, staring at the woman on the bed in front of me. Even injured, scared, and probably half-delirious, she'd still realized that I was the same wolf she'd operated on after seeing my fur and the shoulder wound. Would she remember when she woke up?

Did I want her to?

It'd be easier if she forgot. If this was just a random act of violence. Better still if she believed that I was into something dangerous. Then she'd stay far, far away from me, no matter how much it made my heart ache and my wolf go nuts with the mere thought. She scrabbled and clawed inside me, desperate to curl up with our proposed mate and lick her wounds clean.

I was about to agree with her when the door creaked open, and Hikaru entered on silent feet. She carried a large folder, a frown on her face as her eyes swept the room, finally coming to rest on me.

"Is she..." I took a breath. "Is she okay?"

Hikaru hesitated too long.

"What is it?"

She wouldn't look me in the eye. "It's not that simple," she said, closing her eyes. "Her arm will heal fine, and the minor injuries are nothing to worry about."

"But?" I prompted her when she fell silent.

"But there's something in her head." She opened the folder and pulled out a scan of something that looked kind of like a brain. "She has intracranial damage. She must've taken a blow or two to the head or something. It's making her brain swell and there's no guarantee she's going to come back from that."

My head snapped up and a growl rumbled from my chest. "No. That's not an option," I snarled. "What can we do? Surgery? Medications? What?"

"Wren, it's not that simple."

"Bullshit! They pull off miracle shit in hospitals all the damned time."

"Yes, Wren, in *hospitals*. I may be well equipped here—for good reason—but I can't pull off this kind of miracle alone."

"Okay, so we get her to a hospital."

She scoffed. "How? The nearest one is hours away and I can't promise you she'll survive the trip." She put the folder on the table beside the bed and turned to me. "Wren, I—"

"Don't!" I said. "Don't you fucking dare say she's going to die! I won't let her."

"What are you going to do? Turn her?"

I stared at her. "That's an option?"

She threw her hands in the air in frustration. "Well, yeah! I know you didn't learn how to be an Alpha from your old pack, but surely you know that Alphas can turn humans."

I shook my head. "If there's a way to save her, I'm going to damned well save her!"

As if hearing the argument, Natalie's body shifted, and her good arm twitched. We both stared at her, waiting for her to open her eyes, for her to say something, but there was nothing more. Either way, it gave both of us a moment to breathe.

"Wren, think about what kind of life she'd have if you did that," Hikaru said. "Think about what it would do to her. She doesn't even know what's going on, and she can't fully understand what you are! And you want her to wake up into this world with no say and no knowledge?"

I shook my head. "No! No, I don't want that, but I want her alive! I need her to be alive. To be okay. I need her, Hikaru." I slumped back down into the chair with my face in my hands. "I need her. I barely know her, and I need her."

"I know, Wren. I know." She let out a long sigh. "I can teach you how to turn someone—since you are Alpha, you can do it. But right now, I don't think it's the best idea."

I wanted to run out of the room, leave it all behind and let the wolf out to run, but I couldn't. I needed the additional blood, the IV. I could almost feel it working, cleansing my veins of the poison inside. The blood bag was about half empty.

Blood bag...blood...

I looked to Hikaru. "What about your blood?"

"What?"

"Your blood! Vampire blood heals humans, right? We talked about it back at the cabin."

She opened her mouth then closed it several times. "We went over this before. It's dangerous. There's a lot of problems that might come with me giving her my blood."

"She can handle it. She's stronger than we give her credit for." I looked to the woman who I wanted for my mate. "She's stronger than even she knows. She stood up to those assholes when she didn't even know what was going on."

"I get that, Wren, I really do, but you need to listen to me right now." She paused, taking a deep breath—something I supposed was left over from when she was alive. "There are risks. Risks that might not make it worth it."

"Like what?"

She ran a hand through her hair. "If I give her too much, she'll turn like I did. And we already decided we didn't want that."

"Okay, I get that. What else?"

"She could become addicted to it." My eyes went wide at the admission. "It's a thing, it happens. Like a drug. I've never had someone become addicted to mine, but I haven't been open to sharing it all that often, either."

I hesitated again. "Okay, yeah, um…"

"Oh! And let us not forget that giving her my blood will allow me a modicum of control over her mind, allowing me to speak with her in her head. And the more she takes, the stronger that connection."

"Fine!" I snapped. "Fine! It's a bad idea, I get that. But if she doesn't turn and she doesn't get addicted, and I can trust you won't abuse any sort of hold you have over her, and all of that, isn't it better than her having to live the rest of her life as a fucking werewolf? Not to mention that I don't even know how to pull it off."

"You may have a point. Though I'm surprised you're willing to risk anyone having any sort of mental influence on your mate."

I growled again. "I am trusting you here, Hikaru. And I want to save her life."

"If this goes bad, it's on you."

"Duly noted."

Hikaru grumbled but stepped to the bed anyway. She took her glasses off, then tapped Natalie lightly on the cheek. "Ms. Donovan? Ms. Donovan, can you hear me?"

Natalie's eyes fluttered weakly. No sound came out of her mouth, but she seemed to react. I wanted to run to her, but I kept my distance. The risk of her freaking out over seeing me was too great.

Her eyes opened just enough that Hikaru could meet them with her own blood-red ones. I could almost feel the power that flowed out of Hikaru's gaze as she said softly, "Natalie Donovan, I mean you no harm."

Natalie's head moved in a vague nod and Hikaru continued. "I need you to drink something. It will help you. But you must drink and swallow it. Understand?" Another nod. Hikaru brought her wrist to her mouth and cut it with a tooth. Blood welled up in the wound and she pressed it against Natalie's mouth. Natalie's eyes were still stuck on Hikaru's, but her mouth and throat moved to drink the vampire blood, and I had to look away.

It was for the best. It had to be. It was the only way to be sure she would survive.

And yet, deep down inside, it felt like I might've made the wrong choice.

CHAPTER TWENTY-ONE

Natalie

Hands and knees. Cowering. Curled up against the thick bark, cuddled by large roots and moss. Pain was everywhere. Every part of me felt like it was on fire. Jeans I wore for hiking, torn and bloody. T-shirt sharing the same damned fate.

The look on his face when he threw me down the hill. When he told them not to help me. When my family abandoned me. When I woke up in the hospital, guarded, told not to say a word about what really happened.

Then, standing over me, a man with a shitty haircut. Others, people I don't know. Chasing me through the trees.

And through it all, a wolf howling. A silver wolf. Huge. Red staining the fur on one front leg. She moved closer, came to me like there was no one else to move through. Everything else disappeared. Only her. Only the wolf.

And then she was gone, replaced with Wren, naked in all her glory. But not naked. No, there was fur running up and down her legs, her arms, her chest and back. Ears atop her head. Tail waving around behind her. Claws and fangs. Blood on her shoulder. Amber eyes staring down at me.

"Please," I whimpered, "please, don't leave me."

She knelt in front of me, sharp claws touching torn clothes.

"You and I," she whispered, "we're mates. We're pack."

I gasped in a massive breath of air and my eyes opened wide under harsh fluorescent lights. Inside my mouth tasted of old pennies. My heart beat almost out of my chest as I fought to relax, an itching feeling in the back of my head. Like someone was back there, whispering something. My eyes caught Dr. Maru in the corner, concerned eyes focused hard on me through her purple glasses.

Stay calm.

I twitched as the words reverberated in my head. The voice. It was Dr. Maru's, but it was in my head. I shook myself, running my hands over my face to try to clear my head.

"What the fuck?" It didn't make any sense. I know what I felt before, I know I saw the bone sticking out of my arm. But it was fine now. No marks, no scars, fully functioning. My head, my legs, everything that was hurt before was better. Better than better, I hadn't felt this good in years.

"Natalie." The whisper came from the corner of the room. Wren was in a plush armchair, an IV in her arm and nearly empty bag of blood on the pole.

"Wren…" I drank her in like a dying girl's final breath.

"Ms. Donovan." Dr. Maru appeared beside the bed, hands in plain sight. "How are you feeling?"

I glanced at her, then looked back to Wren. "I…did I dream all of that? I don't understand what happened."

"What's the last thing you remember clearly?"

I closed my eyes. "I left the clinic. After talking to Meg. I grabbed the truck from the diner and went back to the cabin."

"Anything after that?" Wren asked.

I looked between the two of them the intensity of the moment making me squirm. But worse was the feeling that they knew more than I did.

I shook my head. "Not really. Someone burst into the cabin, but it gets a little fuzzy after all that."

The way they glanced at each other told me everything. Something was up, and Wren was in the middle of it all. My memories and feelings came flooding back. That guy—Jason—wanted Wren to suffer. And then she showed up, all wolfed out. But I felt like she didn't want to talk to me about it now. Like they were both fishing for how much they'd have to say. If they had tried some kind of mind-trick-voodoo on me to take away my memories, I was going to be pissed.

"What is going on in your heads?" I demanded.

"What?" Wren asked.

"What?" Dr. Maru echoed.

"You're giving each other looks, and you want to know what I remember, and all this crap—" I gestured. "But no one is talking to me!" I yelled. "I have questions, too, you know! Like how my arm is fine? Or how I don't hurt at all after all that bullshit at the cabin today? And most of all, why you—" I pointed at Wren. "Why the hell you were covered in fur and claws and a fucking tail?"

"Ms. Donovan, please calm down."

"Don't tell me to calm down again!"

Dr. Maru raised an eyebrow. "I've only said it once."

"Then why the hell did I hear it before? When you told me to *stay calm* inside my head?"

They shared another significant look.

"Stop doing that!"

Dr. Maru shook her head. She looked almost sad as she went to Wren and pulled out the IV needle. "This is about done, dear. I'll leave you two to have a conversation."

I stared at Wren's arm. It barely bled at all before the puncture closed without even a scar.

"Thanks, Hikaru," she said.

"Don't thank me. You know there's no going back from this."

"I know," Wren said, and the doctor quietly left the room.

"What the fuck is going on?"

Wren found the wheeled stool that seemed to be a staple in the exam rooms and pulled it up beside me. I drew back as she brought one hand up to touch mine. The hurt look on her face was breaking my heart.

"Natalie, I'm sorry. I never meant for you to get caught up in all this. I just...I just..." She looked away and I could see tears falling. "I just wanted my own life. A life outside of everyone and everything else."

"Wren, what are you talking about?" The tears did me in. I couldn't stop myself from reaching out, tilting her chin up so I could look her in the eyes. "Please tell me what's going on."

She cleared her throat a couple of times and I patiently waited for her to begin.

"I'm a shifter," she said finally. She looked everywhere but at my face. "A wolf shifter. Most people call us werewolves and it fits, I suppose."

"So that silver wolf I saw," I murmured, "that was you." It wasn't a question, but Wren nodded anyway.

"Yes. It was." She shook her head. She lifted her shirt, showing off a nasty-looking wound in her shoulder. "It's why I left so abruptly after dinner. My wolf wanted—needed—to run. When I give her the reins it's like—"

"Like an escape," I whispered, "like being free from everything, if only for a little while."

Her eyes went wide. "Well, yeah. How did you know that?"

I grimaced. "Because I've spent years dreaming of that kind of escape. Anyone who wants a life *outside of everyone and everything else* either yearns for or knows the feeling." I didn't tell her that I could almost feel what she was trying to describe deep down in my gut. The way I'd felt her coming for me at the cabin, or the way it physically hurt when she left that morning without me. But that was all unreal, right? How could I be feeling these things?

She nodded slowly, with an understanding look in her eyes. "Yeah." She took a deep breath. "So, we were running and enjoying the night. Then the gunshots happened. I got lucky and they missed me until that last one that got me in the shoulder." She shook her head. "I've been shot before, but never like that. It was agony. But my wolf was stronger than me. She ran. I think I nudged her in your direction because I was sure you could help us."

"Because I work at a vet clinic."

"Yeah." She hesitated. "And for other reasons."

I raised an eyebrow. "What reasons?"

She shook her head again. "Anyway, you helped me. I couldn't shift before you pulled the bullet out and then you gave me that sedative. When I woke up you were passed out beside me, and I was half-shifted, and I knew I had to get out before you saw me. I put a blanket on you, took the bullet, and left. I went back to my Jeep and slept in the back."

"But I woke up in bed, not on the floor."

"Yeah, because I came back at first light and tucked you into bed. I needed to make sure there was no evidence of, well, of what I am."

I stared down at the bed for a long moment. "Then you made me breakfast."

"Then I made you breakfast."

I leaned back with a sigh. Mind racing, I had no idea what to think. I should be going nuts, getting angry at such a blatant retelling of a fucking fanfic or something! I mean, werewolves were real? What the hell?

But it was all just a little too rational. Too logical. After what I'd seen today, Wren with fur and those men turning into full-on wolves. The way Wren tracked Meg in a speeding car with only her nose. It all made sense.

"This is...I don't even know."

Wren smiled. "All things considered, you're taking it surprisingly well."

I laughed. "There are people in this world who are more likely to believe in what you are than what I am." I glanced down when her eyes darted to mine. "Oh shit. That slipped out."

"What does that mean?"

I shook my head. "Nothing. Nothing. Never mind. It's nothing." Now was not the time to tell her I was transgender.

"Natalie..."

"Wren, please. Not right now, okay? One massively world-shattering revelation is enough for today."

For a long moment I wasn't sure she'd agree, but then she nodded and let out a breath. "Okay, okay, I got you."

I heaved a sigh of relief. "Thank you." My gaze drifted over to Wren's face as she looked up at me from the low stool. Her beautiful green eyes, those gorgeous lips, a pert nose that looked out of place on her more rugged features. I glanced down to her mouth and couldn't help but wonder what it'd feel like to press my lips against hers.

"Natalie," Wren said.

My eyes swept back up. "Huh? What?" I shook my head. "Oh, yeah."

She smiled. "Did you have any more questions? I mean, I just told you that I'm a werewolf."

I gave her a shy smile. Maybe it was the adrenaline from today, or something else inside me, but this time when my eyes fell on her lips, I felt a surge of courage. "Wren…do werewolves…I mean… can werewolves…um…" I shook my head with irritation. "I want to know what it's like to kiss one."

She stared at me for a long moment, and emotions warred across her face. She stood and I leaned in, putting us at exactly the right height.

I don't know who moved first, but a second later our lips connected, and I was drawn deep into this mysterious woman. Soft, warm, with a hint of coffee in there. I melted into that kiss as it deepened, her tongue probing. I opened for her, letting her take me, take everything I could offer her.

And she did.

My mind flickered back to seeing her at the cabin door, bag of greasy food in her hand. She'd been on my mind since, the first thing I thought about when I got up, the last thing before I went to bed. Kind. Funny. Easygoing. And somehow, she seemed to want to spend time with me. I mean she offered to come over and make me dinner! Who does that if they aren't interested in a person?

And her lips. I ran my hands over her back as she gripped my hips, pulling me into her. I slid my fingers underneath her shirt, shivering as I caressed her bare skin. Her moan against my mouth sent flares of heat through my body, settling down in my core as I resisted the urge to thrust against her. A part of my mind warned me away from that action. I had my own secrets, and she wasn't ready for them. I wasn't ready to tell her.

My body didn't seem to care. Instead, as she drew her hand up my thigh, I couldn't control myself. I gasped as she kissed her way down my throat, my neck, my shoulder. She pulled the neck of my shirt aside and her lips touched my chest, a cluster of kisses at the top of my breast. Without thinking I slid my legs around and wrapped them around her waist, urging her closer as she groaned under my hands.

"Natalie." She breathed into my ear and used her teeth to pull lightly on the lobe as I cried out.

"Wren."

I thrust my hips forward into her, wanting to feel every part of me against every part of her. Wren moved her hand up farther, and then hesitated. She looked at me for permission to continue.

Oh shit.

"Ahem."

We leapt apart, my legs letting go as she moved a good three feet away. I sat up on the bed. Dr. Maru stood by the door, arms crossed over her chest, a smile playing on her face.

"I realize you two are intent to enjoy each other's company, but there are things we need to talk about, Ms. Donovan."

"Really? Like what?"

"I'm certain you noticed your lack of wounds," she replied. "And there might be a few other side effects of your healing that we need to discuss."

I glanced to Wren, who'd moved up beside me and rested her hand lightly on my shoulder. "It's okay," she said softly. "Hikaru knows what she's doing."

I nodded and sighed. A wave of exhaustion rolled over me and I closed my eyes for a moment. The image of the bed back in the cabin floated in my mind, enticingly soft and comfortable. A second later, Wren was on the bed in the cabin with me, our limbs entangled, our lips pressed together. I shivered.

"Okay." I moved my hand up to pat Wren's. "But only if Wren stays with me."

Dr. Maru smiled. "I wouldn't even consider otherwise." She came to the side of the bed with a small clipboard in her hands. "Okay, so, this is what you need to know." And she talked. I listened. And listened. And listened.

"Wait, so you're telling me that I could have been turned into a vampire?" I demanded, a little creeped out at this point.

"That was a possibility, but we both decided that it was worth the risk," Wren said.

I looked back and forth between them, feeling my temper rising again at the idea of people making decisions for me. I calmed myself with a few deep breaths. They saved my life.

"Is the blood why I could hear you in my head?"

Dr. Maru nodded. "That will fade in time—as long as you don't need more of my blood. I don't recommend it either."

"Because then you could turn me."

"Precisely."

I looked to Wren. "Can you turn people?"

She stared at me for a long moment before she turned to Dr. Maru.

"It's possible, but not widely done."

"Why not?"

Dr. Maru shrugged. "No idea. You'd have to ask the wolves."

I turned to Wren. "Don't look at me," she said. "Hikaru knows more about all this than I do."

I shook my head. This was just too damned much. I winced as pain shot through my forehead, and for a second, I thought I was about to have a panic attack.

Easy, Natalie.

I glared at Dr. Maru. "Out loud, please."

She had the decency to look sheepish. "Sorry."

"So, when can I get out of here?"

"I want to keep you for another hour or so, just to make sure my blood won't have any lasting effects."

I sighed, turning to Wren. "Are you sticking around?"

She gave me a smile and took my hand, bestowing a kiss on my knuckles. "There's nowhere else I'd rather be."

CHAPTER TWENTY-TWO

Natalie

I settled down in a cushy loveseat with my mind weighed down by everything I'd learned today. Werewolves. Vampires. Ghouls. A whole world and society of people that no one thought existed. And beautiful Wren, whom I was falling for far too quickly, was a part of that world. And now she was letting me stay at her house until the cabin was repaired.

"Water?" Wren asked, standing over me with a worried look. "Coffee? Something stronger?"

"There are days when I wish I drank alcohol."

"No time like the present."

I gave her a sly look. "Are you trying to get me drunk, Ms. Carne?"

Her hand slid across my shoulder, and I shivered. "I don't think I need to go quite that far. I mean, you're already in my house, aren't you?"

"Touché." I watched her move through the open concept ground floor to the kitchen on the far side. Not unlike the kitchen in the cabin, it was spacious with dark wood cupboards and an island with a couple of stools tucked under the lip. It all looked slightly more worn than Rory's cabin, but not run-down. Comfortably lived in, I'd call it. The loveseat sat adjacent to a longer couch in the living area and faced a rustic-looking gas fireplace with a television mounted on the wall above.

I was staring at a framed painting of a wolf in a dark forest, when I heard the icemaker on the refrigerator start clunking. "Damn it." Wren cursed before she came back to the couch, bearing two glasses of what looked like water, one with ice and the other without. She shrugged. "Fridge ran out of ice."

I smiled and took the glass with the ice. The only good water was ice water, in my opinion, and it was like sipping from a damned glacier lake as it slid down my throat. I may have inadvertently made a suggestive noise at the pleasant feeling, and that earned me a cocky smile from my potential date.

She joined me on the loveseat and took a sip of her own glass. I stared at those lips as they pursed and she took another slow sip, her eyes locked on mine. Then the incredibly stupid image of her lapping up the water like a wolf flitted through my mind and I choked. She caught my glass before I could throw it all over her as I coughed and tried to catch my breath.

"Are you okay?" she asked. She set both glasses on the coffee table in front of us. "Did you swallow a piece of ice or something?"

I shook my head, still coughing and trying not to look like someone who didn't deserve to be here with her.

"No—" I coughed again. "No—No." I coughed one more time, my throat raw and aching. "It went down the wrong pipe."

Classy, Natalie, real classy.

She wrapped an arm around my shoulders as the coughing slowly subsided, her hand gently kneading my upper back and neck as I sank into her touch. She was warm, warmer than I would have thought. Her body radiated a heat that made it like touching a warm blanket after a cold day of standing in the snow.

But no matter how much I wanted to stay within that warmth, I didn't think I could. Was I ready for this? Wren had been honest with me, and I knew that at some level I couldn't just throw that trust aside. But being a werewolf was kind of cool. Being me...well, that seemed to be too much for people. People like my parents. Like Misty. I didn't want to go through that again. I wanted someone who wanted me for who I was.

And that brought up another thought. I was supposed to be here to get over my breakup with Misty, not jump into a whole new relationship within a few days of being here. Never mind that doing something with Wren seemed like a dangerous proposition. That world that she came from, I didn't know if I could be a part of it. Or if I wanted to be.

All I really knew, could really say, was there was something about Wren that made me want her so damned badly. And somehow that made me even more scared. The deeper I got in with her, the worse it would hurt when she decided she didn't want me anymore.

I stirred against her and pulled away. She let me go without argument. Definitely another point in her favor.

"You said you have a guest room?" I was unable to look her in the eyes as I said it. She took a long moment to answer.

"Yeah, it's upstairs beside the master bedroom." She moved herself to the other side of the small couch, reaching for her glass again. "Are you tired?"

"Exhausted."

"All right." I followed as she stood, grabbing my glass as she led me toward the stairs. I caught the barest glimpse of her face before she turned away. She was hurt. I wished I could explain to her why it had to be this way, but would she listen? Or would she kick me out if she knew the truth?

She pointed to a door off the kitchen. "There's a small bathroom there." She pointed to another door beside the stairs that led to the second floor. "And the basement stairs there. I mostly just use it for storage, nothing interesting."

I nodded, acting like I got a tour of beautiful women's homes all the time. She led me upstairs, pointing out the master bedroom and the room where I would sleep. "And this is the master bathroom." She pushed open a door and I almost choked on my gasp.

"How do you ever leave this place?" I asked, staring at the gorgeous Jacuzzi bathtub that took up most of the room. A door on the far side looked like it opened onto the master bedroom, with two sinks and mirrors across from the tub. A standing shower stall stood in the far corner, blocked by a small partition. "Seriously? I would live in that damned thing."

She grinned at me for a brief second before it faded, then gestured back at the guest room. "The bed should be made and ready to go—I usually keep it cleaned up in case someone needs to crash for the night." She stepped back as I entered and flipped on the light. The bedroom was plain but cozy, with a comfy blanket atop a queen-sized bed. A small vanity dresser sat against one wall and a desk was pushed into the corner by the window that jutted out from the house, with a small, cushioned seat that a bookworm like me could fall in love with.

I looked back at Wren. "Your home is amazing," I said.

She gave another brief smile. "Thank you." She looked around her, lovingly touching the wall beside her. I watched her hand and imagined it running up my stomach to my chest. "It's the first place I ever had that felt like a real home."

I ached to reach out and wipe the sadness out of her eyes. "Wren."

"Don't," she said quickly. "I get it Natalie, I do. What happened today was inexcusable. You got hurt, badly, and I never wanted that to happen to you. You must be terrified to be with someone like me." She took a deep breath. "I thought we both felt something at Hikaru's, but I understand if you are having second thoughts."

I shook my head. "Wren, please! We do have something. I swear we do. It's just..." My throat closed up with anxiety and I couldn't get the words out, no matter how hard I tried. I fumbled my way through a few weird noises before I gave up and turned away from the door.

There was silence for a long time before I managed to get myself under control. "Wren, I'm sorry." I looked back for a reply, but the doorway was empty.

Wren was gone.

❖

"I think we need to talk," Misty said. I looked at her over my shoulder. I hadn't even heard her come in the door.

"Of course, honey," I said, pausing my game and putting the controller aside. I patted the couch beside me. "Come sit, tell me what's up."

She walked around so she could see me but didn't sit. There was a look on her face that opened a pit in my stomach.

"We're over, Natalie."

I stared up at her. "I'm sorry, what?"

"I said it's over," she snapped, "don't draw this out."

"But wait," I began, but further words seemed to stick in my

throat. I cleared my throat and wondered what the hell was going on? "What did I do? Did I do something wrong?"

She frowned. "Look, we've been together for like eight years. I don't know anything else and neither do you. We had a good run, but now I want something new."

I could only stare at her. "What?"

She folded her arms. "I spent last night with a real woman," she said and it was like a physical blow to my chest. *"I know what I'm missing now, and I want more of it."*

"B-but, Misty—"

"I don't want to be stuck with a tranny for the rest of my life!"

I jolted awake as something thumped into the bedroom. A short cry slipped out of my lips as I huddled on the bed.

Stuck with a tranny.

The words echoed in my head as my vision cleared enough to see a figure standing in my room, frozen near the door.

"Wren?" The word came out in a choking cry.

The woman in question drew back, then straightened in the darkness. She stayed by the door, keeping her distance.

"It's okay, Natalie," she whispered. "I just brought your things from the cabin. I figured you'd want them tomorrow."

I gasped in big gulps of air as I waited for my heart to stop pounding in my chest. Wren turned to leave when I leaped up, the T-shirt I'd borrowed from her hitting me at mid-thigh as I ran to her.

"Don't leave!" I cried, throwing myself at her. She spun and caught me in strong arms, pulling me in until my head was pressed against her chest. I listened to her heartbeat, concentrating on the soothing rhythm. "Please don't," I whispered.

I clutched her tight like she was my only lifeline. I could feel her solid body through the thin flannel shirt she was wearing. The button on her jeans poked into my stomach as I looked up at her and the darkness washed everything with shades of gray.

"Natalie," she murmured, "you need to rest. You had a—"

I shook my head. "No!" The word came out far harsher than I'd meant it to.

Misty's words rolled through my mind again and I let out a sob, clutching to the one lifeline I could find in this new and scary life I was building. "No," I whispered, "no, I'm sorry. I'm so sorry."

Two strong hands pushed my shoulders away enough that she could look down at my face. "What are you sorry for? You didn't do anything."

I shook my head. "You—I—I pushed you away!" I heaved out a breath. "Because I was scared. I'm so scared. But you saved me. You came for me. And I…"

Stuck with a tranny.

I heard those ugly words again and felt like I'd been struck. But I needed to explain to Wren.

"I need to be honest," I said with a shudder.

She stared down at me like she was looking for something in my eyes. I tried to give her whatever she needed. I wanted to. I needed to. She'd done so much for me. And that kiss before was enough to convince me that I wanted to tell her.

It was time to rip the Band-Aid off and go for it.

"Wren, I—"

She cut me off with a tight squeeze. "Come with me," she said, taking my hand and dragging me out of the room. Her room was larger than the guest room, with a king-sized bed on a low frame that made it easy to sit on. More wolf art was scattered around the walls and there was a large stuffed wolf sitting in the middle of the bed, between two sets of pillows. Only one set looked like it got regular use, the dent in the mattress on the same side. A small TV on the wall blended in nicely with a small shelf underneath. The rest of the walls were covered in bookshelves stuffed full of the largest collection of books I'd ever seen outside a library.

I blinked as light suddenly flooded the room, then proceeded to dim. I glanced at Wren, who had her phone out and was manipulating the bulb with it. She smiled at me and nodded to the bed. I hesitated, then sat down. She stood in front of me, her smile still plastered on her face, but it didn't quite reach her eyes.

"Okay," she began. She took my hands and dropped to her knees in front of me. "I know today has been rough. I know that you were kind of thrust into this world without knowing what was going on, without being able to choose whether or not you wanted to be. I get it, and I am sorry for it."

I shook my head. "It's not that, I promise you. This is all kinds of exciting. It's like there's something interesting in life again. I haven't felt like that in a long time, honestly. I always wanted there to be something more to life, and now you've given that to me."

She nodded her understanding. "But there is something big coming between us, and it's not on my side."

"No, it's not. It's me," I whispered. "I've got baggage that isn't fair to make you lug around."

She gave me a lopsided grin. "You do realize I'm pretty damned strong, right? I can handle some baggage."

I let out a soft laugh, feeling the tears begin welling up in my eyes. I looked away, and after a few seconds, found myself staring at her knees. "Not this much."

"Try me."

I sighed and rubbed my face. Strong grips on my wrists stopped me. Wren's hands clenched tight, sending a jolt of warmth and need through me, and her eyes shone with desire.

"Please, Natalie. You can tell me."

Misty's voice rolled through my head again, an agonizing ghost of the recent past that had all but destroyed me.

I gasped out a cry and Wren drew me into her, wrapping powerful arms around me like I was the most important thing in the world to her. She was different too, wasn't she? Maybe she'd understand. Maybe she wouldn't kick me out.

"I'm a...um...I'm a...well..." I tried to get the words out, but they were stuck in my throat. "I mean I'm...I'm kind of..." I let out a long-suffering sigh. "Oh, fuck it." I looked up into her eyes as she looked into mine. "Wren, I'm transgender."

Her expression didn't change. Not one bit.

"And?"

I stared at her. "What?"

Her smile was something I wished I could distill and bottle. "Natalie, honey, I already knew you were trans."

"How?"

She tapped her nose. "The scent. I realized it that first day in the diner." She shook her head. "It has honestly never bothered me, and anyone who lets it bother them isn't worth our time."

"My scent?"

"Yeah, it was just a little different, uniquely you." Her hand moved to my neck, fingertips caressing as it moved up to my chin. I shivered. "Natalie, I—"

She didn't get a chance to finish. I lunged forward, pressing my lips against hers like I could devour her. She moved into me, arching her back as she returned the kiss. Her breath was warm against me, making desperate need ignite with soft gasps and muffled moans. She wrapped her arms around me, casually lifting me into the air. I pulled back to look at her as dilated eyes took in whatever I could offer her.

"You are wearing far too much clothing," I grunted between kisses.

"Remedy that," she groaned into my cheek before her teeth caught my earlobe and pulled slightly. My moan filled the room, a sound I didn't even know I could make. I reached for her shirt, fumbling with the buttons. Then suddenly I was airborne, flying backward onto the bed. My hand caught on her shirt, buttons popping out around the room as the flannel opened. She glanced down then looked at me, an eyebrow raised.

I gave her a grin. "Oops."

She was undressed in record time, crawling up the bed on hands and knees like a predator who's trapped her prey. I shivered as she bared her teeth at me, a growl reverberating through the room. I sat up, grabbing for her, tasting every bit of skin I could reach, then started all over again. Strong hands grabbed the oversized T-shirt and pulled it over me in one swift move until I was as bare as she was.

"Natalie," she moaned as my lips found the sweet spot where her neck and shoulder met. She pulled back, raking her gaze over me with an indulgent smile. "You are so beautiful."

If the words had come from anyone else, I'd have questioned their validity, but not from her. The way her eyes twinkled, her lips parted, her fingers stroked over my skin. Her, I was willing to believe.

"Wren," I gasped, my hips writhing beneath her. "Please!" She only smiled at me, shimmying her underwear down her legs. She slid downward, teeth scraping down my stomach as I shivered. They caught on my panties, dragging them down as I moaned her name again.

I followed her movement, sliding my legs to either side to bring her to me once more. She grabbed my wrists with strong hands and drew them above my head as she leaned into my lips again. The kiss burned away the panic in the pit of my stomach at seeing what I hadn't had surgically removed standing at attention between us. I cringed as her eyes drifted down to it, but she only smiled and pushed me onto my back once more.

"No more fear," she whispered, "I think you're beautiful—so should you." She pressed my wrists to the pillow over my head and leaned into my ear. "Keep these here for me, would you?"

My words wouldn't work so I nodded and gasped as she raked long fingernails down to my chest. She found my nipple and sucked it in, pulling the skin taut as I arched my back into her. She straddled my hips once more and gyrated, working me into position.

Then she took my…my clit into her, and I screamed her name as she rode me, sweat glistening on both of us as she worked my nipples until they were hard under her fingers. More than once I brought my hands up and I wanted to give as good as I got, but each time she caught me easily and pushed them back down.

"Slow down, darling," Wren said, her voice low and sultry. "This one's for you. Then we'll see what you can do when you're really riled up."

I gulped in a breath and gave her wordless agreement as I let her take control. Then, for the first time that I could remember, all the pain and fear and panic that permeated my very bones began to fade. The guilt that I'd internalized inside my mind was washed away until there was nothing left but absolute, wonderous peace.

CHAPTER TWENTY-THREE

Natalie

I woke slowly, nestled in warmth and peace and staring at a pair of yellow eyes. Yelping, I threw myself backward before realizing the eyes were attached to the head of a cute stuffed wolf, staring at me from the far side of the pillows.

Then came the crash and I bolted straight up, pulling the blanket up to cover me.

"Ow." Wren's voice drifted from the side of the bed. I glanced down.

"What are you doing down there?"

She shook her head, pushing herself up on her arms and legs. "Someone," she said, her voice still thick with sleep. "Decided to push me off the bed."

My face heated and I scooted back over, unable to look her in the eye.

"Um, sorry."

"No worries. I've had harsher wake-up calls than that."

"Yeah, me too." The words slipped out before I could think about it. Wren's weight shifted me on the bed, and I let myself fall to the side into her waiting arms. Safe. Peaceful. Desire, and feeling desired. All these things were what I felt being close to Wren, and I never wanted it to end.

"Did Alton scare you?"

I looked around. We were still alone. "Who?"

She nodded to the stuffed wolf that was looking at us. Those glossy eyes looked a little too judging for my liking. "Alton, my wolf."

"You named your stuffed wolf Alton? Like after the cooking show host?"

She gave me a grin that I swore could knock years off my life in all the best ways. "He was the inspiration to get into cooking for me." She reached over me and grabbed the wolf, holding it tight. A tiny jealousy flared, and I tried to push it back down. "I mean on top of other reasons."

I watched her as she closed her eyes and cuddled her stuffy. Sometimes, that's just what you need. The comfort and care of a familiar presence in your life. The jealousy of Wren's other loves tried to rear its ugly head again, but worse was the sudden thought that I barely knew anything about Wren at all. Sure, she was a werewolf, and she could cook. She showed up in Terabend five years ago and bought a diner and a beautiful house on the outskirts of the town.

And she worked my body last night like an instrument she'd spent years playing and perfecting.

I let out a shuddering breath with the memory and Wren pulled me close with her other arm. I ended up staring into Alton's yellow eyes once more, but the comfort and caring kept the negative emotions at bay.

"What's going on in that mind of yours?" she murmured in my ear. "Your face looked all serious for a second there."

I shrugged, feeling her body move with me. "I have a lot going on in my head," I whispered.

"About your ex?"

"Yeah, and other things." I blinked at her and looked into her face. "How did you know?"

Her fingers ran down my cheek and I nuzzled into them. She lifted my chin and I fell deep into those emerald eyes of hers.

"You talk in your sleep, darling."

"I do?" She could probably feel the heat burning up my cheeks.

"And it didn't all sound pleasant. It seemed like you had two or three nightmares last night after we fell asleep."

Nightmares of the past. If she was right, then sleeping next to her kept them from waking me up like usual. If that was true, I never wanted to sleep without her again.

"I've had nightmares since I was a kid," I told her. "More like night terrors. They got really bad through my teens but leveled off when I left my—I mean, when I got older."

I clenched my teeth together before I said more. Cuddling with her after a wonderful night together was not the time to recall all those old wounds of mine. But those arms wrapped around me made it hard to resist. It felt like the night before had reopened my old wounds, leaving me raw and bleeding, but healing properly. Could I have done it by myself? Or was I meant to be with Wren?

Maybe she felt the tension, maybe she was intuitive, but when her cheek came down to rest on my head, I had to fight to hold back tears.

"It's all right, darling," she whispered against my hair. "It's all right."

I shook my head, wet trails down my cheeks. "No, no, it's not." I ran a hand across my face, trying to clean it up. "Last night was so perfect. It was beautiful. And now I'm curled up with you, and all I can do is cry and feel like I'm not worth all this effort!"

"Hey." Wren's voice was sharp as she moved her head back. She lifted my head to look at her again. "That's not true. You are worth everything, Natalie. Whoever told you otherwise was frightened of the amazing, gorgeous person you are."

I scoffed but couldn't get out any words.

"Do you know how rare it is to meet someone who not only knows who they are, but also acts on being that person? You are so brave, so sweet, and you are worth every effort in the world."

Maybe, maybe her words could start to heal me.

"You were so brave yesterday. Even when I told you not to, you came and demanded to help someone you didn't even know. If you hadn't gotten Meg out of there, things might've gone different." She hesitated for a long moment. "And then they came after you. Because of me. But you never blamed me for it. You didn't get mad. You fought against people who were nothing but monstrous." She gave a long sigh. "Now you've accepted the person—and werewolf—I am." She planted a soft kiss on my lips, and I couldn't help the moan that slipped out. "That is what makes you wonderful, Natalie. That's what makes you worth every bit of effort."

I hiccupped as I sniffled, trying to keep my face mostly clean for her. "It sounds like you really like me, wolf-girl." I managed to give her a smile, and she returned one of her own.

"I have been waiting for you for a long time," she said easily. Then her eyes went wide and one of her hands flew to her mouth.

I pulled back. "What do you mean?"

She shook her head. "Nothing. I...nothing."

I took a deep breath and shivered, pulling out of Wren's amazingly warm arms. I pulled the blanket around me as I searched for my underwear and the shirt I'd borrowed.

"I'm going to get a shower," I told her, "and then we're going to sit down and talk about something that isn't traumatic or life-threatening, how's that sound?"

She laughed. "Only if you let me treat you to breakfast—" She cut off, glancing at her phone. "I mean lunch at the diner."

"Deal." With a wink and what I hoped was some sort of sexy flourish that I probably did *not* rock, I spun and headed for the bathroom and that beautiful shower in the corner. Maybe the hot water would help me feel like a new person.

A new person who deserved the kind of caring that Wren was showing.

❖

True to her word, she took me to the diner after we'd washed up and gotten dressed. It wasn't until after she'd jumped in the shower that I realized I could have asked her to join me in the first place. Cursing myself for letting bad memories get to me too much, I opened my suitcase and pulled out a simple pair of jeans and a black Lacuna Coil T-shirt.

Wren's eyebrow raised when she saw what I was wearing, and I shrugged. Misty had never been into the same music as me. She stuck with Top 40 pop and refused to even consider going to the concert with me where I bought the shirt. It wasn't the first time I realized just how much she didn't really want to be with me.

It was almost two in the afternoon when we walked in, getting a smile and wave from the woman behind the counter. It wasn't Meg—which made sense when I thought about it. Wren introduced her as Alisha, and the woman seemed very quick to shake my hand with a welcoming smile. The moment we were settled in one of the booths in the far corner, she disappeared into the back for a quick second, then came back out with another woman and an older man.

Wren groaned and waved them back to the kitchen. I hid my smile behind the menu, pulling my phone out and putting it on the table.

"Kids," she murmured low enough I probably wasn't supposed to hear it.

"Aww," I gushed, "they just want to see you happy." The flush that invaded Wren's cheeks was worth the ribbing, even as she used the same tactic with the menu to hide her face.

"They're just excited." She paused like she was looking for the right words. "I've had partners, once in a while, but I've never really had a date, I suppose."

"Really?"

"My secret makes it hard to date, casually or seriously, unless they're hip to my world. You know?"

"Oh, yeah, I get that entirely." More than she probably realized. Valid fears and all that. I grinned at her. "Wait, so is this a date?"

She flushed even more, and I couldn't help but chuckle, the sound coming out low and wanting.

Wren cleared her throat. "So, see anything you want?" She blanched when she realized what she'd said.

"Oh, definitely." I let my eyes roam over her. Hey, I didn't want to disappoint her.

"Brat. I meant on the menu."

I shook my head. "Well, your picture isn't on here." I pouted. "If it were, then maybe I'd be able to decide easier."

I'd never have spoken to Misty this way, especially not in public. She hated displays of affection that she didn't initiate. She hated innuendo. And most of all, she refused to acknowledge who I was in public. If I was having a bad day with passing, then I was only her *friend*.

As the memories slid to the forefront of my mind Wren's eyes caught mine with a soft look. "Hey," she said, "come back to the present."

I shook my head to clear the bad memories and focused on the woman in front of me. I gave her a small smile. "Thank you."

"Of course." She put down her menu. "I know what it's like to live with memories you don't want to remember."

I nodded and started looking at the menu, trying to keep the fuzzy little feeling of joy in my stomach from running rampant. How different things were with Wren—and in the best of ways. Three days ago, I'd have never considered having anyone like her in my life. Now? I didn't know how I'd live without her.

As if the universe knew I was happy for a change, my phone started buzzing and singing a cheery pop song that made my body go numb. I stared at the caller ID, at the five letters that made me want to throw the damned thing in the nearest large body of water.

Wren looked from the phone to me, biting her lower lip as she frowned. "Natalie?"

I shook my head. "I should take this." I grabbed the phone and stood up. "I'll be right back."

"What did you want to eat?" she asked as I headed for the door. I turned and tried to give her a stunning smile that she had to see right through.

"You pick," I said, "I trust you."

I answered the call the moment I was out the door. "Hello?"

"Hey, baby." Misty's voice was almost nauseatingly sweet over the line. "I feel like we haven't talked in months!"

"Because we haven't. Because you broke up with me and kicked me out."

"Oh, come on, Natty, you know I didn't mean anything by it!" My grip on the phone tightened as she whined. "I wanted to try something new! Something different, you know what I mean? Like, we'd been together for years. It was time for something new."

"So, you had to tear me down to do that? Throw me out so I'm homeless?"

She scoffed. "Well, I wasn't about to bring girls home with you moping on the couch all the time. I mean, come on, I have a heart."

I laughed. "Really? Where the hell do you hide it? It's not in your damned chest."

She sounded like she was going to argue, but suddenly stopped. Instead, I heard her take a deep breath and I couldn't hide my surprise.

"Misty?"

"I deserved that," she said. She sounded apologetic. "Maybe I didn't do things the right way. And I miss you, Natty. We were always so close, thick as thieves, and now I don't even know how to function without you."

I opened my mouth to tell her off, but what came out was, "You don't?" Goddess, I sounded pathetic.

"Of course not, baby! You were my compass rose! The one person I could count on to guide my way through life! I can't do this all without you."

My heart started pounding in my chest. Was she saying what I thought she was saying?

"Misty…" I clutched the phone tighter, barely able to catch my breath.

"I need you, Natty. I need to see you. I need to come to you."

"I'm not in the city."

"I know, I talked to Rory. She said you were on vacation." She let out a weird scoffing laugh that was so familiar. "I can't believe you took a vacation without me, baby. I would've been beside you in a second if I'd known."

"It was kind of spur of the moment, you know?"

"All I know, baby, is that we're so damned good together." Her voice lulled its way into my brain, and I remembered the nights of passion, the nights where I trembled for her touch, and she made me beg for it all. The days that were wonderful and complete and amazing. The way she took me in after what my parents did. Years of good memories. "And besides, we both know that you can't take care of yourself, right? I mean, how long has it been since you shaved? Is your five o'clock shadow showing yet? You know I take care of you, Natty. You know I'm the one you have to thank for being the gorgeous woman you are."

She was right. That's exactly who she was. I couldn't have done all of this without her—couldn't do all of this without her. She was right. I never should've come here.

But Wren.

That quiet, rational part of my brain that often got ignored pointed at the memories of last night. Wren had saved me. Of course, if it weren't for her, I wouldn't have been in that situation, but that was thinking far too much into it. And I hadn't quite worked out all my feelings about all I'd learned in Terabend. Could I be a part of all of this? Did Wren want me to be?

But Wren had accepted me. Fully. Entirely. Misty had kicked me to the curb the second she wanted something different.

"I will always take care of you, Natalie." Misty's voice had gotten low and sultry. "No one else will do it like I do, you know that, baby."

I stood in the parking lot, frozen, trying to figure out what I was supposed to do.

"Just tell me where you are, dear. I'll take care of the rest."

I shook my head and tried to think clearly. "Um, Rory is letting me borrow her family's cabin for a little while, you know, to put myself back together."

I could almost hear her smile over the line. "Perfect, baby. Some alone time in the middle of nowhere is just what we need."

I started to shake. "No. I don't want you to come here. I don't want to see you."

"Natty! You don't mean that! I know you don't. You can't do this without me! I'm the only person who ever supported you. I'm the only one who's ever loved you for what you are!"

I clutched my free arm around my stomach, shaking and trying not to sound like I was crying into the phone. "But—"

"But nothing!" The scorn in her voice slammed into my chest like an anvil. "Stop blubbering and stuttering and get over yourself! No one else will ever want you and you know it!"

My knees wobbled and I almost fell when suddenly there was a strong arm supporting me. Wren's hand found my hip and kept me upright while her other hand took the phone from me.

"Who is this?" she growled.

I could hear Misty's outrage. "Who the hell are you?"

"I'm Wren," my protector snarled into the phone. I leaned into her, trying to draw in some of her strength. "Natalie is my beautiful date for the day, and your phone call is interrupting. So, we're going to let you go now."

I stared at her, the rage making her body vibrate at odds with the smile she flashed me.

"What?" Misty screamed. "That fucking bitch is cheating on me? No one cheats on me! No one!"

"Oh, sorry, they're delivering our food. We're going to have to let you go."

Misty started to scream something else, but Wren hung up the call before I could make it out. I stared at the phone in her hand as she held it out to me. I didn't want to look her in the eyes. I didn't want to see the pity or annoyance that she had to be feeling. The sad little trans woman who can't say no to the toxic relationship. The one who needed a big strong werewolf to stand up to her ex. I took my phone and started to turn away, entirely prepared to walk my way back to the cabin so I could take the truck and leave.

A strong hand on my arm stopped me. "Nat." Wren pulled me in close and wrapped her strong arms around me tight. "It's okay, darling. I've got you."

Wrapped in those soft arms, there was nothing I could do but start bawling. She held me, rocking back and forth as I cried out all the fear, the frustration, the need, and the disgust that I even considered going back to Misty for a second there. She held me until there were no more tears, and I was only heaving in massive gulps of air as I keened into the empty air. It almost felt like my own version of the lonely howl I remembered hearing those first couple of nights at the cabin. I wondered, if Wren were in wolf form, whether she'd join me in my cry.

"I've got you, Natalie," Wren whispered over and over again. "I've got you."

And for the first time in a very long time, I believed it.

CHAPTER TWENTY-FOUR

Wren

It was a good thing I only spoke to Misty on Natalie's phone that one time. If I'd caught her scent from meeting her in person, I couldn't promise I wouldn't do something drastic. When we returned to our lunch, my darling woman spilled her guts, telling me everything that happened between her and her psycho ex-girlfriend.

The worst part of it was that she'd probably never have become the person she was now without knowing Misty. The girl was Nat's only support during her teenage years, and that evolved into a dangerous codependency that threatened to destroy them both.

But now Natalie had me, and I had my mate.

I shuddered at the thought. I couldn't even fathom yet what it really meant. I only sensed how intense my wolf's feelings for Nat were. But when I was given a moment to think, I couldn't help but remember that she was human. Could I really mate with a human?

Growing up in my pack, I knew that to mate was supposed to be for life. In the Cardinals, they tended to assign wolves to each other, dictating the dominant and submissive bullshit that was so ingrained into our culture. The dominant wolves, wolves higher in the hierarchy and closer to the Alpha, were gifted with promises of wolves they considered submissive, the ones who didn't care, or weren't high in their standing in the pack. These were the wolves that weren't active about fighting their way up a brutal and flawed system. I watched the way the so-called dominants treated the submissives and knew I couldn't be a part of that world, that way of life. It was one of the many reasons I wanted to be a lone wolf, with no one and nothing to answer to. And no one expecting me to abuse them on a regular basis.

My Alpha had promised me to someone else, back in my old pack. This was before I was old enough to even understand what this meant, and before I grew into my nature as an Alpha. I'd been promised to the pack enforcer, Craig Reid. Once I became Alpha, I was out of his reach, and he had been hounding me ever since. No one could force me to mate, now that I was an Alpha.

Maybe other packs were different. I had to hope they were, but I didn't have a lot of experience. To me, a mated pair were supposed to be something special, something more than just one wolf having complete control over another. We were only given a single mate in our lifetime, and that person would complete us. That was the lore anyway. Sounded like a crock of shit for most of my life.

And then Natalie happened.

I needed more information. I needed to learn so much that I never had the chance to. Hikaru seemed to know a lot, but I needed to hear it from a wolf's mouth, not a vampire's.

These were the thoughts on my mind three days after our date at the diner. Misty hadn't called again, and Natalie seemed to be recovering well from everything that had gone down. Heather had almost finished cleaning up Meg's home—penance for being part of the group that attacked her in the first place, and Zeke and some of his family had almost finished fixing up Rory's cabin.

I almost didn't want to tell Nat that she could go back to the cabin. My bed was much more comfortable with her in it. Any room we were in together was more comfortable for me. From the moment we met, whenever we were apart, there was this feeling in my gut, pulling me in her direction as if she were a part of me that I was missing. I couldn't even describe it if someone asked. All I could say was that she completed me.

"Wait, what did you say?"

Natalie looked at me and cocked her head. We were sitting in my tiny office in the back of the diner, chatting as I filled out paperwork and tried to put together a supply order. I was trying not to be distracted by my thoughts—or the beautiful woman sitting on the other side of my desk.

"I was talking about the person I met in the woods by the cabin," she said. She smiled at me. "Were you not listening?"

I shook my head. "I was, and I wasn't." I put my pen aside with a sigh. "The paperwork has never been something I enjoyed about all this."

"Yeah, but isn't it nice to own your own place? No bosses to tell you what to do, and a flexible schedule, including making sure you have time to run off some steam from time to time." She raised her eyebrows and I laughed. I resisted the urge to throw a pencil at her.

"Har-har," I said. "Now tell me about this person. Do I have to be worried?"

She burst out in laughter. "No! Of course not. It was just a surprise. I mean, I was totally lost, and then suddenly there was this...person. And I mean, yeah, they were dressed for hiking and all that, but it didn't suit them."

"No?"

"No way. Everything looked totally out of place on them. It's like they should've been wearing a power suit and bossing people around in one of those shiny conference rooms in a skyscraper with windows that look over the city and all that."

I smiled. "You've thought about this a lot."

"What can I say? The clothing makes the person."

We had a good laugh together, something so comforting I never wanted to let it go.

"So did you get their name?"

"Yeah. It was, um, Vadi? I think. Sounded exotic."

I froze. "Did you say Vadi?"

"Yeah, that's what they said. I told them I was lost, and they showed me the way back to the cabin."

Vadi. Natalie had already met Vadi. It had been two years of living here before I got to meet them, and I thought that was a short time. They weren't seen often in town, but all of us supernaturals knew that it was thanks to them that we had Terabend as a sort of sanctuary. Sure, I controlled this county as the Alpha werewolf, but that didn't put me anywhere near Vadi.

But that gave me an idea. I couldn't go to Vadi about werewolf business—what the hell would they care, as long as their territory was kept safe? But outside of the county was another pack, with a leader who controlled the surrounding area outside of Terabend and Greyland County. Kendra Harper was the Alpha of a much larger area. She had knowledge. She'd been around a long time. If I played my cards right, maybe I could get some answers and advice.

"Hey," Natalie said, "where'd you go?"

"What?"

"In your mind, where did you go?"

I shook my head. "There's a lot on my mind."

She nodded, then glanced to the office door. She closed it, cutting off the noise of the kitchen, then came back to the desk. I raised an eyebrow, willing to see where this was going.

"I have a question," she said quietly, "about the whole *rawr* thing." She made a motion with her hand like a fanged maw chomping down on something. I stared at her, then glanced at the door. Private enough, I hoped.

"Go for it."

She hesitated. "Wren, what does mate mean for a werewolf?"

That word from those lips. There was nothing that sounded better.

I clutched at my desk as my wolf tried to push her way to the forefront. Fur rippled over my bare arms for only a second before I regained control. Nat scrambled back away from the desk. She looked so afraid.

I had to fix it. I never wanted her to be afraid ever again. Especially not of me.

"Where did you hear that word?" I asked. I made my voice as soft as I could make it.

For a second, I thought she wasn't going to answer. Eventually, she peeled herself off the far wall and inched closer. Her fear permeated her scent, and I hung my head in shame.

"I mean, you said it." She shook her head, like she thought she sounded crazy. "In my dreams."

I stared at her. "You've been having dreams?" I'd dreamt of her too, the night she took the bullet out of my shoulder. Had she shared that dream?

"Yeah. It's always a dark forest with huge trees that have very few branches low down. I start alone, or sometimes in the middle of a nightmare, but when you and your wolf show up, it changes. It becomes something more, and you're always..." She drifted off with her eyes closed like she was reveling in the memory. "Before

I woke in the clinic, you were talking to me. You saved me from a nightmare. And then you said that we were mates. That we were pack."

The blood drained from my face. Hikaru had said something about dreams. That we'd both have them. I needed to know more, but I didn't have access to the lore. Maybe it was time to get it.

For wolves, mate could mean a lot of things. Simple mating— having sex—was commonplace for wolves to do with basically whomever they wanted. And whoever wanted to do it with them. But that wasn't what she was asking about.

No, from the way she said it, and my heart lurched as I considered the idea, she was talking about the mate bond. A special bond between two wolves that lasted a lifetime. It was something that no wolf would ever choose to do with a human like her. It was taboo. It just wasn't done.

I couldn't tell her that.

"I don't know what it means," I said, sounding far too insecure for my liking. "I wish I did. I really do."

"But this is a wolf thing, isn't it? How don't you know?"

To tell or not to tell. If this were anyone else, on any other day, I wouldn't go into it. But I knew Natalie well now, and I wanted to know her better. And she'd shared with me her own past with Misty. It was only fair I did the same. Telling this all to a human, I couldn't say if this was a good idea or not. But she trusted me, the least I could do was trust her.

"I'm not even sure where to start," I said. "I grew up in and out of foster homes and orphanages. I have no idea who my parents are or even if they're still around. From what I know, it only takes one parent being a werewolf to have a wolf pup." Natalie let out a small gasp, then took the chair in front of my desk, reaching out to me. I put my hand in hers, taking comfort from her. "My first shift was when I was twelve. I was so scared. Terrified that I'd hurt someone, that I was a monster." I tightened my grip and she clasped her hands around mine, her thumb rubbing patterns into my knuckles. "So, I ran away from my foster home. I spent a while on the streets before someone from the local pack, the Cardinals, found me. They took me in, let me be a part of things, of the community." I sighed. "It started out really nice."

"But it didn't last?"

"No, not even close. The dynamics between wolves in that pack—in most packs, I guess—revolve around being dominant or submissive. I saw the way most of the dominant wolves treated the other ones and it was absolutely terrible. And the submissives had no one to stand up for them, because it was the way the pack worked. The way the whole wolf shifter culture worked, I guess." The memories reared their ugly heads, and my voice was hard with anger. "I knew I couldn't be a part of that when my nature came to me."

"Nature?"

"After puberty, after we learn to control our shifting and come to terms with our wolves, our natures reveal themselves. Most wolves just...come of age, I guess. They come into their own and gain better control over their wolves. They're considered adults after that point. When I came of age when I was nineteen, my nature as an Alpha awakened and all the wolves who thought they could control me suddenly couldn't." Natalie nodded and I smiled. For someone who only learned of this whole other world a few days ago, she was taking in knowledge like nobody's business. "When I became an Alpha, things changed. The pack didn't know what to do with me, and the current Alpha, Ronan, was scared that I would challenge him." I laughed, but there was no humor in it. "He tried to kill me. Well, to have me killed. He refused to put through a proper challenge."

"So, what happened?"

"Eventually, I made him a deal. He paid me, and I got the hell out of there." She looked almost concerned and I waved my hand. "I got enough money to leave and make a life for myself out here, and he didn't have to worry about his wolves not coming back to him because he was a weak asshole who was afraid of a twenty-year-old Alpha."

She took a moment, and I could see her mind working through everything that I'd said, taking it all in and filing it away like she was a damned computer.

"Is that why you don't have a pack? Because of what you saw when you were with—what did you call them? The Cardinals?"

"Yeah. And yeah. I didn't want to force anyone into a life like what I saw, and how could I possibly have a pack under me when I never learned how to be an Alpha? A leader? So, I came out here, to an unclaimed area, and made myself a home."

"Holy shit! And they just let you go?"

"Ronan promised he would, but he didn't hold up his end of the deal. I've had to deal with wolves from my old pack coming in and making trouble for a few years now. But it was never anything orchestrated like what happened to you."

"You think that asshole was working for your old pack?"

"I know he was. Jason was the brother of the wolf I was promised to before I became an Alpha." I shook my head. "I don't know what the plan is, or when the other shoe is gonna drop, but I know Craig isn't going to just let his brother's death be for nothing."

"This is sounding really complicated. Why go through all this trouble? If Jason had killed you, what would have happened to Terabend?"

"I don't know," I admitted. "Jason didn't seem to be the sharpest tool in the shed. I doubt he could put together a cohesive plan for taking and keeping my territory. And he wasn't an Alpha, so there's no way he could hold it. Someone else would come along and take him out no problem."

"Only Alphas can make a pack?"

"As far as I know. I mean, he could have a bunch of people with him and call them a pack, but the real power that binds the pack together comes from the Alpha. Even as dominant as he thought he was, he wouldn't have any real control over the others."

"So why come here and attack us?"

My heart fluttered when she said *us*. "I can only think it's something about his brother. Craig wasn't happy when I became an Alpha and didn't want me to leave the pack. Ronan made him stand down the day I left. He was almost feral." I shook my head again. "But it's been five years. You'd think he'd be over it by now."

She was quiet for a long moment. Her mouth turned down in concentration as she closed her eyes. "Maybe," she said slowly, "the idea was just to destabilize you, not outright kill you."

"But why?" I asked. "It was a waste of time. He didn't succeed, and only served to warn of possible other attacks in the future. Never mind sacrificing himself."

She shook her head. "Not unless the point was to try and destabilize your power base. And I honestly doubt he meant to get himself killed," she said, "but his attack would have given Craig an idea of what kind of pack or defenses you had ready to protect your territory." I stared at her for a long moment, speechless. "What?" She shrugged, giving me a small smile. "I play a lot of strategy games. If I were looking to take lands for myself, I'd consider small attacks that would probably be unsuccessful but would gain intel and sow chaos."

"Fuck." I stared at her. "You're scaring me." She gave me a wide smile as I added, "It's fucking hot."

She reached out over the desk and pulled at my shoulders until I leaned over enough for our lips to meet. I could feel the smile behind hers as I let her take what she wanted, loving every simple point of contact. Her lips, her mouth, her tongue, her hands, every piece of her was gloriously soft and sweet. I had to push down the desperation that threatened to overwhelm. The office was not nearly big enough to be able to really enjoy what I was getting desperate for.

The kiss ended but we stayed close, foreheads touching softly as we smiled. Her eyes were half-lidded with relaxation, and she had this smirk that made me want to hide it between my legs. I was almost about to make that happen when something knocked against the office door. We sprang apart like teenagers caught doing something dirty.

I cleared my throat a couple of times before I could find my voice. "Come in."

Leslie opened the door but didn't enter. Instead, Heather walked in, and I knew my surprise was written all over my face.

"Heather," I said, "I wasn't expecting to see you today." I looked past her to Leslie. "Thank you, Leslie." She nodded, giving me a questioning look, before she walked away. "I'm assuming this conversation should have the door closed?"

She nodded, then glanced at Natalie.

Shit. "Nat, can you give us a moment?"

"Sure."

But Heather shook her head. "No, it's okay. She knows, right? She's close to you, she can hear this too."

Natalie smiled and backed away from the single chair, leaning comfortably against the far wall with the bulletin boards and staff schedule. Heather closed the door and took the chair, and I settled in back behind my desk.

"What can I do for you?" I asked.

"I wanted to let you know that Meg's house is cleaned up," she reported. "The damaged furniture has been removed or repaired. The back door is whole again. When she's out of Dr. Maru's care she should be comfortable going right home."

I was thankful that Heather had done such a quick job. "That's good to know." I hesitated for a second, then decided to speak my mind. "Thank you for doing that. I appreciate your help, and that you decided to stick around."

She shrugged gracefully. "I had a lot to atone for."

"I understand that, but you know I wouldn't have chased you if you left town."

"I know, but I can't do that. I need help."

I raised an eyebrow. "Is this about why your scent is off? I mean, you smell like a wolf, but there's something else there."

She nodded and looked away like she was almost ashamed.

"It's okay," I said. "You can tell me. You know you can. It's why you stuck around, right?"

"Yeah." She took a deep breath and looked me in the eye. "Well, I guess...I guess I should start at the beginning."

"If you're ready," I said. Natalie was silent behind her.

"My father was a werewolf, but my mom is human," she began, "that gave me a fifty-fifty chance of coming out furry, I guess." She looked down at herself, her words softening a little. "I guess I got lucky, depending on how you look at it."

It wasn't unheard of for werewolves to have children with humans—sex happened, and people got pregnant. There was no special mate bond needed for that.

"The signs started showing not long after I was born. I don't know how it works, my mother didn't go into details. But the minute she knew that I would be a wolf like my father, she...I don't know. She went crazy. She hired someone—a witch or something—to put a curse on me." She shook her head, her breath coming out in a scoff. "A fucking curse. Can you believe it? She cursed her own fucking daughter."

"What did this curse do?" Natalie asked, her voice soft with caring. I bit my lower lip at the sound of it.

"It locked my wolf up," Heather said. "Caged it inside me. I can't shift. I don't have the strength and speed even in human form that our kind has. I am—effectively—human."

I looked her in the eyes, knowing there was more to the story. "But you can feel her, can't you."

She nodded and wiped a hand over her eye like she was fighting back tears. "Yeah. I feel her. For the longest time I thought I was going crazy. I felt like there was this whole other person inside me, trying to get free. Trying to talk to me. To communicate somehow. Like I'm half of who I'm supposed to be. But every time I tried to bring it up to my mother, she would brush it off. Ignore what I was saying, how I was feeling. I'm normal, she'd tell me. And I should be grateful for it."

Natalie made a sound somewhere in between a scoff and a gasp. I glanced at her and saw she had the makings of tears in her eyes too. It took half a minute to realize she must've gone through something similar in her own life.

"How did you find out you were a werewolf?" I asked.

"A long story I'm not ready to get into," she replied. "But I found out and I confronted my mother. She told me everything. Then I ran away. Found myself in a new city, with no one who knew me. But then the wolves found me, and I guess I smelled enough like one that they let me join them."

"That's when you joined the Cardinals."

"Ronan promised he'd help me break the curse. Free my wolf. But then I got labeled a submissive and was considered the lowest in the pack. I had to wait months to get to even talk to him again. He barely remembered me the second time I got to talk to him."

Just another example of why I didn't want a pack like everyone else's. "So, you think an Alpha can help you?" She nodded. "I...I don't know how. I don't know how to do much. I don't know *how* to help you."

"I know. I'm not expecting miracles here. I'm just…I'm just looking for someone to want to help."

I leaned back in my chair, taking in everything that she'd said. I wanted to help her. I needed to help her. I had claimed her as one of my people, and after everything that had happened I realized that I needed people. I needed a pack. If I wasn't going to have one, clearly, I was going to build one around me anyway.

"I don't know how to help you right now," I said. I sat forward and held a hand out. She took it without hesitation. "But I promise you I will find a way."

CHAPTER TWENTY-FIVE

Wren

I pulled the door of the Jeep closed, then started the engine and rolled down the window to look out at Natalie's smiling face.

"Are you sure you don't want to come with?" I asked. I wasn't looking forward to being apart from my beautiful girlfriend, even for a few hours.

"No." She shook her head. "Dr. Maru wants to give me a checkup after everything last week. And you need to go get some answers for Heather."

I shivered thinking about it. She had been more than forthcoming about what had happened and what she needed from me. Now I needed to do what was right for her by learning everything I could.

"Are you sure this is a good idea?" Nat asked softly. "I mean, won't they be mad at you for showing up on their lands?"

I shook my head. "Generally, if a wolf is passing through it's not a big deal. It's always a good idea to pay respects to the Alpha, but not much else. If I was planning to stay for a while, then it would be different. Either way, I need to go see the Alpha, so they'll know I'm there anyway."

She held her hand out to me. "Right. Well, make sure you come back to me, all right? If not, I'm going to have to come after you."

I brought her knuckles to my lips. "Nothing could keep me away, darling."

I loved the way she blushed and swore I'd need to find more reasons to make it happen.

"Have a good trip."

"Say hi to Hikaru for me. And let Heather know I'm going to figure this out for her. She's going to be okay."

Natalie nodded and I pulled the Jeep away from my house, watching her in the mirror until I couldn't see her anymore.

The second I hit the highway I slammed down the accelerator. The quicker I got around the lake to Silva, the better. That strange pull in my gut grew stronger, more uncomfortable, the farther from my mate that I got.

"Shit," I muttered, cursing myself for thinking about her as my mate again. "I don't even know what that really means."

But whatever was happening between us, it was far too real for comfort.

❖

Terabend was a small town. Hell, I didn't even know if it could be promoted from village status or not. With a little over a thousand people living there, it was quiet but wasn't quite so small that everyone knew absolutely everyone. The perfect place for displaced supernatural creatures to hide in plain sight—more or less.

Silva, on the other hand, was the epitome of a tourist town. The population had to be easily four or five times that of Terabend, with most of the residents working to ensure the town's appeal to the tourist trade. The main street along the highway had motels, hotels, gas stations, and plenty of fast-food restaurants. But drive a few blocks toward the lake from the highway and you could find the real reason to come here—the boardwalk.

Parking lots lined the street closest to the beach and then there were wood plank paths laid out between them and the buildings. Along the boardwalk was everything a tourist would need for a day at the beach. Swimwear stores that doubled as gift and souvenir shops, a few restaurants that catered to families, ice cream shops, and more rustic fairs and arcades. It was exactly the kind of place I was thankful Terabend wasn't. But then, we weren't nearly so close to the lake or a swimmable public beach.

I turned off the highway away from the beach. I didn't want to bother with the heavy traffic or the crowds on a beautiful day in the summer. Though the idea of seeing Natalie in a two-piece, soaking wet as she climbed out of the water...

I shook my head. Not the time for daydreams. No matter how

much my wolf and I both wanted nothing more than to spoon into my beautiful Natalie, to press my lips into her neck as I gave her the pleasure she desired, or to sink my teeth into her collarbone as she moaned and screamed my name.

I slammed on the brakes. The Jeep squealed to a stop far too close to the sedan in front of me. The red light gave me a moment to catch my breath, pushing those thoughts down and away as far as I could. My gut roiled at the idea of not thinking about her. It still ached with the distance between us, and my wolf prowled deep inside, agitated and wanting.

Ten minutes later, I was pulling up to a pair of wrought-iron gates manned by a single security guard. The second I rolled down the window I picked up the smell of a wolf. Multiple wolves, though there was only one I could see. Dressed in a security guard uniform, he moseyed out of the guardhouse and stepped up to the car.

"Name?" he grunted, giving me a hard look with eyes that almost glowed amber.

"Wren Carne. I'm here to speak with your Alpha."

He furrowed his brows at me. "One moment." He stepped aside, pulled out a radio, and spoke into it. A moment later he returned. "All right. Pull up to the main house. Someone will be there to escort you."

I nodded my thanks as the gates opened. The road was lined with trees that tried too hard to pretend to be a wild forest. It was all a little too perfect, the trees spaced too evenly to be anything more than planned out. There were scars in the ground, like trees had been cut down and stumps removed to make everything look manicured and almost perfect. They lined the road for most of the way before thinning and opening into a large, empty lawn that led up to a picturesque mansion.

I shuddered with the thought of running in those trees. It felt too much like being in a zoo, in a cage. Give me the Canadian wilderness any day.

Two wolves awaited me as I climbed out of the Jeep. Both tall, with stoic looks, and wearing simple shorts and thin shirts. They looked like they were ready to shift at a moment's notice. I stepped up to them calmly, looking them in the eye and letting them know exactly who—and what—I was. They resisted at first, but after a moment of silence they both looked down and away in submission.

They might not be my wolves, but I was an Alpha, and they knew to show me respect. The shorter of the two, a woman with long dark hair tied into a tight braid pulled from the top of her head, gestured to the door.

"The Alpha will see you now," she said, "please, follow."

I nodded and they led the way through the manor. Throughout the house were more wolf guards, dressed like those leading us, positioned all over the place. It was overkill, like Kendra was expecting an attack or something. Did she think I was here for just that? I had no interest in her territory. Hell, apparently, I could barely handle my own.

They led me up to the second floor and down a long hallway that was lined with painted portraits of people. Every single one had a look on their face like they were looking at the viewer like they were nothing but prey. My escorts seemed to shrink under the painted glares.

The double doors at the end of the hall opened as we approached. It was hard not to groan and shake my head at the theatrics. Like I needed to be shown that I was in the presence of a powerful Alpha, one who'd ruled her lands for decades.

If she thought all this would cow me, she had no idea who she was dealing with.

Kendra Harper sat behind a large ornate desk in the middle of the room, large windows at her back as she lounged in her over-stuffed office chair. Her short, graying hair only enhanced the stern look that seemed to fall naturally over her face, and her clean-cut, fitted dress shirt and slacks worked heavily in her favor. But the moment her penetrating gaze roamed over me, she visibly relaxed. She shared a warm smile like we were old friends and was quick to vacate her chair and come around the desk.

"Wren Carne." Her gravelly voice traveled across the too-big office. "Alpha of Greyland County. To what do I own this pleasure?"

I bowed slightly to give the Alpha her due, as was called for. The guards who'd led me here retreated beyond the office doors, leaving us alone.

"Alpha Harper, I appreciate you being willing to meet with me on such short notice."

Kendra waved a hand in the air. "Oh, darling, you don't need to be so formal. We're neighbors, there's no reason for us not to have a healthy relationship."

Sure, that's why the show of force on the way up here.

She stopped in front of me and offered a hand. I took it, giving a firm shake. "I don't disagree. Five years is too long between visits."

She smiled. "Well, I had to meet the wolf who decided to stake a claim on a territory next to mine." For a second, that smile pulled away from her eyes and the look was cold. Terribly cold. "Though I can't say you haven't been a good neighbor."

Vadi had told me once how Kendra had requested access to Greyland County. She had not been pleased to be rebuked.

Kendra ushered me to a chair in front of her desk. I acquiesced, accepting the seat as she reclaimed her own chair on the other side.

"I needed a new life," I told her. "And Terabend has given me that."

"I'm glad to hear it. So, what brings you to me today?"

I hesitated. It was hard to admit my spotty knowledge of my own kind, but I was between a rock and a hard place. Never mind the whole mating thing going on with Natalie, but there was also Heather's curse that I needed to help her with. She was mine now, and I needed to do whatever I could for her.

I pushed away that thought. As I wondered when I'd claimed Heather as one of my people, I looked up at Kendra's smiling face, and tried to be selective about what I said.

"I need some help," I began. "Information, really."

"On what?"

"On us."

She raised an eyebrow. "Come again?"

I gripped the side of the chair tightly. "Let's just say that my education when it comes to my own kind is spotty at best. Even as an Alpha, I find I don't always know what I am doing, or what I'm able to do."

I told her about the fight at Callum and Heather's campfire, when Natalie and I rescued Meg. I tried my best to explain the supernatural wind that I had called up, which had dragged Callum to the borders of my lands as I banished him.

"I heard about some wolves causing trouble in Terabend." The lack of surprise brought with it the worry that she had something to do with it in the first place. "I also heard that several humans were involved."

I grimaced. "They were, but it was handled."

"Yet you truly did not know what you were doing when you banished the wolf?"

I shook my head. "No, and now I'm finding there are things I need to deal with, but I don't know how."

She slipped on a sly smile. "Would one of these things be the young person whose scent is all over you?"

I couldn't hide my surprise. "How do you know about her?"

"My dear, the scent wafts from you as if it were perfume. Does she know just how much you think of her? How much your wolf wants her?"

"I—" I didn't even know how to answer her. What did I feel for Natalie? I'd known her for all of a week now. How could I be sure this was all real. Was this even possible with a human? It wasn't done in my old pack, but was there good reason for that? If mating was forever, was that something Natalie wanted? Something we could handle? Would she want to be turned? "No. She doesn't. And I can't afford to think about it right now."

"No? The idea of mates for us wolves is not something to push aside. Believe me," her eyes flickered to the side briefly, "I know how important it is."

"I don't know what I'm doing with her. I really don't."

"You feel the girl in your gut?" I nodded. "And you can't stand to be apart from her for an extended period?" I nodded again. "And are you having the dreams?"

I snapped to attention. "The dreams?" It was her turn to nod. "Yeah, I've been having dreams. And so has she."

She nodded like she knew exactly what she was speaking of. "And where did this wolf come from?"

I shook my head. "She's human."

I expected to see a smile bloom across her face, but instead she went completely cold, her emotions shut down and eyes narrowing. That scent in the air was definitely fear.

"You need to talk to her," she said slowly, her voice as cold as her visage. "And you need to understand the risks of mating with someone like her."

"Risks? What do you mean?"

She shook her head. "To put something like a mate bond onto a human is nothing short of monstrous. They can't handle it. The power, the feelings. The magic—"

"Magic?"

She laughed without mirth. "What do you think allows us to do what we do? It's not exactly within the laws of physics as we understand them."

"What happens to human mates?"

She shook her head. "It never ends well. Trust me. You cannot have mates from two different worlds. At best they die long before you do because they aren't as hardy and don't live as long. Worst case? They get killed because they're your mate and because someone else decides that they are weak."

"I'd protect her!" I snarled.

"Of course you would," she said. Her tone was admonishing but not degrading. "But you can't be with her every second of every day. I mean, you're hours away from her right now! You can't protect her forever and from everything."

"I'd find a way."

"Wren, please listen to me. Humans cannot handle this. Most of them can barely survive the mate bite! I assure you, going further with this girl will not end well. You must either turn her or let her go."

"I...I..." My throat closed up, keeping all the words in.

Kendra took a deep breath, seeming to shake herself out of whatever had come over her. "I speak from experience, my dear. Make a better choice than I did."

"What do you mean?"

She shook her head. "I fell for a human once. He...was taken from me. I have carried that loss in my heart ever since."

I tried to imagine what that would be like, to lose Natalie to whatever life might bring. My wolf howled mournfully, and I shook with the anxiety of the idea. I would never let anything happen to her. But what if I wasn't there?

"I will figure out what's going on with her on my time," I said. I wished I felt more confident in that idea than I really was. "But I have something more pressing right now."

"Do tell."

As much as I hated telling someone about what Heather had told us in confidence, I needed to know what I could do to fix it. "I have a pack member." I tried hard not to shudder at the implication of being in charge of someone else's life. "She was cursed by a witch when she was a child. Her wolf is locked inside her."

"That's…" Her face went pale. "That's terrible, absolutely barbaric. How is she even coping?"

I had to shrug. The strength Heather had was amazing for what she was going through. I couldn't even imagine it. But I sat and told Kendra everything I could without going into too much detail. Heather had never had a chance to run with her own kind or to howl at the moon. I wanted to give her that. She trusted me to help her.

"She has been told that an Alpha can help break her curse," I said at last. "And I want to help her. She is one of mine."

Kendra stood, wandering away from the desk. I kept an eye on her, but she seemed to be lost in thought. Did she even know how to help me? This kind of issue couldn't come up often. It would mean a war between shifters and witches. The last war between preternatural creatures was several centuries ago, that I knew of. We were all too worried about involving humans in a fight that could mean the end of everything.

She ran her hand along a tall bookshelf, and I stood from my chair to move closer. Most of the shelves were filled with leatherbound books that looked like they hadn't been touched in decades. Kendra pulled a book out. The dust cloud that followed made her sneeze twice, and I couldn't stop my smile.

"Here," she said, holding the book out to me. "Honestly, you should've been allowed to study a book like this the moment your Alpha nature surfaced. Any Alpha worth their salt should've done better by you."

"They did what they did. They didn't offer the information, and I didn't exactly have a leg to stand on in demanding the knowledge. Not the way I left."

"Be that as it may, this book will help you. You might even find a solution to your own wolf's problem."

"What is the book?"

"An old journal from an Alpha who managed to combine a number of packs into a strong family. They wrote it to help train new Alphas how to lead a pack so that they were the strongest and most put together that they could be."

I took the book, handling the old leather with care. The damned thing felt like it was going to fall apart in my hands. "Is this it? All I need?"

"I don't know. I've never found myself in your position, my dear."

We were going to do this. We were going to help Heather. And Natalie was going to be beside me the whole time.

"Thank you, Alpha Harper." I lowered my head formally, offering her a little more than the standard amount of respect considering our positions. "I truly appreciate your assistance."

She chuckled. "It's like I said before, Wren. You are a fantastic neighbor, and I don't want that to change."

I turned away, biting my lip. I didn't talk about the past much, or what I wanted from life, but maybe of anybody, she'd understand.

"I never wanted a pack. Never wanted people to put their lives in my hands. But then people started saying I was an Alpha. They acted like it was set in stone that I would lead a pack."

"It's a burden that we all bear, despite what we might wish for otherwise," she replied sagely, her eyes soft and sad. "Having another to share it with helps. Find your mate—it makes everything else in life worth it."

"Shit." I clutched the book to my chest. "I'll think about it." I couldn't bring myself to say what I wanted to say. Yelling at her to stay out of my love life was not the diplomatic way to end this. "Thanks for your help."

"Anytime, my dear, anytime."

I was out the door before she finished speaking, ignoring the guards on either side of the door and making my way back through the manor. The book stayed clutched tight against me. I couldn't wait to get back to Terabend and crack open the journal. I tried to focus on the things that I might be able to learn from it to help Heather, and not on what Kendra had said about Natalie.

But no matter how hard I tried, I couldn't shake a nagging feeling. Maybe Kendra wasn't wrong. Maybe Natalie couldn't be mine.

Both my wolf and I howled in mourning at the mere idea.

CHAPTER TWENTY-SIX

Natalie

The waiting room was empty when I walked into Dr. Maru's office. I almost hadn't come. It was a close call between this and turning the other direction to follow Wren around the lake. It hurt so deep inside to be apart from her, something I'd never felt before. Sure, I missed Misty when she wasn't around, but it was nothing like this. I felt like I could barely function without Wren.

Not that I could say anything about it to Wren. I was already coming off clingy as it was, breaking down in her arms the other day. She had other things to worry about than me.

Like Heather. I couldn't imagine what life was like for her, knowing there was something inside her but that she wasn't able to let it out. I stopped for a moment, realizing what I'd just been thinking. Maybe I knew how she felt better than I thought. When she was talking with us yesterday, I stayed close, hoping my hand on her shoulder gave her some sort of strength and comfort. No one should have to go through life without feeling that from someone else. If Heather was going to be important to Wren, I wanted to help take care of her.

Of course, I wanted to take care of Wren too. I got the sense that she was going to make that difficult. How could I show her that she didn't have to do everything alone anymore? I could be there. I could help. I wanted to help. I needed to be useful.

"Good morning, Natalie." Dr. Maru's voice broke into my thoughts and my head shot up. She was leaning against the wall near the exam rooms, giving me a once-over with eyes hiding once again behind the purple lenses of her glasses. I smiled at her, and she moved forward to offer me a hand. "I'm glad you made it. I wasn't sure if Wren was going to monopolize your time."

"She had to head out of town for a few hours."

"Her loss," she chuckled, "but I bet it's getting hard to be away from her, huh?"

I stared at her. "How did you know?"

She sighed. "Come on, we should talk in my office."

I remembered the way there, but she led me anyway, closing the door behind us as I took a chair in front of her desk. I rubbed my hand hard against my leg, the friction and repetitive movement helping keep my focus on the present.

Dr. Maru took her chair behind the desk, taking off her glasses and setting them aside.

"You two really haven't talked about any of this, have you?" she asked.

"That's not true," I argued, then stopped and thought about it. "I mean, I know she's a werewolf. And we talked yesterday about her past and what she knew about...about..."

"About being mates?"

My other hand, the one not rubbing my leg, started twitching. "Yes. Mates." I shook my head a little too vigorously. "I don't even know what it means, and she doesn't either! But it's all I can think about sometimes. That word is worked into my brain, and she wasn't even the one to say it first! Well, I mean, she was but she really wasn't. You know?"

Dr. Maru stared at me for a long moment. "No. I don't quite understand. What do you mean she was the first to mention it, but wasn't?"

I flicked my hand in the air, the stimming helping to wean off the anxious energy. I was not going to have a panic attack. I was *not* going to have a panic attack.

"It was in my dreams," I said, unable to look at her. "I know, it sounds fucking crazy. But I've been having dreams since I met her, and she's always there. She protects me, takes care of me. And she told me we were mates. So, I asked her about it yesterday and she said—" I had to take a deep breath and force my hands to stop shaking and rubbing. "She said she didn't know. Didn't have the knowledge. It's one of the reasons she left today. She said she's going to speak with another Alpha and see what she can learn." I didn't mention Heather's predicament. That wasn't my story to tell.

Dr. Maru rubbed a hand across her face. "I do not get paid enough to deal with werewolf romance." She groaned, and I couldn't stifle my laughter. Not something you hear someone complaining about every day. "Look, there's a lot of stuff that Wren doesn't know. She's going to have to learn if things keep happening like everything last week. She's not going to be able to keep her head down and her territory off the map for long if people keep coming by to try to take it from her."

That made sense. Wren hadn't even wanted anything to do with a pack, but she couldn't face every challenge alone. I stopped myself at that thought. I played far too many video games because I was looking at it like that. It wasn't real life. Instead, it was battles to be fought and people to take care of. What the hell was happening to me?

"Having a mate will make her stronger, and also make the pack stronger. A wolf's mate is usually their perfect match. Each one fits the other, complements the other, and boosts each other in every way. At least, that's what the lore likes to say. I'm sure it's not that convenient."

"But how do you know if you have the right mate?"

"Because supposedly mates are chosen by the Mother of Wolves." She did the air quotes thing with her fingers at those words. "I don't know how accurate it is, but the stories go that there is one true mate for every wolf. Not all of them find that person, or sometimes they settle for something less. But when true mates find each other, even if they fight it, there's little that will keep them apart in the end."

I shook my head. "But I'm human. How am I supposed to be able to help her run a pack?"

"Beats me. But maybe you are exactly what she needs to find the strength to move on from her past and make a proper life, at ease with all of who she is." She glanced away for a moment as if considering something, then caught my eyes again. "I don't know how much she's told you, but she didn't have a good past."

"Neither did I," I said, but it only meant that I could understand letting the past rule you.

"Then you know what it's like to try to find life after that. Wren wears her past on her sleeve, using it like an armor to keep the world out." She hesitated. "You know, since she met you, I've never seen her so open. Maybe that's part of what you could do for her."

I shook my head again. "But there's so much she doesn't know about me. My past, my family, my parents." I took another deep breath to push down the anxiety. "Everything that happened to me. How can I help her when I can't help myself?"

She grimaced. "As cliché as it sounds, you need to follow your heart." I held a hand to my chest, feeling my heartbeat and aching for Wren to be at my side. "And that stirring inside that's making you pine for her."

"How do you know so much?"

"I'm very observant." We shared a smile and lapsed into silence. It gave me time to think over all the new information.

A mate. That's what my dreams told me I was. Someone strong enough to support my Alpha, even for all my own flaws. Would she help me through them? Would she help me feel like the worthwhile person I only ever felt like on the really, really good days? Could I have forever like that with her?

Dreams. It was all just dreams and wishes. Things weren't that easy, and they never would be.

"How does it work?" I asked softly, desperate for more before my brain could spiral into anxious oblivion.

"When the two of you are ready, the stronger wolf performs the mate-biting. Usually, it's done during coitus. Then the mate bites them back. After that, well, your guess is as good as mine."

"Fuck," I groaned, slouching in the chair.

"What?"

I pulled the neck of my shirt to the side and revealed a line of bruises that I'd been proud of only a few seconds before. I remembered Wren's mouth on my skin, sucking and nibbling and—I cut myself off before I started moaning in the damned doctor's office.

"I mean, do love bites count?"

Dr. Maru barked out a laugh. "No, no. If she did the mate bite, you wouldn't be questioning it." She shook her head. "But it looks like she had fun nonetheless."

My cheeks heated as I pulled my shirt back into place. "She wasn't the only one," I murmured.

"I can see that." She gave a small sigh. "No, the mate bite requires her to call on her wolf in the moment. It won't be made with solely human teeth."

I stared at her. "Would I be able to survive something like that? I'm mean, I'm only human."

"It's...not widely accepted in most of shifter culture," she said. There was something on her face that made me think she wasn't pleased about that. "But there have been human mates to werewolves before."

"So, it would be bad if Wren had me for a mate?"

"Why do you ask that?"

I took a moment to try to find the right words. "Because I don't want to cause any trouble for her with the other wolves." And suddenly I couldn't be sitting there anymore. I leapt out of the chair and paced in the open area behind the chairs. I mumbled to myself but couldn't even figure out what I was trying to say. Or think. Or feel. It was all too much, just too much. I hadn't even known her for a week, and yes, I didn't want to be away from her, and I needed her, and wanted her, and she took care of me and protected me, and—

"Stop!" I shouted to break the run-on sentence in my head. "Just stop. It's too much, it's all too much."

Then there were arms around me, small but strong, and a warmth helped settle everything that was roaring inside. Dr. Maru held me close, her eyes at the level of my neck. But even knowing what she was, I didn't have any fear of being that close. I trusted her. And I trusted Wren with all of my heart.

"I'm sorry," I murmured.

"Don't be," she replied just as softly. "But if I could offer a little advice?" I nodded dumbly. "Don't worry about all this. It can all be talked about and figured out in the future. For now, focus on you and her and how much you want to be together. Focus on your relationship and let everything else fall into place when it's ready."

I took a deep breath, then a second, then a third. Only then did

I trust my words enough to say something. "Don't borrow trouble," I whispered. "My dad always told me that."

"In this particular case, he's not wrong." The way she said it made me think she had a pretty good idea of why I didn't often try to willingly remember my father's advice.

She held me for another long moment before we separated. She grounded me. It was something very few people could do. Rory was one of them. Wren another. How was I getting so damned lucky?

"I really do like her, you know?"

She laughed, doing a small jump to sit on the corner of her desk instead of behind it. "I can tell. And like I said before, you're good for her."

I cleared my throat a couple of times, sniffling to hold back the waterworks that threatened to flood the room.

"So," I choked out after a moment. "I'm pretty sure you didn't ask me to come in to discuss my relationship."

She froze, going so still it looked like she'd replaced herself with a statue. It was uncanny, disturbing, and I couldn't help but hope she'd move again. The more disturbing thought was that this was the first time I had ever looked at her and seen something that wasn't quite human. Even the reddish eyes were easier to handle.

"No, no, there was something else." She moved off the desk, avoiding my gaze. "I have your tests back, the ones I put through after your recovery."

I nodded in understanding. "Is there something wrong?"

"I want to preface this with something," she began. "I have never had the pleasure of treating someone who is transgender. But I am learning, I am researching, so please have patience with me."

"Of course." I'd had doctors straight-up refuse to see me because I was trans. Already Dr. Maru was way ahead of the pack. "So does this have something to do with me being trans?"

She didn't answer at first, keeping her head low as her hands fretted away at a loose thread on her chair.

"It does, I think." She gave a long-suffering sigh. "It looks like my blood did more to you than I was expecting."

"What do you mean? I'm not..." I started to panic again. "I'm not going to turn into a vampire or something, am I?"

"No. No, not even close. You would've needed to be much

closer to death for that to have the best chances of happening. I mean, it was a possibility, but wasn't likely."

"Okay. So, what's wrong then?"

"What medications do you take for your transition?"

I hesitated at her directness but didn't let that stop me for long. "Testosterone blockers. And I use patches for my estradiol. Why?"

It was a long few minutes before she told me.

"So, I guess you don't have to be on those things anymore," she said as she handed me a large file folder with my name on it. I picked it up and started flipping through all the papers in there, understanding nothing. "My blood changed your body chemistry. You're producing higher levels of estrogen instead of testosterone now."

"Wait, what the fuck are you talking about?"

She shook her head. "I didn't know that was even a thing it could do, honestly. I've never had to put that much blood into someone who was on hormone replacement. Something I'll definitely keep in mind for the future."

"No way. I don't understand." I stared down at my feet, taking deep breaths in an effort to push away the impending anxiety attack. "Does this mean my body is different?"

"No, I'm sorry." And she honestly sounded so. "Your body is still the same, it's only your hormones that are different now. That might affect your body to some degree more than the pills you were taking, but you don't suddenly have a womb or ovaries or whatnot."

I nodded, knowing well enough that even magic—or vampire blood in this case—was not a cure-all that I truly desired.

"Eight years," I murmured, unable to tear my eyes away from the ground. "I've been on these meds for eight years, Doc." I shook my head. "I don't know how to not be on them. They've been the key to being who I really am for so long, and now you're telling me I don't need them anymore?"

"I'm sorry, Natalie." And she truly did sound apologetic. "I don't think you should up and toss all your pills and patches as soon as you get back or anything like that. I want to run more tests and would like to take more blood, just to make sure my findings are right. But if I am, then I guess you won't need them anymore."

A pair of feet appeared in my line of sight and a hand raised my chin up until I could see her face.

"Natalie, I want you to tell me how that makes you feel."

"What are you, a psychiatrist?"

"One of my many medical specialties, though it's a decade or two old."

I rolled my eyes. Of course. Vampire.

"I don't know how I feel," I said. "I don't know how I should feel, or what I think." I took a deep breath. "I was prepared to be on these things for the rest of my life. I had this idea of how life was going to be. I chose to be nonoperative, to not have surgery…"

I drifted off, staring up at Dr. Maru. I realized that I was left staring into the red irises of a centuries-old vampire—who had given me as much of a miracle as anything in this world could.

"I'm scared. I'm scared it will be taken away from me. That it's all a joke or wrong or that it will reverse itself or something. I'm afraid it'll just be one more thing that I think I have in my life that gets snatched away."

"Well, I promise you I will do whatever I can to ensure this is not taken away from you," she told me. "Do you believe me?"

I nodded, unable to form the words I was sure she wanted to hear. I took a deep breath, trying to soothe the nerves that had been clawing around my insides. This was good news, not bad. In fact, it was amazing news. The kind of news that would literally be considered a miracle under any other circumstances.

But there was still one question I needed answered.

"Should I tell Wren?"

She shrugged and released my chin before she moved back behind her desk. "If you feel it necessary. Probably eventually if you two are going to be together."

"Do you…do you think she'll be happy about it?"

She was quiet for a long moment. "I think that she'll be happy about it if you are. Has she given you any reason to think otherwise?"

I shook my head. "No, no. She's been perfect. Absolutely perfect." My heart swelled just thinking about it. Goddess, I missed her. I wished she was here beside me. She'd reach out, hold my hand, make sure I was okay. Maybe a kiss…

"Natalie."

Dr. Maru's voice broke me from my thoughts, and I smiled sheepishly. "Sorry."

I left the office with a slight spring in my step and a second warning from the good doctor not to toss my meds just yet. She'd taken more blood to double-check things, but I was in too good a mood to care. Now all I needed to do was tell my Alpha about this.

I smiled. My Alpha. Definitely had the right ring to it.

CHAPTER TWENTY-SEVEN

Wren

I knew I needed to sit down and talk with Natalie. I knew we had to discuss what the future would bring and why we felt so connected. I knew that I couldn't just force her into something like being my mate for life without making her aware of all the risks and other things that could happen.

I knew that.

But the moment my eyes landed on her again at the diner, I couldn't even begin to care. I charged in, ignoring everything else, then took her hand and pulled her to me. My wolf almost purred at the surprised laugh that burst from her as I dug my nose into her collarbone, taking in that scent of her. The scent that made me want to tear her clothes off and take her right here on the bar in front of everyone.

"I missed you," she said, and I pulled her closer, tighter, like we were one person.

"I missed you too."

Mine! my wolf howled.

My sentiments exactly.

Her lips touched mine in a voracious meeting that bards would sing about for ages to come. Until something cold and wet slapped me in the face. Natalie shrieked as we parted, and I spun around to find whatever was attacking us.

Alisha stood behind the bar, a spray bottle in her hand. She gave us a stern look. "Get a room," she said, spraying another jet of water that barely missed my cheek. "Or don't and let me charge admission."

I held up my hands in surrender. "I get it, I get it. Sorry."

Natalie's apology echoed mine but was full of laughter. I handed her a napkin off the bar, and she wiped her face with it.

"You realize we aren't cats, right?"

Alisha raised an eyebrow. "Still works, doesn't it?"

"Yeah." Natalie chortled. "And since we're not cats, we might actually learn our lessons."

"I don't care either way," Alisha said, "but whatever you decide to do, do it off my floor."

"Your floor?" I couldn't keep the smile off my face.

"That's right, my floor. At least until my shift is over."

I opened my mouth, but Natalie moved in front of me, giving Alisha a sloppy salute. "Yes, ma'am." She grabbed my shirt and tugged me to the door. "Come on, kitty, we need to talk."

When we got outside, I turned and pushed her up against the Jeep. "Did you really just call me a kitty?" Her smile sent heat blooming through me, down between my thighs, where it ached.

"I couldn't very well call you puppy or wolfy, now, could I?"

"You're just getting yourself in deeper trouble, girl," I snarled. She didn't look the least bit afraid.

"Oh no, whatever shall I do against the big, bad wo—"

She finished the word inside my mouth before she started to moan as I pressed myself against her. Her arms wrapped around my neck, and she hoisted herself up so her legs could tuck around my waist. She let out a throaty growl.

"Seriously—" She panted as I kissed my way down her neck. "We—we need to talk, Wren."

"So, talk," I murmured into her glorious skin. She tasted like apples and peaches and summer and everything wonderful that I'd missed out on for so long.

"Not here! It's sensitive!"

I sucked her skin into my mouth and nipped at it. "If I take you somewhere private, the only thing you're going to be saying is my name."

"I...can live with that—"

I opened the door and shunted my mate into the passenger seat, then ran around to the driver's side. The engine was started, and I had peeled out of the parking lot by the time she got herself situated.

She barely got her seat belt on before I hit the highway and sped down the asphalt.

For the first time in…ever, I regretted the time it took to get from the diner to my house. Sure, it was only ten minutes, but with my libido roaring, it felt like the longest ten minutes of my life.

Even my wolf was riled up, but not in the usual way. There was no danger, no worry, only a desperate sense of needing to be close to Natalie and to have her with us. She wanted Natalie as much as I did, and as much as that scared me, I couldn't argue against it.

"So, Dr. Maru gave me some interesting news." Natalie's voice in the car made me jump a little. I realized I'd fallen too deep into my own thoughts and was barely paying attention to the road, never mind anything else.

"Oh? Do tell," I said, smooth and suave as always.

"Yeah, so I—um—I guess I don't need to take my meds anymore."

Panic shot through me at the words. "What do you mean? Is something wrong? Did something happen?" If something bad had happened to her, I'd be able to smell it, wouldn't I? If something had changed? I just wanted her to be herself, the beautiful woman that I was enjoying getting to know. Why would she need to stop her meds if they were working so wonderfully for her before?

I watched her shake her head in my periphery. "No, no, it's nothing like that. She thinks that her blood somehow…changed my body chemistry. Like I'm producing the right hormones and everything now instead of having to supplement." I felt her hand on my arm and covered it with my own. "I didn't mean to worry you."

I started to shake my head but stopped. The truth was I was worried for a second. Worried that something had gone wrong. "I'm sorry," I said, and truly I was for reacting the way I did immediately. "I know how important your medications are for you and who you are. I was scared that something was going to take that away." I slowed the Jeep down before I drove past my turnoff. "Especially because it was me who told Hikaru to give you her blood. If that's the reason you couldn't…"

"No, Wren," she said. "It's not your fault, and I would never blame you anyways. You did what you had to in order to make sure

I survived. I'd never fault you for that. But this is a bit of uncharted territory. No one could have predicted that her blood would do this to me, so I'm not even certain what's going to happen."

"What do you mean?"

"I mean if it's maybe temporary or permanent, if I'll have to continue to supplement with my meds, or it I can stop taking them altogether. Things like that. Dr. Maru took more blood and we're going to work together on this over the next little bit."

I parked the Jeep in front of my house. Neither of us moved as I cut the engine.

"I thought it was important that you know," she added quietly.

"Why?" I asked, honestly curious.

"Because you're important to me. And you accept and support me in all of my transition goodness." She looked down at her feet, her voice going soft, timid. "Is it bad that I told you?"

I took her hand in mine and pressed it to my lips for a quick kiss. I put my other hand beneath her chin, raising it until I could see her face and look her in the eye. "No," I said, "it's definitely not bad that you told me. I want to know everything about you, Natalie. I want to be here for you in everything, whether it has to do with your transition or not. I think you are an amazing, beautiful, strong young woman who knows what she wants and is so damned courageous."

She blinked several times, and I could see tears welling up in her eyes.

"How can you think that? You barely even know me."

I wiped away a tear with my thumb and smiled at her. "I know enough. I know you helped to save someone you didn't know. I know you stood up to monstrous people when you had no idea what was going on. And I know you accepted me for who and what I am with barely a word of concern." I leaned forward, placing a soft kiss on her lips. Her eyes closed and her breath hitched as she opened for me, but I didn't take the kiss deeper. "I think you're amazing, Natalie Donovan. I think you're perfect."

Except that you're human.

I didn't say that part. I was still trying to figure out what that meant for us. I pushed away Kendra's voice in my head, warning me about humans and making her my mate, and focused on the present. I wanted nothing but the beautiful woman in my arms, and from the way she looked at me, the way she pressed her lips against mine, it was safe to say that all she wanted was me.

❖

The day had passed into night by the time I woke, cuddled under the covers with a beautiful woman on my arm. Her lips puckered slightly, eyelids fluttering in slumber. The world felt right, being here with her. Like this was where we were supposed to be.

And it scared the hell out of me.

Watching her for a long moment, I couldn't bring myself to wake her up. She was peaceful, content, and I didn't want her to awaken into my crazy inhuman world.

Slowly, I pulled my body out from under her. A sigh escaped her lips as she nestled into the pillow that was still warm with our scents, but she didn't awaken.

I padded away from the bed, then headed downstairs. The book Kendra had let me take sat on the kitchen island, waiting to be looked at. I tried to have a staring contest with it. It was two minutes before I blinked, losing to something with no eyes.

"Focus," I whispered. All this mate stuff had to get pushed to the side. Heather needed help and she was a part of my pack. My responsibility.

For the first time, that idea didn't make me want to throw up.

My eyes flitted over page after page. Apex Alphas, Omega Wolves, Territory Bonds, Turning a Human. I paused on those pages. It was so tempting, but I shook my head. I couldn't look at that, not yet. It wasn't even something I was sure Natalie wanted to consider. Would she want to be like me?

Every few topics seemed to be written in a different hand, like the journal had been passed around for a number of Alphas to fill in their thoughts and knowledge. Other topics seemed to have arguments going on right there on the page, when one Alpha disagreed with another. It was almost a comical look at how our history was expected to be passed down. Talk about archaic.

Then I found the pages about the pack bond. I'd heard of that bond before. My old Alpha would only bond with the dominants in the pack. He treated it like a special reward, one the submissives couldn't reach. Instead, the submissives were controlled by the dominants, usually by being forced to take on a mate bond. It was those kinds of archaic practices that made me not want a pack. But now that I had one, I had to look into doing things my own way. With Heather now, I thought I could do that. I could handle a pack bond with her. One person, maybe two, just to start. Maybe I could be an Alpha.

A tear rolled down, startling me. I wiped it away angrily. This was stupid, getting worked up about all of this. I was just doing what was right. Helping people who deserved it. That's all. That's what this was.

At the thought of Heather, I could feel something in my gut stir. It was similar to the feeling Natalie gave me, but softer, less intense.

Duh. This was the pack bond. Feeling her, I focused on that sensation until it became almost like a tether between us. Then I pulled on it.

The effect was almost instantaneous. I felt Heather jerk awake, her confusion traveling back down the tether. I eased up, trying to send apologetic feelings to her. No idea if it worked or not. Either way, I could still sense her, and a few minutes later, she was moving, coming closer to my house.

Moments later, there was a soft knock on the door, and I went to open it. Heather stood on the step, eyes downcast, her head tilted to the side to show her neck in submission.

"You called, Alpha?"

I ran a hand through my hair and growled. "You don't need to grovel to me. You know that."

She looked up, sheepish. "It's habit, sorry. I never met a dominant wolf who didn't enjoy seeing their submissive wolves being submissive."

"You know I'm not like that."

She shook her head. "You don't understand. That's the way it is in a lot of packs. Submissive wolves are treated like crap if they don't fall in line with what the dominants want."

I pinched the bridge of my nose. "This is why I wanted nothing to do with a pack. Ever."

"Well, too late now." She glanced behind her at the sedan I'd lent her. "Unless you want me to go, that is."

"No, no. It's just too much crap in too short a time, you know?"

"It can't help that you met your mate too."

I threw my hands in the air. "Does everyone know about this? Was there a freaking Google Meet about it? A Facebook event?"

I returned to my seat in the kitchen, Heather following me as she laughed softly. "It's not the first time I've seen a wolf going through heat for their mate."

I waved a hand. "We are not talking about that right now."

"Yes, ma'am." She looked around the kitchen. "If you don't want to talk about that, then why did you call for me?"

With a long sigh, I explained my mistake—my testing of the bond between us. I told her how it felt different than Natalie's, and maybe we could use the pack bond to figure out how to break her wolf out of the chains holding it.

She stared into the distance as I finished. Like she was trying not to have too much faith that we could figure something out.

"Heather," I began, "I am going to find a way to help you. I promised before, and I don't break promises."

Her shrug was nonchalant, but I could see the war of emotions in her eyes. "No biggie. Honestly. I've lived with it so long, it's like second nature."

"You say that, but I can sense how you really feel." I grinned. "The pack bond doesn't lie."

Groaning, she stood and started pacing between the kitchen and living room.

"I just don't want to get my hopes up, okay? I've had people telling me for years that they would help me figure this all out. That they would help free my wolf. And guess what? My wolf is still locked away deep inside me. I've never even had a chance to meet her, you know? I've never shifted, never felt the wind in my fur, my paws running across the ground. I missed out on all that because my mother wanted to punish my father!"

I settled a hand on her shoulder and pulled her into a hug. "It's okay. We'll figure this out. I won't stop until we get it fixed. Okay?"

She sniffled. "I didn't even know, you know? That I was a wolf. For the longest time all I felt was like something was missing, being kept from me. Like the life I was living was somehow…wrong." She shook her head.

"We'll make it right. I promise you that."

I pulled her in close, her head pressing into my shoulder. She shook several times, sniffling into my shirt. It didn't matter. Tears and snot washed out of clothing just fine.

Someone cleared their throat and we leapt apart. Natalie was standing at the bottom of the stairs, a small smile playing on her lips. "Am I interrupting something?"

It took everything inside me not to throw her over my shoulder and take her back upstairs.

"Sorry, Nat," I said, "didn't mean to wake you."

"We were just going over some research," Heather added, "and trying to fix me."

Natalie nodded sagely, a finger to her lips as she moved into the kitchen and took my vacated stool. "I remember you saying that your mother hired a witch to lock your wolf away, right?" Heather nodded as I wondered where my mate was going with this. "Well, have you ever considered going to another witch to try to break the curse?"

The silence that filled the room sat heavily on us. I glanced at Heather. She glanced at me, too many emotions crossing her face.

Natalie gave us that little smile again. "I'll take that as a no."

"Fuck. I didn't even think about that."

"I mean, it might work. If we find someone strong enough," Heather added.

"But if your wolf doesn't want to come out..." I began.

"You can take care of that," she was quick to point out. "If we can strengthen the pack bond between us, then you'll be my Alpha properly. You can call my wolf to you, to make me shift."

I glanced from her to my mate and back again. "Holy shit, I think we have a plan."

Heather squealed and threw her arms around my neck, hugging tight. A second later, she was across the kitchen and pulling Natalie into the same hug.

"I know I'm not supposed to get my hopes up," she sobbed into Natalie's shoulder. "But this might actually work. I've never been this close before!"

"Shh," Natalie soothed her, "it's okay. We'll see this through, okay? We'll take care of you." Her eyes caught mine over Heather's head. "We're both here for you, okay?"

My heart broke to see her fulfilling the roll of Lupa, the Alpha's mate. The Alpha was strength and command, the Lupa was compassion and love. Together the pair would take care of the wolves in their pack. And my mate was already acting like the perfect choice.

Heather pulled back and Natalie gave her a pat on the back a few times before she stopped sniffling again.

"So," she began quietly, turning to me. "Know any witches?"

I frowned. "Um, no. No, I don't."

"Me neither, to be fair," Natalie added.

Heather shook her head. "Not me. Guess that means a road trip."

Natalie smiled. "I'll get the snacks."

Chapter Twenty-eight

Natalie

I awoke buried within Wren's arms and snuggled in as close to her as I could. Her legs shifted, one thigh pressing between my legs in the perfect spot that made me gasp a little too loudly. Wren didn't even open her eyes, but the smile that bloomed over her lips told me she was nowhere near as asleep as I'd assumed she was.

"Open for me," she murmured in that voice that made me want to do whatever she said without question.

And I did. I lifted my legs apart, and her thigh entered the gap in the perfect angle that it hit the most sensitive part of my clit. I moaned into the pillow and Wren chuckled before twisting us both until I was on my back and she was atop me.

"Good morning," I said.

"It certainly is."

As her hand leisurely traveled down my body, I decided it was a wonderful idea to sleep naked in this giant bed with my gorgeous girlfriend. No underwear or clothing to get in the way of spontaneous morning fun-times. I stared up into those beautiful emerald eyes and rose up enough to capture her lips on mine.

Her powerful arms raised her over me as she stared down, a gleam in her eye and smile on her lips.

"Stay," she commanded, then rolled off the bed to the side. I didn't go to follow her, despite how much I wanted to, but I did watch as she started digging through her nightstand. A moment later she pulled out something dark with several straps and something that made my jaw drop.

"Wren?" I gasped and stared at the not large but still slightly intimidating dildo that she was affixing to the harness.

She paused, looking up at me. "Are you okay with this?"

I nodded vehemently. "Very, very much."

"Have you done this before?"

"A couple of times…" I said, remembering too much of my life with Misty and the things she frowned upon.

Wren smiled, and it chased the bad memories out of my head. She handed me a small bottle of lube, then climbed back on top of me, pushing me up so I was sitting up. The dildo stood at attention over my chest, and I had to resist the urge to put my mouth on it.

"Lube me up," Wren said, her voice a low growl that sent electric shivers to every part of my body. I did as she asked, using a generous amount of lube on the dildo, feeling it dripping off onto my stomach. "Good girl," she said, then backed off me. "Now flip over, on your knees."

I moved faster than I think I ever moved in my life, and a second later, I felt the tip of the dildo.

"Is this okay?" Wren asked from behind me, and my heart soared. I nodded enthusiastically, not trusting my words to come out as something coherent to human—or werewolf—ears.

The moan that slipped out of my mouth echoed through my head and the bedroom as she pushed inside me. I'd never felt anything like it before. Fingers wrapped in my hair and pulled my head back and I moaned again, panting like I had lost all control over every part of my body.

"Wren," I gasped as I felt her hips touch my ass. "Please, Wren!"

She backed up and thrust again, building up speed as she went until I cried out and had to reach down with one hand, touching myself.

"Good girl," Wren grunted, "touch yourself for me."

I moaned and gasped as her fingers tightened in my hair again and pulled deliciously tight. "Oh fuck! Wren, please!"

"Please what?"

"Please! Bite me!"

Wren froze halfway into me. "What?"

"Bite me!" I begged her. "I'm your mate! Make me yours, please!"

I tried to look over my shoulder at her, but her grip tightened in my hair, and I gasped. She began moving again, filling me with the dildo as I continued to touch myself and I tried to find my words. She leaned against me, her breasts pressing against my back. Her mouth touched my shoulder, my neck, and planted soft bites in places I couldn't see.

"Come for me," she whispered in my ear, "do it now."

And as if I were waiting for her permission, the orgasm that hit me had me seeing stars. I faltered, falling to the bed as Wren eased the dildo out and slid to the side. She rested a hand on my side, and I looked up at her, taking warmth in her soft smile.

"Rest, darling," she said, "I'm going to clean this up."

I nodded and she disappeared from the bed toward the bathroom. My bottom ached, but it was a good sore, and I felt so damned good I could just stay in bed for the rest of my life. But the longer she was gone, the more my brain decided to betray me.

Why had Wren hesitated? Dr. Maru had told me how the mate bite worked. There was no reason for her not to do it, right?

I tried to push those thoughts out of my head. It was just surprise that made her freeze. That's it. That's all it was.

At least, that's what I was going to tell myself. Even so, I still grabbed Alton the stuffed wolf and cuddled up with him as I heard the shower turn on in the bathroom. It didn't do much to stop the fear that started spiraling in my head.

❖

I waved good-bye as once more Wren's Jeep left her cabin without me. I understood. I wasn't that clingy girlfriend who couldn't be away from my lady for more than a few minutes at a time. I refused to be that person.

The wolves had gone off on their search for a witch, leaving me here alone to try to understand what had happened this morning. Since then, she had been a little more distant than normal. Or it was just something that was in my head. I mean, from the outside looking in, it probably was no different, but with the way my mind was spiraling, I was certain something was wrong.

If I really thought about it—a dangerous idea for someone like me—she had seemed almost different since the moment she returned from Silva. Maybe that time away had given her a chance to think clearly about dating me. Maybe there was something wrong with me.

Was it Heather? As jealous as I felt of their closeness and the fact that Heather was part of Wren's pack, I did not feel that Heather was competition. I could feel Wren's strong emotions. I had no idea how, but I could feel them. And they didn't spike when she saw Heather like they did when our eyes met and neither of us could look away.

The farther Wren traveled, the more my abdomen ached with her loss. I groaned and went back into Wren's cabin, as much a home to me now as my apartment with Misty had been. I glanced at her liquor cabinet, considering for a brief moment, before shaking my head. It wasn't worth it. I was never one who could hold my alcohol. I had never been able to build up a tolerance.

The cabin was far too silent for comfort, and I found myself wandering around. In Wren's bedroom I stared at the huge bed that still smelled like her and resisted the urge to curl up with nothing but the pillow and little wolf Alton. Then I caught a glimpse of the leather-bound journal Wren had been poring over for the past couple of days.

Was it something in that journal that was forcing Wren to back away from me? Did it tell her something that made her scared of whatever this was between us? It was all happening so fast, so hard, that it was almost difficult to believe. Whatever it was that made Wren what she was—and it was still hard to believe—had brought the two of us together, I was certain of it.

The lure of that damned journal was too great. I grabbed it and slipped into the armchair on the other side of the room, putting my feet up as I flipped slowly through the pages. The topics sounded unbelievable to my human mind. The first topic was already frightening: Apex Alpha Werewolves—wolves that had a fourth, monstrous form that could take them over during times of great mental or physical distress. Wren was pretty hot as her hybrid form, barring the claws that could tear me to shreds, and adorable as a full wolf. It was hard to imagine her as a monster.

I flipped through more pages. Omega Wolves were a rare opposite of an Alpha wolf; Pack Bond—something that happened between the Alpha and their pack when both parties allowed it. As I read the info, it was similar to what Wren and I had, but I wasn't a wolf. Then, near the back of the book, was a topic that read True Mates.

If I wanted to know what was going on with me and Wren, and everything, this would be a way.

"True mates," I spoke aloud as I read. "Or fated mates. Each wolf has the potential to meet their one true mate. An Alpha's mate, or Lupa or Lupo, is often considered a once-in-a-lifetime opportunity. There is a mate for every wolf, but there are no guarantees that they will find each other—" I cut myself off when my eyes caught something interesting. I couldn't read it, though. It said more about mates, but whatever had been written had been crossed out so vehemently that the rest of it was illegible. In the margin beside the scratched-out words was a scrawled handwriting.

"Humans cannot be mates. They cannot handle the power, the magic. Humans must not be subjected to our magic." I read aloud, already feeling the tears welling up in my eyes. The rest of the page finished: "Finding one's true mate is extremely rare, with only the luckiest wolves finding them. This has brought rise to the belief that true mates are a gift from the Mother of Wolves and not to be taken lightly."

Was that what Wren was worried about? Being stuck with one person as her mate for the rest of her life? Or was it because I was human? Or transgender?

Was that the reason she was pushing me away? Because I was...different?

I wiped my eyes, scanning the couple of pages again to make sure I didn't miss anything. "The bond between true mates does not require the mate bite to start, but it must be done to bring the bond to completion. In some cases, true mates have developed mate bond characteristics even shortly after meeting, such as tapping into each other's senses—" Well, that explained what happened in the forest when I was running so damned easily. "And feeling each other's emotions and sharing in great physical pa—" I shut the journal and tossed it back onto the bedside table.

I wondered if Wren had read this already. If so, why hadn't she mentioned this to me? Maybe she was just tired, and I was reading into things far too much. Maybe I was just seeing things, projecting my own feelings onto her because she wasn't as present as she had been a couple of days ago. Of course she wasn't. She was an Alpha, and one of her pack had a problem that she had to take care of, and that was important too. I couldn't be mad at her for helping someone else. And I knew it must be difficult to take all these new things in stride.

I shook my head and left the bedroom. I grabbed my keys and phone and then headed out to the truck. I couldn't just sit here doing nothing or I was going to fall apart. There was nothing wrong between us. I believed that. I needed to believe that.

Because if there were something wrong, what would I be able to do to change it?

❖

I was beginning to feel like I spent more time at the diner than I had at either Rory's or Wren's cabins by now. I was tucked into the booth in the far corner, nursing my third—fourth?—glass of Coke.

I knew there were things that I should probably be doing. I knew there were things that I could go out to find to do. But even with the best of intentions, I found myself here, desperate for something that reminded me of Wren. The entire diner smelled like her—or she smelled like it, anyway, but it didn't matter. I was comfortable here. I didn't want to wait at home like I was nothing but her pet.

Though that wasn't a terrible daydream either.

I hid my blushing face in my hands as the image popped into my head. Me, kneeling on her bed, wearing nothing but a thick leather collar that had a tag dangling from it. Proclaiming me as her property. My thighs started rubbing together almost of their own volition, and I quickly banished all of those thoughts before they could get me into trouble.

"Hey, Nat, you okay?" I glanced up at Alisha, who was standing behind the bar. She gave me a sideways smile. "Just checking on you. Don't want the boss lady to come back and think I wasn't taking care of her beau."

I laughed with her, but it was far too forced for comfort. "Don't worry about it. I just miss her."

"You've got it bad, girly."

I sighed. "You have no idea."

"Let me know if you need anything."

I started to say it was all good when the scent of food drifted from the back room. "Yeah, I mean, I could use a burger and fries if that's cool."

"No tomato, no onions?"

I smiled. It tickled me that she knew how I liked my burger. It wasn't like I was in here *every* day. "Yeah, thanks."

The distraction of food was a welcome one and I did my best to savor it, pulling up an e-book on my phone to try to take my mind off Wren and everything else that was tumbling about in my brain. That's why I didn't look up when the bells on the diner door rang and clacking heels stomped around the diner.

"Natty!"

My head wrenched up with a terrifying crack.

"M-Misty?"

The woman standing beside my table was tall with the five-inch heels that she always wore. Long blond hair artfully hung down just past her shoulders. Her face was contoured until her cheekbones looked sharp enough to cut steel. Lips, ruby red and full, parted slightly with every breath as ice-blue eyes moved up and down me and the seat I was in. Her clothes, like her makeup and hair, were immaculate: jeans that were tight enough to bounce a quarter off her ass, a tight tank top that showed off her chest and stomach, and a classy three-quarter-sleeve denim jacket.

Everywhere she went, she wanted to be the center of the universe—and most of the time she succeeded.

"I can't believe you're sitting in the middle of this one-horse town, and I can't believe you made me drive all the way here to rescue you!"

"R-rescue me?"

"Duh! I mean you left the city without a damned word!" Her voice was loud and almost a screech, earning stares from the couple of other diners and from Alisha behind the counter. I caught her eyes and gave the smallest twitch of my head. This was my mess. She didn't need to get involved.

"I left because I needed to get away."

She laughed, the sound full of scorn. "Yeah, get away. From what, Natty? Me? Well, clearly that isn't working so well. I mean, look at you!"

I looked down at my loose jeans and simple T-shirt. Sure, not the most feminine of outfits, but it was comfortable.

"You look like you're not bothering to put any effort in! Like you don't care if people see you as a woman anymore!"

"Of course I care," I said, "but I don't need to go all-out all the time to please everyone else. I am who I am, and that needs to be enough."

She laughed again and I could feel my heart pounding in my chest—and not in the good way. Flashbacks of my life bombarded my mind, and I could feel myself tearing up as I lowered my eyes.

"And what are you eating?" She continued like she couldn't care less about what her words were doing to me. "A burger and fries? Do you know how many carbs and fat there are in all that? What happened to the diet we had you on, huh? We wanted you looking your best, remember? The meds did such a number on your body. It was me who helped you through all of that."

"Yeah...I know. I know you did." My voice sounded far too soft and weak.

"Then you remember how much we sacrificed, Natty. How much *I* sacrificed for you. We were in this together, Natty. I can't let you throw all that away!"

I wanted to yell at her, to scream at her. I didn't throw it away. I had let myself think I was in a healthy, loving relationship with a woman who wanted me to be my true, honest self. It wasn't that, but I had thought it was all I could ever have. Now, with Wren, things were easier. At least they had been. But no matter what I wanted to do, I couldn't even lift my head to look at her.

"Excuse me." A woman's voice cut into Misty's tirade. "Ma'am, it would be appreciated if you could take a seat and keep your voice to a more reasonable volume."

Now I did look up, watching Misty turn upon the newcomer. She was shorter than Misty, brunette hair cut into a cute pixie that helped frame a sweetheart face. She wore a brown sheriff's deputy uniform, complete with badge and a pistol in an unsnapped holster.

"Oh, I'm sorry, Deputy Dawg! Am I making life a little more

interesting around here? A taste of what you're missing on black-and-white TV?"

The deputy looked my way. "Natalie, is this woman bothering you?"

I was about to shake my head when Misty screeched: "Of course I'm not bothering her! I'm her girlfriend!"

The deputy's face turned cold toward Misty, a hand on the butt of her weapon. "Ma'am, I don't know who you are, but you are not Natalie's girlfriend. I'm going to have to ask you to leave."

"Excuse me? Why should I have to leave?"

"Because you are disturbing the good people of my town, and you need to leave. Now."

"I'm not going anywhere."

"Go, now, or I will personally escort you out at gunpoint. Then we'll get into my squad car, and I will drive you out of town and leave you by the side of the road to walk back to the city." She gave Misty an evil smile. "How does that sound?"

"Fine. Fine! I'm leaving!" She turned back to me. "I'll see you later, Natty. I'll help you put yourself back together. I promise."

She stormed past the deputy and out of the diner. Applause started from the other diners the moment the door closed behind her, and the tension in the air dissipated. Yet in my head I still couldn't help but think about all that Misty had seen me through. Starting my transition, living with her and her family for years before we moved out together. They had saved me from my family. I owed Misty so much. It made me feel sick. I pushed the half-finished burger and fries away and rested my head on the table.

"I'm Danaan Rias. Wren's told me all about you, Ms. Natalie. That's how I knew that woman was *not* your girlfriend," the deputy said as she slipped into the seat across from me with a soft smile. "Are you okay?"

"Sure. You know, I'm just fucking peachy. Wren is off dealing with something that I can't really help with, my toxic-as-shit ex-girlfriend just made a scene in the middle of Wren's diner for the whole town to see, and I've got shit to deal with that Dr. Maru tells me is fucking important." I slammed my forehead against the table hard enough to make sure it hurt. "Plus, I'm pining massively for my new girlfriend, the gorgeous owner of this diner, who I only met like two weeks ago and now there's shit going on between us that I have no fucking idea how to fix." I looked up at her, knowing there was a red welt on my head. "So, yeah. I'm just fine. How are you?"

"I think it's safe to say better than you." She smiled and offered me a napkin. "You've got something on your forehead."

The napkin came away with a few drops of ketchup and fry crumbs. "Thanks, Danaan."

She shook her head. "Call me Rias. Everyone does."

I looked her up and down. "You're one of Zeke's?"

"Not quite. I am a deputy of this fine county's sheriff's office, but I'm not one of Zeke's family."

I raised an eyebrow to her. "Wait, you know about all the…"

"Yup. Hard not to with the number of us in town." She laughed. "You think Wren and Hikaru and Zeke are all we have here?"

"I mean, that's all I know of. And Heather, of course."

She reached over and stole a fry from my plate.

"So, what're you?" I asked, lowering my voice to make sure the conversation stayed private.

"You can't tell?"

I gave her a blank look. "Should I be able to?"

"I guess not." She stole another fry. "I just figured, you know, you seem to be so damned popular with us supernatural folks that I figured you'd be able to tell with a look."

My gut clenched. Suddenly, I could feel Wren and her frustration and impatience tightened in my stomach. And underneath those feelings, there was a sense of fear. Had she felt my response to Misty? I shook my head to quickly dismiss the thought. I was overthinking it. I had to be. But even if that were true, I wasn't being stupid. Wren was putting up walls, and I didn't know why.

"I'm not that popular," I muttered. *And getting less so every day*, I added silently. I shook my head, trying to clear those kinds of thoughts. I needed to be better.

"What?"

I shook my head. "Nothing. So, are you going to tell me, or do I have to guess?"

She smiled. She lifted a hand and waggled her fingers in the air. "I'm a witch."

I stared at her. "Are you fucking kidding me?"

Chapter Twenty-nine

Wren

"You have got to be kidding me."

I stared at Natalie and Deputy Rias. Together with Heather, we had commandeered the kitchen table in the deputy's home, a simple bungalow set back in a massive yard that encroached on the wild forests surrounding most of the town.

"There was a fucking witch here the whole time and we didn't even know?"

Rias shrugged. "You didn't ask."

I glared at her. I was already pissed about what had happened with Misty, and finding out about the witch wasn't making it easier to focus.

I'd never seen her out of her deputy uniform before, but her choice of baggy cargo shorts and tank top suited the warm night. I could admit that she looked good, but my eyes were constantly drawn to my mate. Natalie was still in jeans and a T-shirt, and my mind was pulling off her clothes bit by bit. Revealing her underwear, her bra, seeing if they matched, and then getting a glimpse of what was hiding beneath them.

I shivered and pulled my attention back to the situation at hand.

"I've been here for years. How didn't I know that you were a witch?"

"Again, you never asked. And I don't exactly go around advertising. The term *witch hunt* takes on a very real meaning for people like me."

"That makes sense," Heather interjected. "We spent most of the day in the city, hunting down leads on a coven to try to get them to help us." She grabbed a piece of pizza from the open box in the middle of the table. "News flash—they weren't interested."

Rias chuckled, but there was little amusement in the sound. "Yeah, that sounds about right. If it's the coven I'm thinking of, they don't have the best track record with helping anyone, really. They work for themselves and only themselves." Her face darkened as she pushed around a leftover crust on her plate aimlessly. "They tread real close to breaking the Rule of Three."

I glanced at Heather and Natalie. I wasn't exactly a practicing pagan or Wiccan, but even I'd heard of the Rule of Three. That what you put out into the world comes back to you in threes, both positive and negative. But the way Rias said it felt more significant than just a simple karmic balance.

"So why are you out here, on your own?" Natalie asked. "Or is there a coven here that no one told Wren about?"

I scowled but the other girls had a good laugh.

"No," Rias said, "no coven. I left the last one I was in a long time ago." She paused for a moment. "Let's just say I didn't approve of the direction they were taking things. I needed to get out of there, so I came here."

Natalie nodded, and the conversation continued, but their voices faded into the background for me. I could focus on nothing but my mate. Her upset feelings from her confrontation with Misty had riled up not only me, but my wolf too. *She* wanted to hunt down the stupid bitch that would talk to our mate like that. The fear and despair I'd felt over our connection had torn me apart. It had hit when we'd been tracking down the coven and I nearly shifted then and there, ready to tear out the person's neck. Heather had to pull me away from the witch, who was certainly not about to lend help to someone they called a rabid wolf.

We weren't mated yet. I knew that. But this connection with her had grown all on its own. One day it wasn't there, the next suddenly I could feel what she was feeling, could feel where she was. I'd never heard of anything like this before. Even Heather couldn't recall another wolf ever speaking of it. It was like a pre-mate bond. A partner bond, maybe. Once my heart knew who she was to me, that was when we were connected. Was it as strong on her end? As I stared into her eyes and she met mine, I wanted to say yes.

But she was human. She was human and that meant I couldn't have her. Could I? She'd begged me to bite her, to make her my mate. And by the Mother, I desperately wanted to. My wolf wanted her. *I* wanted her. But the book said she couldn't. Kendra said she couldn't. I wasn't going to risk her just to make her my mate.

Something hit my shin under the table, and I blinked, turning to Heather. She glared at me before turning back to Rias.

"So do you think you can help us with this?" she was saying.

"There's a good chance, yeah. But I'd have to get a look at the inside of you, see what's in there keeping your wolf all locked up."

"Okay. How do we do that?"

Rias stood, dusting pizza crumbs off her hands. "Come with me. I have an altar in the other room I can use to help. I'll take a look, then we can see what's what."

Heather looked at me as if asking for permission.

"Go ahead," I told her. "Anything we can do to help, just ask."

"Just stay out here," Rias said. "Too many people around can muddy up what I'm doing."

"Oh, I think they'd much prefer to stay out here," Heather said as she followed Rias out of the kitchen.

The moment they were gone, we were out of our chairs and clinging to each other. I dug my nose into the side of her neck, taking in that beautiful blend of smells that was my mate. Like pine trees and fresh baked bread, like cinnamon and just a hint of spiciness. It filled my nostrils and I groaned loud enough for her to gasp against me.

"Wren," she cried as I planted kiss after kiss up her neck until I claimed her mouth. I caught her bottom lip in my teeth and bit down until she whimpered.

Mine, my wolf howled.

Ours, I agreed.

"Wren! Please!" she gasped again as I released her lip. "We need to talk."

"I know," I leaned over and whispered in her ear. "I know what happened. I'm so sorry. I should've been here to help. I should've been here to protect you."

Her lips touched my cheek then moved down the side of my neck. Her teeth nipped at my skin.

"It's not…" she began, as her mouth moved against my skin. "Not your fault. I should be—" She gasped as I moved my hand over her breast and flicked her pebbled nipple. "I should be stronger."

You're perfect. The words were on the tip of my tongue, but I couldn't get them out. She was perfect. As I pressed lips to flesh and played with the sensitive parts of her chest, I knew she was absolutely perfect for me in every way.

Except one. She was human.

It wasn't fair. She couldn't know the dangers of being involved in my world. She'd already had a taste of them, and that was far from the worst it could be. What if another pack tried to attack us? Or worse, hunters? No matter how peacefully we lived, there were always those who thought people like us shouldn't exist. I didn't want her to have to deal with that.

"It's okay," I whispered into her ear. I bit the lobe and tugged softly. "You're wonderful just as you are."

She sighed into me, pressing herself tight to me as her leg found its way between mine. She lifted her knee until I was rubbing against her and growling under my breath.

The things this girl did to me.

"You're mine," I growled, "all mine."

"Yours!" she gasped, and I pushed her back and took control again.

I trapped her against the kitchen wall and lifted her shirt until I could get proper access to her beautiful breasts. With one hand, I kneaded her breasts, trying to give equal time to each, as I moved the other hand down and quickly undid the button on her jeans.

"Wren!" she moaned. She leaned forward in an attempt to capture me, but I pushed her back.

"No. I am going to make you mine."

She writhed against the wall and her hands flailed uselessly as I touched her clit and wrapped my hand around it. It was trying to stand at its full length, and I smiled. She was already wet, and it was easy to start focusing on the parts I knew were going to drive her wild.

And they did.

She thrashed and moaned and clamped her hand over her mouth after a particularly loud cry when I bent forward and took one of her nipples into my mouth. I brushed it with my teeth and held it gently as I pulled away from her body. She stopped breathing for a good few seconds before I let it fall.

"Wren," she whimpered, "please!"

"No, darling." I moved into her again, working her into a fervor as I wrapped my other hand into her hair and pulled her head to the side. "You don't come until I tell you to come, understand?"

She whimpered again as I drew my teeth along her neck and collarbone and nipped at the skin there. I pulled the collar of her shirt down her shoulder, which gave me better access as I left a trail of mouth-shaped bruises from ear to arm.

"Wren!" she cried. Her eyes were wide open. I glanced at them, seeing the golden reflection of my own eyes in them. Arousal filled my nostrils, and I could feel my body reacting. Fur grew along my arms and legs, my ears moved to the top of my head, and my teeth lengthened and sharpened. Fear flashed across Nat's face, and I buried my head in her neck, focusing on the scent of her, and not how scared she suddenly was. "Please, Wren!" she gasped as I continued to pleasure her with a hand now furred with small sharp claws. "Please! Bite me!"

I pulled my head back and stared at her.

"Bite me!" she pleaded again, her eyes closed, as her body writhed under my ministrations. "Please!"

I leaned into her again and rubbed my body against her. I placed my mouth to her ear and whispered, "Come for me. Do it now." My low voice sounded like a hungry growl.

I moved down to her collarbone, my mouth wide with sharp teeth and ready for the bite. She wanted it. I needed it. We were mates. It was meant to be. Wasn't it?

Humans cannot handle this. Kendra's words echoed in my head. *Most of them can barely survive the mate bite! I assure you, going further with this girl will not end well.* I pulled back as she began to shudder and cry out and wetness exploded over my hand. *You must either turn her or let her go.*

Then I was across the room. I wiped my hand on a napkin as Natalie collapsed against the wall. She slid down to the floor with a soft gasp, disheveled and eyes out of focus. I loved seeing her so wrecked. But as her vision cleared and she stared at me, I could see the beginnings of tears in her eyes. I took a step forward but stopped myself. I couldn't do it. I was too close to biting her before. I couldn't let that happen.

Humans cannot handle this.

Those words were going to haunt me for the rest of the night, but there was nothing I could do. I couldn't bite Natalie. She couldn't be my mate.

"Nat," I began as she slowly started to get herself put back together.

A second later, the door opened, and Rias returned with Heather following. They looked from me to Nat and back again. Heather chuckled and shook her head while Rias went to the counter and picked up a roll of paper towel, then tossed it to Natalie.

"Really?" She directed the question at me. "You couldn't wait?"

There was no good answer, so I shrugged. "Sorry."

"Well, get cleaned up," Heather said. "We're doing this tonight."

"Tonight?" Natalie gasped.

Rias nodded. "No time like the present. We can take care of it in the backyard, but I'm going to need you, Wren."

I glanced at Nat. "What about Natalie?"

"I want to be here." The words dropped out of her quicker than she could think about it. I raised an eyebrow.

"It might be dangerous."

Rias seconded my comment.

Nat shook her head, standing and turning her back to us all as she put herself back together. "I don't care. This is my family too."

My heart all but broke at her conviction.

"Okay," Heather said, "but if it goes bad you run into the house and barricade yourself, understand?"

She nodded, her eyes a little wide.

"Good," Rias said, "then let's get this done."

CHAPTER THIRTY

Wren

Together we cleared off the concrete pad that Rias used in lieu of a back deck. On either side of the yard was a large, nine-foot privacy fence preventing the neighbors from being too nosy. The back of the yard encroached on a field that led to one of the many wild forests of pine trees found along the foothills approaching the Rocky Mountains.

I couldn't help but wonder who else in this town was hiding secrets. Like me, like Rias, like Hikaru. I knew Zeke had family here, parents and a few siblings and cousins, but in five years I felt like I'd barely scratched the surface of this place.

Maybe I didn't want to.

It's not like I went out of my way to ask around, to find a community. I didn't want anyone. I was a werewolf with a huge chip on my shoulder. I don't even know what Hikaru saw in me that day or why she let me buy her building.

"Wren." Rias's voice broke me from my thoughts.

"Are we ready?" I glanced around. Rias had drawn a large, unbroken circle in chalk on the concrete. Heather waited inside it, legs crossed, hands fidgeting like she couldn't stop them.

"We're ready," she confirmed. She beckoned Natalie over, who had been standing a little away from the non-humans. "I can't just delete the spell that is keeping her wolf locked up. It doesn't work that way. But what I can do is weaken it."

"What do you mean?" I demanded.

"Think of the witch's spell like a cage inside Heather, and her wolf is trapped inside the cage, okay?" We both nodded. "I can't just unlock the cage without knowing exactly how the witch did it in the first place. But I might be able to bend the bars enough to let the wolf out."

"Is this going to be dangerous?" Natalie asked in a small voice.

"Potentially, yes." Rias caught my eye and held it. "That's where you come in, Wren. Her wolf has never known freedom. She's going to be scared, and that can be dangerous. I need you to help."

"How?"

"When I'm ready, I will call for you. I want you to break the circle and do whatever Alpha magic you can to make sure her wolf comes out peacefully." She gave us a wry smile. "Preferably before she rips my throat out."

"But I don't—" I began, but Rias was already taking her position inside the circle beside Heather. A warm hand touched my shoulder. Natalie was there, a soft smile on her face.

"You can do this, Wren," she said. "You can be exactly the Alpha Heather needs right now."

"Natalie—"

She shook her head before I could continue, moved away and positioned herself behind Rias, outside the circle. Heather's eyes flicked to her, and she gave my mate a brave smile before focusing on the witch.

"Okay," I said, "let's do this."

I don't know what I was expecting. Maybe some flashy lights, loud sounds, strange symbols. Something that gave presence to the invisible power I could feel swirling around us all. I glanced at Natalie. Her eyes were wide, and she stared into the circle.

I had to forcibly push my thoughts away from my ma—Natalie. I couldn't think of her like that anymore. I just couldn't do it. If something happened to her because of me, I'd never be able to live with it. I certainly wouldn't be fit to be an Alpha for anyone.

Rias's lips were moving, but even my hearing couldn't pick up any words. Was it the circle blocking her voice? Not knowing made me growl under my breath. If I was going to do this whole Alpha thing, there was a lot more I needed to learn. That book from Kendra was a good start. Maybe if I asked, she'd help me with everything else. She was kind when I went to her, not like what I was expecting. I hated to ask for help, but she did offer.

Heather cried out and I focused back on my wolf, ready to break the circle. Rias's eyes were open, wide with fear, but her lips kept moving without sound.

"Heather!" I shouted and Rias's eyes flicked to me. The barest shake of her head made me stop. It wasn't time, I couldn't break the circle.

Heather snarled, fur growing on her skin one moment then receding the next. She opened her mouth to howl, fangs jutting out from her jaws in slow, agonizing spurts.

"Shit!" I shouted, drawing Natalie's attention. "She can't control the change! Rias is in danger."

"What do we do?" she cried.

Rias was still chanting, and I couldn't do a thing about it. If she didn't stop and get herself to safety, there was no telling what might happen when Heather's feral wolf broke free. But she wouldn't stop. I took a step closer to the circle, earning another baleful glare from Rias.

"We have to!" I yelled to her. "I can't let her hurt you!"

Again, Rias shook her head. The movement made Heather's stormy gray eyes focus on the witch in front of her. Her face began to elongate as her teeth and fur still couldn't decide whether or not to stick around.

Shifting was painful enough, but being stuck in limbo with everything going in and out was something I wouldn't wish on my worst enemy. I had to do something.

"Heather!" Natalie cried, standing just outside the circle behind Rias. She waved her hands to draw Heather's attention. Heather's wolf-gray eyes slipped toward Natalie and narrowed. A low snarl rumbled through the backyard. "Heather, it's me. It's Natalie. I am the Lupa of your pack and you will listen to me."

All my focus turned to Natalie, along with my wolf's. Hearing Natalie claim to be our Lupa almost tore my wolf from my control. How did she even know that word? Was this more about the connection between us? Who was this astonishing woman?

"I am your Alpha's mate!" she screamed over the rush of wind and power that circled around us all. "You will hear me and you will stand down! The one in front of you is a friend of the pack!" Heather's eyes locked hard onto Nat, and I saw Nat's throat bob as she swallowed her fear. "She is a friend, and you will not hurt her, understand?"

They stared at each other for so long I lost track, but then Heather sat back on her haunches, her head lowered and to the side. Natalie had asserted herself as dominant over her, and Heather accepted it. How was this even possible?

She caught me staring at her and gave me a small smile. "It's okay," she said, "it'll be okay now."

My head jerked into a nod, but I still couldn't understand what I'd just seen. No wolf would ever be submissive to a human. It was taboo. It was unheard of. It didn't happen.

"Natalie…" I whispered, but she didn't hear me.

"Wren!" Rias's voice was oddly modulated as it reached out from the circle. "Now! Break the circle—draw out her wolf!"

I shook myself and charged into the circle. Heather was lying on her side on the ground while her body started the shift, then shifted back again and again. Her wolf was trying to break free, but Heather was fighting her wolf. I knew how frightening the first time could be.

I knelt beside her, taking her face in my hands as I forced her attention onto me. I could feel my wolf creeping to the surface as I stared into her wolf's gray eyes.

"It's okay, Heather," I murmured. "It's okay."

She shook her head in my hands. "No! No!" she cried. "I don't want to hurt anyone!"

"You won't," I told her. "It's only you and me, and I won't let you hurt anyone."

Rias and Natalie had retreated back into the house, but a glance back told me they were watching from the window.

"Can't fight!" Heather gasped.

"Don't fight."

She convulsed hard enough to pull her face from my hands. I moved in beside her, gripping her neck and forcing her eyes to mine again.

"Don't fight it. Let her come!"

Suddenly, a wild energy burst from me and engulfed Heather and everything around us. She gasped and cried out, but not in pain this time. The air filled with pheromones and endorphins, and I had no idea what was happening, but I could feel Heather inside me on a primal level I never thought possible. Fur erupted over my skin once more. My ears moved up the sides of my head, and my claws and teeth lengthened. Heather mirrored my shift and bowed down on hands and knees in front of me. Her clothing tore as her body contorted and she screamed as her bones broke audibly, only to be fused back together in a different shape.

She threw her head back and screamed, "It hurts! Oh, Mother, it hurts," loud and long, until it turned into a howl.

In my half-shifted state, I put my mouth beside her ear and said words without thinking. "Let her come. Free her. Release her." I turned and placed my lips on her cheek. "Twenty-three years is far too long to be trapped, Heather. It is time to be free."

She arched back and howled into the night sky—her shift almost completed. But then it stopped, like it wasn't enough. She was stuck, almost a wolf, but not quite. Her whimper broke my heart, and I grabbed her mostly canine head and pulled it to me. "Be free, wolf."

Seconds passed and there she was, a rusty-furred wolf standing on unsteady legs in front of me. She was smaller than me, more angular, but her fangs were just as sharp and her claws as threatening as any other wolf shifter. I smiled and she shook her head and ruffled her fur.

"Welcome, sister," I murmured.

She flung her head back and howled into the night sky. Moments later I joined her, having shifted through the clothing that kept my wolf trapped. Our howls rang through the air, melodies of life that ripped from our hearts.

And then we ran. We ran across the backyard and into the wild fields behind Rias's house until we left all the trappings of civilization behind.

❖

The moon was invisible in the darkness of the witching hour by the time my wolf and I padded up to the back door of my house. Heather had been safely returned to the motel room she was staying in for the time being, and I allowed my wolf to lead me back home. The connection with Natalie pulled at us. She was home and waiting for us. My wolf couldn't wait to see her. *I* didn't want to go inside.

We took our time wandering in and out of the tree line around my cabin. Desperation made the need for my mate's touch almost unbearable, but could I push this relationship further? I had almost bitten her before—almost completed the mating bond.

I didn't even try to hold back my whimper. There had to be something I could do. Some way to fix this all. What if I turned her? Would she want that?

The diary had the information. It was a long shot—would she even survive the turning? Would she even want to try? I couldn't make that choice for her.

I shifted back to skin with a long sigh and let myself in the back door. Natalie glanced up from her seat at the kitchen island. She wore nothing but a thin tank top and shorts. A glass of ice sat melting on the counter with something amber pooled at the bottom. A sniff of the air said it was my good bottle of whiskey—and it wasn't her first glass.

She smiled and her eyes roamed up and down my body. "Sexy wolf." She laughed and her eyes shone with mirth. "Come here, sexy wolf. It's time you got your reward."

I shook my head, but still stepped closer to the beautiful woman in front of me. "Natalie, we need to talk."

She snorted. "Why start now?" She waved a hand in the air. "We can talk later." She sauntered over to me and wrapped her arms around my neck. "Right now, I need my Alpha."

"Nat, I need to know how you knew those words you used tonight. You called yourself Lupa. Where did you learn that?"

She shook her head and stumbled a little with the movement. "Your little book. I read a bunch of it. The word was in there—it came out of my mouth." She pulled herself tighter against me. "No more talk. Only pleasing my Alpha."

The words rattled in my mind, reminding me of what happened in the woods only a week ago. This was real. She was my true mate.

But she was still human. I couldn't have her.

My body had other plans. Without thinking, I captured her lips as she dug her nails into my neck. Sweet pain flooded through me with a rush of endorphins, and I picked her up by the waist. She wrapped her legs around me and I swept an arm across the counter. I set her on the island and in two quick swipes tore away her shorts and shirt, leaving her in nothing but tatters as she tangled one hand in my hair.

"Say it again," I murmured into her ear.

"My Alpha," she cried, and electricity shot from my lips on her skin, through my core, and down between my legs. Sweeter words were never uttered, and I needed to reward my mate.

The logical, reasonable part of my brain seemed to be on vacation as I latched my mouth onto her nipple. She arched back as I sucked and pulled it in my teeth. Her gasp was music to my ears, and I felt the fur ripple across my body. My wolf stirred near the surface as I moved to worship her other nipple and she gave me another of those sweet moans.

"My Lupa," I whispered, feeling my fangs elongate, my ears reach the top of my head. I pulled her to me, her face to my breasts and she returned the favor on my nipples with a fervor. "Mine!" I cried out around the long teeth. I pulled my head up and back, keeping away from her neck. But she worked my nipples like a professional as her hand slipped down between my legs.

She slid her fingers inside me and I reared back as she found the exact perfect spot and kneaded her fingers into it.

"Natalie," I whispered. "Mine. My mate. My Lupa." The words slipped out before I could even think about it. My wolf took control and growled as we both cried out in bliss. Then my mouth came down to her shoulder, my sharp teeth dripping with saliva.

It was the speed of thought that saved us both. I pulled my wolf instinct back and tore myself away from my mate. A second later I was across the room, the same response as at Rias's place earlier. Except this time, as Natalie came down from whatever high she was on, she stayed seated on the counter.

"Natalie…" I said, but the rest of the words failed me as tears fell from her eyes.

She leapt off the island, legs unsteady, but she stuck the landing before she picked up the tattered ruins of her clothes. She shook her head without a word and tossed the clothes aside angrily before turning to glare at me with red, wet eyes.

"Why are you doing this to me?"

"I don't mean to—"

"I don't care what you *mean* to do, Wren!" She ran a hand through that gorgeous hair of hers. "Two weeks we've been together, and I swear I feel closer to you than I ever did to my ex after years! I feel you inside me, Wren!"

"I know. I feel it too."

"Then what is this? What is wrong with me that you keep pulling away?"

I shook my head. "There's nothing—" I stopped myself. Wasn't that the whole problem? She was human. It wasn't fair.

She slammed a hand down on the island counter. "Talk to me! Please! I'm falling apart trying to figure out what is going on! Why are you pulling away from me?"

"Because I can't do it…"

"I want you, Wren!" She filled the silence between us. "I *love* you. I want to be with you, and I want to be a part of your pack. I want to be your Lupa. We are true mates. You have to feel it too!"

"I can't!"

"Why the hell not? I want you to bite me, Wren! It's in every part of my body. I need you! I am your mate! Please!"

"But I can't, Nat! I can't bite you!"

"Why not?"

"Nat—"

"Why?"

I spun, lashing out at the overstuffed armchair behind me. My claws rent through the fabric and stuffing flew into the air as I let my frustration out on the furniture. "Damn it, Natalie!" I shouted. "I can't do it, okay? I just can't risk biting you!"

From the look on her face, I figured she'd back off. Maybe cool down a little, maybe not. Instead, there was murder in her eyes as she stalked to me. Even though my fangs and claws were still out, she didn't seem to care about the danger.

"Tell me why," she demanded, putting herself easily within biting distance. My wolf roiled inside, desperate to finish what we started, but I pulled her back. "Tell me why and I will leave. You'll never see me again." My stomach clenched so hard I almost doubled over. "Just tell me what's wrong with me that you can't bring yourself to want me."

I blurred away from her and put both living room and kitchen between us. My claws scraped deep furrows in the island counter.

"Damn it." I didn't want to tell her. If I said it out loud, it would be true. It would be too much for both of us. If I put the words out into the universe, then there'd be no going back.

"Why, Wren?"

"Because we're from different worlds. Because you aren't like me." The words dropped from my mouth before I could rethink them. "Because I can't let you be a part of my world. We can't be together." I refused to meet her eyes.

There was no sound from across the room. When I finally got the courage to look up, Natalie was turned away from me, her shoulders shuddering.

"Nat, please. I don't want to lose you." My words seemed to push her into motion. She didn't look at me as she grabbed her keys and phone from the table beside the front door and walked out. I started after her. She was naked except for a few tatters of her clothes that were left. I couldn't let her leave like that.

I stopped in the doorway as the clinic truck reversed and turned, and headed down the gravel road away from me. Tears poured down my face as I threw my head back into the air and let out a single, lonely howl.

CHAPTER THIRTY-ONE

Natalie

I knew I was driving way too fast, but it didn't matter. I could barely see anything through the tears, but I didn't care anymore. If something happened, so what? Who would care? Who would even notice that I was gone?

Rory popped up in my mind, but I shook my head. Sure, yeah, she'd be sorry for a little while. It would suck to leave her in the lurch at work. And my stuff was all still at her place, too, so it'd be work to get rid of that. I made a note to ensure I cleaned my things out of my boss's apartment before anything happened to me. That settled, I focused on getting back to Rory's cabin.

Yes, I realized I was naked when I got in the truck. No, I didn't much care at the moment. I needed to get the hell out of there before I did something we'd both regret. I had some clothes still at Rory's cabin, things that had been forgotten when Wren had brought the rest to her place. Now I was thankful for that, because everything I left behind, I was giving up for good. It's not like she'd even want to see me again.

Because you aren't like me!

Her words wouldn't leave me alone as I drove. And all the while, that stupid feeling of her in my gut ached more and more the farther I went. I guess it was a big deal that I'm transgender. Yeah, I'm not like her. I thought that she'd be able to look past that, but clearly I was mistaken. If only it hadn't taken her two weeks to figure that out.

Could've saved a lot of heartbreak if she'd been honest at the start.

Even as the thought entered my mind, I shook my head. That wasn't Wren. This wasn't Wren. Maybe she was being put up to this. Thinking of any situation that would force Wren to throw me away made for a fun game for all of two minutes before my stomach heaved and I felt like I wanted to throw up.

"Wren!" I sobbed, trying my best to keep a clear eye on the road.

But she didn't want me. One more in a long line of people who didn't want me. Somehow this was worse than my father's beatings. It hurt worse than Misty breaking up with me. It hurt so much—I couldn't think of another pain to compare it to. My heart felt shattered into thousands of pieces, scattered over kilometers of blacktop until there was no way to find them all.

I'd come here to figure out who I was. I found a place to belong, someone to belong with. And now there was nothing.

I didn't remember the rest of the drive. I barely registered pulling up outside the cabin beside a very out-of-place dark colored sports car. I climbed the front steps in a haze and let myself in.

"Well, it's about damned time!"

I hit a wall made of Misty's nauseating voice. "Misty?"

As if summoned, she appeared in front of me. Her eyes roamed up and down and I cringed, trying to hide myself with my hands, but not having any luck.

"That is disgusting. Do you want everyone to see that stupid thing between your legs? Get some clothes on."

I didn't move.

"What the hell are you doing here?"

She let out a harsh laugh. "What do you think? I told you that I came back for you. It's time to go back together."

"You broke up with me. You kicked me out."

"Yeah, and now I see that you clearly can't function without me." She scoffed, waving a hand at me. "I mean honestly, Natty, what are you thinking?"

"Don't call me that!" I said, "I hate when you call me that. You know that."

She shrugged. "Whatever, Natty. Get dressed and let's get out of here. We'll put everything right." She moved toward me like she was going to pull me into a hug. My stomach cramped with nausea and I backed up.

"Get the hell away from me!" I screamed.

She backed off. "Wow, no need to get all menstrual on me."

"You don't get it, do you?" I was done with this shit. Done with Misty, done with Wren, done with Terabend, and everything else this stupid vacation brought down. "You abandoned me! You decided you were done and now we're fucking done! I don't want to be with you anymore, Misty!"

"Natty, I—"

"No! Get the fuck out of here!"

I heaved in deep breaths, trying to contain the panic that was rising inside. Misty took the moment of silence to move in close, and before I could think her arms were around my neck and she forced her lips onto mine.

Three things happened at the same time: My panic ratcheted up ten notches, freezing my muscles as she pressed herself against me. My mind knew that her lips were nothing—*nothing*—like Wren's and I didn't want her touching me anymore. And the big picture window beside the front door shattered inward.

Wren, covered in silver fur with long claws and fangs and tall ears, stood in the shattered glass. A low growl spread through the room as I found myself able to move again. I pushed Misty away a second before Wren moved, slamming bodily into Misty and tearing her away from me.

She screamed as Wren slammed her against the wall with a roar, one clawed hand holding her aloft by her throat and neck.

"Wren!" I shouted, but she ignored me. Her other hand came up and she drew a single claw down Misty's cheek. It left a trail of blood, and Misty's eyes went wider than I'd ever seen them before.

"W-w-who?" She barely managed to get the word out before Wren's hand convulsed on her throat and she choked.

"Wren! Let her go!"

She shook her head, wild mane flailing behind her. "No!" she growled. "She hurt you!"

"You hurt me, you bitch!" I yelled. "Let her go!"

Her golden eyes flicked over to me, and I saw the heartbreak in her eyes. "Nat," she said.

"Let her go," I said one more time, putting as much of an order into my words as I could. "Put her down and get the hell out."

She dropped Misty, who fell to the floor like a sack of potatoes. She turned and faced me, naked except for the silver fur that covered most of her body. "Natalie, I'm sorry."

"Save it! Get out—"

My words were cut off by Misty's scream. "Oh my God! What is that! What the hell is going on?"

Before I could say something to calm Misty down, Wren lashed out. The back of her paw smashed into Misty's face and sent her sprawling. She didn't move again.

"What the hell did you do?"

Wren growled. "She hurt you. She made you panic."

"What do you care?"

"Natalie—"

"No! Fuck you, Wren! You fuck me, then you dump me? Because I'm fucking trans?" I shook my head. "You don't get to jump through the fucking window and attack someone after that!"

Something I'd said made her cringe, and suddenly the fur and claws disappeared, leaving nothing but smooth, naked skin. Wren's green eyes wouldn't meet mine as she looked anywhere but at me.

"It's not that!" she cried with a shake of her head. "I swear to you, Natalie, it's not that you're trans, I promise. There's nothing wrong with you. It's me. I swear to you that I love you, that I need you, but I also can't bear to lose you. I can't protect you. I can't make sure no one will come after you again if—"

"Fuck you, Wren," I snarled, moving past her toward the stairs. "*You* get to explain to Rory why the window is busted. *You* get to deal with whatever the fuck you did to Misty. I'm getting some fucking clothing on and I'm leaving."

"You're leaving?"

"Yeah. I'm leaving. I don't want to be here anymore, Wren. I can't." I left her in the front room as I headed back to the room I'd claimed when I first came out here. There was a pair of jeans and a purple T-shirt with a unicorn print on it still in the closet, and I pulled on both of them. I hesitated for several minutes, hoping that Wren would be gone by the time I got back down. I needed to get back to the truck.

I went back downstairs. Wren had laid Misty out on the couch, a pillow under her head, and was watching her from the armchair until she noticed me.

"Hikaru is on her way," she said, her voice barely above a whisper. "She'll make sure Misty is okay. And doesn't remember anything."

I snorted. "Yeah, that would be nice."

"Nat, I'm sorry."

I didn't want to hear it, so I made a beeline to the door. I had one foot out the door before she spoke again.

"Please, Natalie. Wait?"

I stopped but didn't turn around. "What more do you want, Wren? What more can you possibly do to me?"

"It's not about you being trans. That was never a problem for me. You are not a problem for me. You have to believe me. I just can't…with a human…" I heard her let out a long breath and could imagine her shaking her head. "Please know, I never meant to hurt you, Nat."

I glanced back over my shoulder.

"Well, you failed."

And suddenly I had no more words. I walked out the door, walked out on the best—and shortest—relationship I'd ever had. Just when I thought I was out of tears to cry, my body surprised me, and I sobbed the entire ride back to the city.

CHAPTER THIRTY-TWO

Wren

I was barely aware of anything as my wolf gnawed on the leg bone of a white-tailed jackrabbit. We lay in our rough den, eating happily as the wind twined its way through the trees. The fur on our back ruffled slightly and we tucked ourselves a little tighter into a ball with the bone loose in our teeth. The scents of pine and leaves and damp undergrowth filled our nose as we slowly started to drift off to sleep.

Then there was a new scent on the wind. It was vaguely familiar, and I didn't pay any heed, but my wolf was smarter and more alert. She bared our teeth, hackles rising, and a low growl rumbled out of our den.

From downwind came the very deliberate crunching of twigs and leaves, making its way ever closer. The smell got stronger and it took longer than I would have liked, but eventually we recognized it to be Heather. We stood and discarded our meal, then left the den to meet with my pack member.

Heather's wolf was smaller than me, with russet red fur from nose to tail, speckled with white and gray. Everything about her screamed speed over power. Three feet from me, she stopped, lowered her head to the side, and assumed a submissive position.

Alpha. I heard Heather's voice echo in my head. It wasn't the weirdest thing ever, but after years of being on my own it was still weird to communicate while shifted.

Heather. I acknowledged her, then let the wolf in me take over. She moved forward, putting her jaws on Heather's exposed shoulder and biting down softly. I had to struggle to keep my awareness focused on what was going on and not slip back behind the wolf, letting her take over completely. *What do you want?*

You've been gone a while, Wren.

I backed away from her, closer to my den. *What's your point?*

People miss you.

And that's a reason to shift by yourself and come into the woods?

It was hard. Really hard. My wolf and I aren't...there's just so much more to learn and work on. I need you back, Wren. I needed to find you. I know you're hurting.

I turned and snarled at her, baring teeth far larger than hers. *You know nothing!*

"Hey!" A voice cracked through the silence of the woods. I spun to see Hikaru, standing downwind from me. How the hell had she gotten here so damned quietly? "Back off, Wren. She was just helping me find you."

My wolf whined as I pulled her awareness back to take the driver's seat once more. Looking between the two of them, I couldn't control the anger rising from my gut. I bared my teeth again and prepared to pounce on the smaller wolf.

You led her here?

Heather's wolf shook as I gazed at her. *She asked me to help find you. She's worried about you. Wren, we're all worried about you. You've been gone for over a month!*

A strong grip on the back of my neck was the only thing that stopped me from tearing Heather apart. I spun to growl at Hikaru, but she only gripped me tighter.

"Go on, Heather," she said loudly. "Get back to your home. I need to talk to your Alpha alone."

Heather looked from me to Hikaru and back again. I could sense her hesitation in leaving me with a potential threat, and I felt bad for trying to attack her.

Go, Heather. Give your wolf control and run for a while. Just remember not to go into the town.

She hesitated still. *Alpha.*

I'll be fine. Hikaru won't hurt me. Go and learn your wolf better. I'm sorry I haven't been there to help.

Her movements were slow and cautious, but eventually she

turned and loped off back into the trees. A moment passed before Hikaru let me go.

I hate you sometimes.

She only stared at me. "You realize it'd be easier to have an actual conversation if you weren't an animal right now."

I knew she couldn't hear me in wolf form, but damned if she couldn't see what I was saying on my face.

It took longer than it should've to find myself in the right headspace to start the shift. It was almost like the silver sickness had returned, preventing me from shifting again. How long had it been? My wolf wasn't much for checking the time or recording days. My wolf was reluctant to step back, but even worse was my reluctance to step forward. Being human again meant thinking about things again. Thinking about things meant feeling emotions.

Emotions were the whole reason I'd been in the woods so long in the first place.

Slowly, I shifted back to my human skin. Shivering in the breeze without the protection of my fur, I glared at Hikaru as she watched without a hint of discomfort.

"What? It's not like I haven't seen it before. I am your doctor."

I grunted at her and made a little seat on a large rock sticking out of the ground a few steps away. When I was as comfortable as I was going to get, I looked back at my old friend.

"Why are you here?"

"We were worried about you. You've been gone too long."

"I don't care."

"Yeah, but other people care about you. And they've been taking care of your business."

I shook my head. "I never asked them to do that."

"You don't get to choose that for others. That's not how life works."

"If they're unhappy that I'm gone, then that's on them!" I picked my knees up, wrapping my arms around them. "I just want to be left alone."

Hikaru shook her head sadly. "I know. I get it, I really do, but you have responsibilities back in town, and you need to pull yourself together."

I launched myself to my feet. "Don't tell me what to do! I don't want to go back there! There's nothing left for me!"

"Excuse me?" I backpedaled quickly at the sudden fury in Hikaru's voice. Her eyes started to glow as angry trails of red spread outward across her face. Her hands went dark, fingers sharpening into long claws far more wicked than my own. "Nothing? *Nothing*, Wren?" She snarled. "I seem to recall a poor, wretched wolf coming to my doorstep with *nothing*." She stalked forward on nimble feet, and I stood petrified in front of her. Only once had I ever seen her go full vampire before, and it was as terrifying then as now. "But now that wolf has a life! She has a diner and staff and a home and, most of all, friends who give a shit about her!" She stopped mere inches from me, claws moving like she was barely holding herself back from shredding my skin. "Even if she was an idiot and broke her own damned heart!"

Her fangs had dropped and were sitting in front of her lip as she bared her teeth at me in a look more terrifying than my wolf's most ferocious snarl. I fought the urge to close my eyes, waiting for her to fall upon me and take what she wanted. Then she turned away from me and took a long breath. Suddenly I could move again, and I backed away into my little den, feeling the bone I'd been chewing on under my foot.

"I had to do it." My voice was so quiet she wouldn't have heard it if she were human.

Slowly, her hands returned to normal, and by the time she turned around her face had cleared up, leaving her with her normal eyes behind the purple-tinted glasses. "If that's really what you want to believe, then maybe you deserve to be left out here."

I shook my head. "I didn't want to hurt her. I just couldn't live with myself if something happened to her because she was with me."

"Wren, you *did* hurt her! You hurt her by driving her away!"

"Yeah, but at least she'll survive!"

Hikaru took a step backward, confusion making her eyebrows rise. "She could have had more than that with you."

I tried to convey a look of *are you stupid?* from my eyes, so I didn't have to say the words out loud. "It's because of the mate bite! Even on the small chance she could survive it, what kind of life could she possibly have with me? I can't risk her getting caught up in all the werewolf bullshit again. Craig still hasn't shown his asshole face, and I know he's not going to let his brother's death go. Everywhere I go I have wolves coming after me. What kind of life would that be for a human?"

Instead of understanding or even pity, Hikaru only looked even more confused. "I don't understand. You drove her away because you didn't want to give her the mate bite?"

"Obviously!" I threw my hands in the air. "She was begging me to bite her, and damn it, I wanted it more than anything. But I couldn't! I couldn't risk her like that! If she died because I tried to make her my mate, I don't think I would've survived it."

"Wren." Hikaru's voice drifted off as her face went from confused to shocked to something like pity. I wanted to claw and tear to make it disappear. "Who told you the mate bite risks the mate's life?"

I blinked at her. "The Alpha of the next county. Kendra Harper. And it's not all mates, only the humans. Humans can't handle the power, the magic that flows into them with the mate bite." As the words tumbled out, my stomach started to twist with each syllable. What if I was wrong? What if I drove Natalie away for nothing?

Hikaru slowly shook her head. "No, Wren. Humans can take the mate bite as well as any wolf shifter."

"No!" I growled, filled with the sudden energy of denial that pushed me to start pacing in front of her. "No. No. No. No. No!" I gripped my upper arms tight, digging nails into my skin until it hurt. I wanted to scream with the frustration, the rage that was building within. "No!" I screamed. "No! Please! Please tell me I didn't...I didn't..." I gasped in deep breaths of air. "Please say I didn't push her away for nothing."

"Kendra Harper lied to you. Or she was told wrong or had a bad experience. I can't say for certain why or what happened with Ms. Harper, but I can tell you that the mate bite is perfectly safe for humans and shifters both." She gave me a small, sad smile. "I'm sorry, Wren."

I turned on her. "How the hell do you know? Why do you know so much about me and my kind when you're a fucking blood-sucker?"

If she took any offense to my words, she didn't show it. "I've been around for a long time, Wren. I've learned things."

I shook my head. "There has to be more to it than that."

She let out a long sigh. "Fine. But this stays between us, do you understand?"

"Why?"

"Because my past is not a story for you to tell others. I'll thank you to keep it to yourself."

I truly thought about it and decided that I needed to know. I needed to know if I could really believe her that her information was better than Kendra's. I needed that assurance, and my silence was a small price to pay.

"Tell me, please."

She took a few steps forward and reached up, pulling the collar of her shirt out and down her left shoulder. I realized this was the first time I'd ever seen Hikaru's pale skin outside the usual parts. And there, snaking down and around and back up on her collarbone, were long-healed marks in the shape of—

"A mate bite?" I whispered.

She nodded. "My mate." Her voice rumbled low in her throat like she was holding back a flood of emotion. "She gave me the bite a long, long time ago."

I stared. "But you're…"

"I wasn't always a vampire, Wren," she said. "No one is. Vampires can't bear children."

"You were a wolf?"

"No." She shook her head. "Human. Pledged to marry the head of our village long before Japan was what it is today. Then I met her." She smiled softly. "My Yasha. She stole my heart, and then she stole me from the village. We traveled Japan for years after she bit me. We were together for a long time, Wren, and we never stopped loving each other."

"A long time?"

"The mate bite is special, you know that. It allows one mate to live as long as the other mate does. Even humans can live for several hundred years as long as their mate survives."

I tried to make sense of all this new information, but felt my head wanting to explode. The only coherent thought slipped off my tongue. "What happened?"

Her face darkened. "We took a ship to the mainland and continued traveling and exploring. Until we reached what's now the Russian part of Europe." A red-tinged tear trickled down her face. "We stumbled on a clan of vampires. They took me, and Yasha tried to save me. But it was too late." She looked away. "They'd turned me. Otherwise, I would've died with my love. And done so happily."

I covered my mouth with my hands. "Oh, dear Mother. I'm so sorry. So, so sorry."

She sniffled and shook her head. "It's the past. I live on."

"How?" I asked. "How do you keep going? I'm almost ready to tear my own heart out, and Natalie is alive only a few hours away. How did you do it?"

"Because she's in here." She tapped her head, then her heart. "And in here. I am the only living memory of Yasha. I have to remember her, otherwise no one will know she even existed."

"You preserve her memory?"

She smiled and nodded. "Just so."

"Fuck." I drew the word out with a long breath before rubbing my hands over my face. "What do I do? How do I fix this?"

"You still want to be with her?"

I glanced down at my body and could still sense Natalie within that well of magic that all shifters had. "I do," I whispered. "I still feel her. I still want her."

She gave me a kind smile. "Then come on. Let's get you back into the world so you can get your girl back."

She threw her arm over my shoulders, and together we walked out of the darkness of the woods. With my best friend beside me, I took my first steps back into the light of the world.

CHAPTER THIRTY-THREE

Natalie

"Shit!" I shouted as the long scratches up my arm stung like a mother. The water was cool against my skin as I ran it under the tap, washing away blood and dirt and whatever else that cat might've had on its claws.

"Natalie? You okay?" Rory's voice preceded her entrance into the exam room. I nodded and hissed when my finger caught one of the gashes. She appeared beside me and gasped. "Holy shit! What happened?"

I grimaced as I soaped up my arm. "Ms. Galar's cat," I said. "Apparently, he doesn't like me much."

"Mr. Nibbles did that to you?" She stared at my arm. "What the hell did you do to him?"

"Nothing!" I said. Guilt rolled through me as she backed off a couple of steps. "I didn't do anything out of the ordinary. It was just a regular check-up. I've done it plenty of times."

"That cat is always such a sweetheart."

I snorted. "Not today, apparently."

She looked me up and down then pulled me away from the sink. "Sit down," she commanded. I wasn't in the mood to argue, so I sat on the rolling stool. She grabbed a few rolls of gauze and antiseptic before going to work on my arm. "I know you've never gotten along well with cats, but damn, girl. This is ridiculous."

I could only shrug. She was right that I was never a fan of cats—they were never fans of me, really. But I'd never gotten clawed like this before. And I couldn't tell Rory that maybe they smelled werewolf all over me, because even after a little more than a month back in the city and with many, *many* showers, I could still smell Wren all over my skin.

"I'm sorry about what happened out at the cabin," she said suddenly, her eyes and hands focused on bandaging me up. She shook her head. "I didn't know Misty was going to go all crazy like that and hunt you down."

I bit my lip. This woman was so good to me, but I couldn't really tell her anything. I couldn't tell her that her old friend was a werewolf, and I'd fallen hard for her and then she pushed me away because I was different. "It was my fault. I slipped and told her where I was. I didn't know she was going to come after me."

She let out a long breath as she finished with my arm. "But that's all over with, right? She's done now?"

"Goddess, I hope so. I never want to see her again."

"So, the cabin did sort of work out for you? Maybe not so much in the end, but the rest of it?"

"It made me think about a lot of things."

She smiled. I couldn't tell her anything about Wren. Even leaving the whole werewolf thing out, I couldn't hurt either one of them. Wren was allowed to have opinions—even if they were the wrong ones. Didn't mean I needed to be around her at all.

"Did you get to swim in the lake?" I gave a noncommittal shrug. "Isn't it gorgeous there? And the town hasn't been turned into a tourist trap, so you're not fighting for space with everyone else."

We hadn't made it to the beach, despite having wanted to. As much as I wanted to think of something good that had happened, all that came to mind was that last night there. The look on Wren's face in Rory's cabin, when she said those last words to me.

"It was nice." She didn't look like she believed me. "No, it was good. I mean, before it all went bad."

She sighed. "I was hoping it would help you, but you seem even more upset than before."

"It is what it is, Rory. It was good—but it was bad too."

"I really wish you'd tell me what happened out there. If I'd known you were going to get hurt, I wouldn't have—"

I cut her off. "It's not your fault. It's mine. All mine." Flexing my arm and testing the bandage, I moved around her toward the door. "I'm going to take off, okay?"

"Yeah." Rory was slow to reply. "Of course. I'll see you at home."

"Sure." I grimaced at the tone as I hurried out of the clinic.

I'd already been apartment hunting so I could get out of her hair. Between that and spending a good chunk of a week at the university's financial aid office, I was trying to make sure Rory had her space away from a sorry sack like me.

And yet, all of those moments were still spent thinking of Wren. Thinking of what we had, thinking of how I could still feel her deep inside. For a while there I thought it had stopped, that she had moved on and I wouldn't feel her anymore. Until a few days ago, when her fear and anger woke me from a fitful nap on Rory's couch. I wanted to get in the truck and drive straight to her. I wanted to make sure she was okay, to comfort and hold her and feel comforted in return. I wanted her. I *needed* her.

Dear Goddess, I hoped that feeling faded soon.

We'd barely known each other for a few weeks, and I was craving her touch more than I'd ever craved Misty's—even after we broke up. And for some reason that didn't bother me as much as I thought it should've.

Frustration ripped through me, and I desperately wanted to lash out and hit something. Out on the sidewalk, surrounded by people, I was impotent in that wanting and made myself keep walking away from the clinic, away from Rory's apartment. I didn't have a clue where I was going, but somehow my feet did.

I stopped in front of an old gym—one I'd frequented a lot over the years with Misty. Until she decided the place wasn't fit for girls like us and took me to one of those fancy places with the spin classes where people yell at you over headache-inducing music. I walked in, knowing full well I didn't have anything on me to wear in there, but not caring. I just needed to hit something—and badly.

"You've got some nerve showing your face in here, Natalie," a voice said from behind the counter as I walked into the gym. I froze in my steps. I recognized that voice.

Gwen was a short woman, barely over five feet tall, but had the attitude of someone twice her size. Her skin was a deep tan color and she had dark hair that curled as if it had a mind of its own. Her green eyes were sharp and never let a detail pass her by. Her lips curled up at the corners as I gave her my full attention, and I let out a long sigh.

"Jeez, Gwen," I said. "Give a girl a heart attack. I thought you were really mad at me."

She laughed, her entire demeanor changing from protective, almost threatening, to completely calm and at ease. "I mean, I should be. You went and disappeared on us. I lost my favorite workout partner."

The shame was unbelievable. After running from my family and finding a new one with Misty, I hadn't wanted to fall down too much on the training and exercise my parents had pushed us into. Self-defense classes, strength training, cardio, the works. Then Misty decided that this place wasn't good enough and started dragging us to some other gym that I'd never felt comfortable in. The worst part was losing my friendships with the people here. Mostly, Gwen.

"I'm sorry." There weren't any other words I could give her. There was nothing I could say, no excuse that would be good enough, for disappearing on her almost a year and a half ago and just letting it happen.

She came out from behind the counter and pulled me into a tight hug. "You can tell me all about it later, okay?"

I nodded, not sure if I could get words out without starting to cry.

She pulled back but kept her hands on my arms. She gave me a long look up and down, smirking. "And I need to see how much you've let yourself go since you were here last."

I grinned. "Yeah? You want your old sparring partner back?"

"Sure! It's the only reason I missed you." She winked.

I glanced down at my scrubs. "I'm not exactly dressed for it."

"I'll spot ya." She ran back around the counter and stuck her head through a doorway there, chatting with someone for a quick moment. She came back with a duffel bag clutched in one hand. She tossed it to me hard enough to bounce off my chest.

"Get in the ring," she said despite her smile. "Bitch."

I shared the smile. "Good to see you, too, Gwen."

"Talk later, spar now," she said, already moving to the boxing ring set up on the far side of the room.

I groaned before hanging my head and heading for the change rooms.

❖

Gwen and I sat on the edge of the boxing ring, legs hanging over the side, arms wrapped in the ropes. We passed a heavy bottle of water back and forth as we panted, and I tried to ease the ache in pretty much every muscle I could think of.

"You're out of shape," Gwen said. She said it like it was a simple statement and not an insult. And she was right. "You used to at least give me a challenge on your worst days."

I grinned. "And on my best?"

She grinned back. "You'd have me on my ass faster than I could see."

We laughed together and I realized how much I had missed this. Jumping from the shit with Misty to trying to make a new relationship work with Wren was a terrible idea. I was still just a part of someone else—I didn't have anything of my own. Not with Misty, and not in Terabend with Wren. These were my friends, and I hated how long it took for me to realize it.

"So, where the hell have you been? It's been over a year since the last time you were in here."

I sighed and took a long swig of water before telling her the whole story with Misty. I wanted to blame it all on her, but I couldn't. I still made the decision to stop coming to the gym, to avoid seeing or talking to my friends because I knew Misty wouldn't like it. I was as complicit as her.

"Bullshit." Gwen shook her head when I told her that it was my own fault. "That toxic bitch made you do it. Yes, you could've said no, but the consequences could've been a lot worse. You understand that, right?"

"I just wanted to stay with her."

"Why? After all that kind of stuff, why?"

"Because I didn't think anyone else would ever want me." My voice was raw with emotion. "She beat it into my head that she was the only one who would ever have me. I couldn't let her go."

"See?" Gwen pulled the water bottle back from me and took a gulp. "Toxic."

"I know that now," I replied.

"So, what've you been doing since?"

I laughed but there was little humor in it. "Oh, the usual. Crashing on my boss's couch, borrowing her cabin for a vacation, falling in love with a werewolf, then coming back here when she decides she can't handle that I'm tran—"

Gwen's eyes were wide with confusion. "What the hell?"

This time my laugh was real, because the look on her face was priceless. I told her about Rory and Wren and everything that happened in Terabend—leaving out the gory details, of course. And the bits about the things I learned there. Rias and Heather and Dr. Maru—their secrets weren't mine to tell. Her eyes were still wide and staring when I finished, and I took the water bottle back.

"B-but werewolf?" She gasped and I chuckled. She had a thing about the supernatural—which was kind of cute in a way that scared me, now that I knew about that world.

"I was just kidding," I assured her. "Wren was certainly the outdoorsy type and loved her flannel, but werewolves aren't real. You know that."

She chuckled weakly and turned away. "Right. Right. I know that. Duh."

I gave her a moment to breathe as I slipped under the ropes. "As much fun as this has been, I need to get—"

Pain flared in my gut, and I fell over, screaming. It echoed through the gym, bringing everything to a dead stop as Gwen leapt to my side. I barely noticed hands touching me, holding me as my legs collapsed underneath me and I screamed again. Sharp, searing pain stabbed into my gut like someone had a hot knife, and I cried out again. My hands searched for a wound, but there was nothing there. But where—

"Wren!" I gasped. My eyes flared open to see Gwen and several of the gym's staff all huddled over me.

"How hard did you hit her?" one of them asked, not a trace of accusation in his voice.

"I didn't do this! She just started screaming."

"Who's Wren?"

"Her ex!"

"What the hell is going on?"

The voices started to all mesh together in my head as wave after wave of pain tore through me, coming from that place in my gut where I could still feel my mate. I saw Gwen's face over me, saying something, but there was no more sound. And a few seconds later, there was no more vision. Then there was no more consciousness.

CHAPTER THIRTY-FOUR

Natalie

I opened my eyes to a far-too-familiar sight. Tree trunks that disappeared into a dark sky, bare ground with foliage that didn't tear into my bare feet. The forest that had haunted me for over a month now, taunting me with what I lost.

"Fuck you!" I screamed and the air swallowed my words before they could echo. "Stop fucking bringing me here!"

Every damned time I was here, Wren couldn't even be bothered to come find me herself. Her wolf would appear by my side after a few moments, but the wolf never gave me any indication that Wren was also here with me. And now?

"I don't want to do this anymore!"

If the forest heard me, it didn't show.

I heard the wolf before I saw her. Normally, she would be playfully sneaking, trying to get around me. It got to be a bit of a game with us—one that never failed to give me a brief smile. But tonight she moved unerringly toward me. She was slow, limping heavily even though her legs looked fine.

Something was wrong.

"Wren?" I whispered as I knelt down in front of her wolf. "Is she okay? Are you?"

The wolf whimpered, high and loud and I took her muzzle in my hands. She leaned into it, tongue lolling out of her mouth as she closed those golden eyes.

"It's okay," I soothed her. "It's okay. You'll be okay."

She whined and whimpered a little and I kept my hands around her. I ran my fingers through her thick fur, untangling matted clumps.

She flinched when I reached her belly, and I pulled my hand away. It was slick with blood.

"Wren?"

"Easy there, beautiful." Wren's voice drawled from behind me. "No need to shout."

I spun and there she was. My mate. My love. Standing in dark jeans and flannel shirt, her hands pressed hard to her gut.

"Wren!" I shouted, pulling back from her wolf and running to her. She met me a few steps later, wrapping a single arm around me as the other stayed at her abdomen. "What the hell is going on?"

She shook her head. "I was hoping I'd get to see you here. I wanted to have a chance to say I'm sorry."

"Wren, please! Tell me what's happening."

She tightened her grip and laid her head on my shoulder. "It doesn't matter, Nat. I'm so sorry. I thought I had to push you away. I didn't think…I didn't know…"

"Tell me what's wrong, please!"

"You're perfect, Nat. You always were. Just the way you are. I'm an idiot. A complete idiot. I just want you to know that."

"Wren—"

She shook her head, nuzzling my neck like a content canine. "I'm so sorry. I know you never asked for all of this, but I promise I was a better person for having known you."

"Stop talking like we'll never see each other again!"

"I love you, my mate. My Lupa. My Natalie."

She slumped in my arms and I couldn't hold her. We fell, her on top of me, and I held her close as something warm soaked through my shirt. Blood seeped from Wren's abdomen, and I rolled us over, pressing hands to her wound.

"No! No!" I screamed. Something soft and furry brushed my back. Her wolf padded slowly past me, lying beside her other half and putting her head on Wren's neck. "Wren! Please don't go!"

She coughed and choked, blood spilling from her mouth as her eyes found mine. "I'm sorry, Nat." Her eyes closed and darkness started to fall around the forest. "Please forgive me."

I didn't get a chance to respond before the world went dark.

"Wren!" I screamed, throwing myself up and out of the bed. Two people who were not the werewolf I wanted to see. "Wren!" I gasped again as I realized whatever covers I'd had on had fallen back—and I was naked.

"Nat!" Rory cried, completely ignoring my undressed state and wrapping her arms tight around me. "Oh, my Goddess, are you okay?"

I shook in her grasp, trying to make sense of everything. Gwen was standing on the other side of the bed, frowning down at the two of us.

"What happened?" I choked out, prying Rory off me.

"You collapsed at the gym," Gwen said, "I brought you here."

"She should have brought you to a hospital," Rory said.

Gwen shook her head. "There was nothing wrong with her."

"It could be internal!"

"I knew it wasn't."

"How could you possibly know that? Are you a doctor?"

"I knew because I knew!"

"Enough!" I shouted, earning surprised looks from both of them. "Gwen did the right thing. I don't need a hospital."

"We don't know what's wrong with you." Rory said.

"I do," I muttered, unable to look at either of them.

There was a long minute of silence before Gwen said softly, "Yeah, I figured it was something like that."

I stared at her. "You know?"

She gave me a wry smile. "You let it slip. I know you meant it as a joke, but…"

"But it's not a joke for you." I nodded in understanding.

Rory looked back and forth between us. "What the hell are you talking about?"

I had no idea where to even start. Then there was there was a knock at the door. I glanced at Rory, who was still looking confused, and she sighed and walked away.

"Gwen, you've been holding out on me."

"Not like I could tell you anything when we met."

"So, you've been holding back on me in our sparring matches?"

She had the decency to look sheepish. "Maybe. It's not like you didn't do well."

"It's fine," I said, "but I think at least you owe me some clothing."

She gestured to a bundle at the foot of the bed, knocked askew when I awoke.

"I'll be outside."

The moment the door was closed, I got out of bed. There was no marring anywhere on my stomach, but I could still feel the stinging pain that made me pass out. The dream came back to me, Wren's body on top of mine, bleeding. I needed to find her. I had to help her.

I dressed and exited the bedroom, already knowing who would be waiting for me out there. Rory stood in the kitchen, preparing four mugs of coffee. When she caught sight of me, she opened the fridge and pulled out a bottle of Pepsi. I nodded my thanks before turning to the newcomers. Dr. Maru sat on the couch, the picture of nonchalance in her sweater and jeans. She waved to me, eyes shining a little over the rims of her glasses.

Heather stood behind the couch, standing protectively over Dr. Maru. Her eyes were glued to Gwen, who was standing by the hallway to the bedrooms. Gwen was staring back at Heather, and the tension between them was tangible.

"You know," I began, as I claimed my bottle of pop, "I thought it was bad when I came out to my parents, but the amount of tension in this apartment almost takes the cake."

Gwen and Heather continued to glare at each other as Dr. Maru quietly accepted a mug from Rory. As the only other human in the room, I felt bad for Rory—mostly because she really had no clue what was happening.

"Enough," Dr. Maru said, her voice a command. "Calm yourselves." She glanced to Gwen and added, "*Both* of you."

Rory looked between all of us. "I feel like I'm missing something here." She focused on Dr. Maru. "I mean, I haven't seen you for years, and suddenly you show up on my doorstep asking about Nat?"

Dr. Maru smiled at me. "We became friends during her vacation. I was worried about her, so I came by."

"With an escort?"

"Heather insisted."

"What are you two doing here?" I asked. I opened my mouth to say more, but I didn't want to put the words out into the world.

"You know why," Heather growled.

"Something happened to Wren." It was a statement, and one that I knew Dr. Maru was angry about.

"I know," I whispered, rubbing my stomach. "I felt it."

"Okay, hold on!" Rory snapped. "What the hell is going on? What happened to Wren? What do you mean you felt it? Why does it even matter?" Her eyes fell to me and widened. "Oh. *Oh!* That's why you didn't want to talk about..." She drifted off for a moment, as if rethinking all the conversations we'd had since I came back.

"Yes," I said. "Me and Wren."

Her face darkened. "She dumped you? She dumped you because you're trans?"

At that, everyone in the room turned to look at me, and I felt the blush creep up my face. "Um, maybe? I mean I thought she did at first, but I don't think she meant it that way."

"It's pretty hard not to mean those words when someone says them."

I fidgeted. "It's not...she didn't actually say the words..." I shook my head. "There isn't time to talk about this." I turned to Dr. Maru. "Doc, we can trust her. Can you tell her what's going on?"

She gave me a solid disapproving look. "Natalie..."

"If we're going to get Wren, we can't exactly make a plan by kicking Rory out of her apartment. So if you want to waste time going somewhere else, be my guest, but I'm staying here until I know she's safe."

"She won't be very safe if she knows—"

"Hey!" Rory said. "You don't get to decide things for me. I can take whatever this is."

Dr. Maru gave me a hard look. "For Wren."

As Dr. Maru gave Rory the CliffsNotes version of everything, I turned to the two shifters in the room.

"Are you two going to fight, or just stare at each other all day?"

"I have no issues with her," Gwen growled.

"I am not leaving Hikaru in a room with this one," Heather retorted.

"I can see we're all going to be fast friends," I said.

"The wolf will be fine as long as she doesn't hurt you," Gwen said, giving me the side-eye. "I hate that you got to know them before knowing who I truly am, but I've been your friend a lot longer than she has."

"Hmph. And didn't even bother to be honest with her."

"I couldn't!" Gwen said, "it's not like I had a fucking option! Our king wouldn't allow it."

"King," I said, musing. "You're a lion?"

She shook her head. "Fuck, cat's out of the bag now, huh?" She looked between me and Heather, wrapping her arms around herself as she backed away a few steps. "No, I'm a panther. There are so few feline shifters we usually form a pride together, and the leaders are our king and queen."

"What she's not telling you," Heather growled, "is that she's a very strong panther. One of the strongest in her pride, I'd wager a guess."

She blanched at the accusation.

"Is that true?" I asked.

She nodded. "I hide it. I don't want the attention that being strong brings. It's just not for me."

She retreated from the conversation, collecting a mug of coffee for herself and moving to the far side of the kitchen. Watching her, I realized some of those mannerisms that made her Gwen were very feline in nature. The thought made me smile.

By the time Dr. Maru was finished, Rory was sitting on the sofa beside her, leaning over with her head between her legs. Dr. Maru was rubbing her back daintily as Rory moaned softly.

"She's a little overwhelmed."

I snorted. "That's an understatement."

"You handled it a little better."

"Maybe. I was in a hospital bed when you told me I'd just been fed vampire blood, after a group of rogue werewolves took me hostage to draw out Wren. What else could I do but handle it?" Rory's head snapped up and focused on me as I spoke. "I don't think I had much of a choice in the matter—especially not after finding out that I'm Wren's mate."

"Oh, oh no," Rory muttered. "I think I'm going to be sick."

"We don't have time for that," Heather said, "We need to find the Alpha."

"Why are you here? She sure didn't come for me," I asked.

"Because you're still connected to her," Dr. Maru said. "You are still her mate, even if she was stupid and pushed you away." My hand went to my stomach again. "When I passed out, was that because of whatever has happened to Wren?"

Dr. Maru only shrugged. "I would assume so. Enough trauma on one end of the connection can affect the other end. If whatever they did hurt her bad enough to prevent her from fighting back, it might've made you pass out."

"I saw her," I whispered. Dr. Maru's eyes focused on me. I raised my voice a little. "I dreamed of her. Again."

"And?" Her voice was too gentle, too knowing.

"She was there. I didn't know she'd be there. I've dreamt of her wolf for a while now, but never her. But she was there this time, and she was hurt and she was apologizing and saying it was all her fault. It was like she was…" I couldn't finish the sentence.

"Saying good-bye?" Heather said what I couldn't.

Rory laughed abruptly. "Sounds like Wren," she cackled. "Saying good-bye is something she sucks at."

Her words helped me shake the melancholy, and I looked around at the ragtag group of allies around me. "So, you came here expecting me to help you find her? After what she did to me?"

My words made Dr. Maru and Heather look at each other worriedly. "You don't understand," Heather said.

I shook my head. "I understand more than you think," I snapped, "and I understand how important she is to you, but that doesn't negate what she did."

"She was given false information," Dr. Maru said. I opened my mouth to argue, but she held up a placating hand. "I'm not saying that absolves her of what she did, I am merely giving you context. She was told that humans can't survive the mate bite. That it would kill you. She tore you and herself apart to make sure you lived."

I stopped myself from responding without thinking. It wasn't easy. The hurt was still so fresh in my head, in my heart. I tried to put myself in her position—knowing what she wanted, but not sure if she could have it. It wasn't fair. Not to either of us.

"What happened to her? Where is she?"

"We don't know. There was a problem with the shipment for the diner." Dr. Maru shook her head. "I don't know where she went, but she had to go deal with it."

I looked between the wolf and the vampire. "What do you need from me?"

"You still have the mate bond," Heather said.

"You can't track her through the pack bond?" I asked and looked to Heather.

"She shut it down as much as she could back when you left town," Heather said. "I can feel she's still alive, but that's it."

"But I can still feel her. I can find her." I looked back and forth between them all again. "I'm not staying back. If you want my help, I'm coming after her too."

Heather shook her head. "I can't protect you if there's too many of them."

"I can protect myself just fine," I said. I turned to Gwen. "Are you coming with?"

She hesitated. "My king won't like it." Then she shook her head. "But fuck it, yeah. I'm in."

"I will do what I can," Dr. Maru added, "but that might not be as much as you'd like."

"We'll take all the help we can get."

Rory stared at all of us. "What can I do?" No one could meet her eyes. "I'm her friend too. I want to help."

I stared at her for a long moment. She'd only just learned about all of this and she still wanted to be there for her friend. I couldn't shut her out. Then it came to me.

"Can you drive the truck?"

Rory smiled and went to grab the keys.

I turned back to everyone else. "Well, what are we waiting for?" They all started to shuffle toward the door. I gave the apartment one last look back, wondering how this had become my life. I wondered if I'd change it for anything in the world, then shook my head. *Not a damned chance.*

CHAPTER THIRTY-FIVE

Wren

After an hour stuck with my wrists chained to the ceiling, balancing on my toes, I could say for certain that I was not a fan of this. First of all, there was the swinging. Moving at all caused my body to sway in some direction I sure as shit wasn't ready for, making my stomach lurch. The weight pulling down on my wrists constantly sent aching pain running through my arms. If it wasn't for a shifter's healing and strength, I probably would've dislocated both wrists and my shoulders by now.

I kept calling for my wolf, hoping that with even a small shift I could make a difference. But whoever had done all this had put a loose silver chain around my neck and over my shoulders. It was loose enough that it hung over my shirt instead of burning skin, but it was still too damned close. The weakness permeated through me, and the absence of my wolf tore a hole in my heart. The silver knife I'd taken to the gut had driven her away, and the silver chain kept her from me.

At least I got a chance to say good-bye. Even if it was in her dream. The forest—our forest. I hadn't seen her since I pushed her away. She was so beautiful, magnificent even. And she was all mine. At least should've been. How did I mess things up so badly?

"Because you decided to be a scared little bitch," I muttered. No one appeared to admonish me for speaking aloud so I decided to continue with the single-sided conversation. "Because you were told something by someone you barely know, and you took it for gospel and decided to tear apart the heart of the one woman who could actually handle you."

I wasn't really one for crying, but I did want to run my hands through my hair a few times. Or even just sit. Just sit and hold my face in my hands and wonder what the hell was wrong with me.

"Okay, seriously, deal with the current situation before you go all pity party on us, okay, Wren?"

Again, I called for my wolf, knowing it was useless. Maybe I was losing my mind. Didn't they say that insanity is doing the same thing over and over and over again and expecting a different result?

"Losing it already, are you, Ms. Carne?" A low, somber voice filled the darkness around me. I stared out into it, only able to see maybe five, ten feet out even with my shifter senses. "I thought you'd hold up much longer than this."

I shook myself, making the chains binding me to the ceiling rattle like Marley's ghost. "There's nothing wrong with talking to oneself," I said. "Especially in my predicament." I looked around, still trying to see where the voice was coming from. It was too damned familiar, but I couldn't place it.

"Well, you only have yourself to blame for this," the voice continued. "You brought this all on yourself."

"What the hell are you talking about? I don't even know you."

"Really, Wren?" Footsteps echoed around the room. "Really? You don't remember me at all?"

My insult died on my tongue as a figure stepped from the shadows. He was taller than me. His salt-and-pepper hair was buzzed close on the sides and left longer on top. He wore dark jeans and a thin tank top under a denim jacket with heavy work boots. But it was his eyes that stopped my response. Those eyes had haunted me for years. Hard gray eyes with flickers of gold that turned almost blood red when his wolf was close to the surface.

"Craig." I tried to hide the fear that was flooding my nerves.

His eyes flared a dull rust color. "Ah, so you do remember. I wasn't so certain you would. Nice to see you again, Wren."

My connection to Natalie suddenly kicked, becoming a ball of energy that helped keep the fear at bay. I drew on the years of sass and banter I'd perfected as an orphan and shot him a wry grin. "Of course I remember the man who thought he owned me for several years."

"I did own you! Four years you were mine! Ronan promised you to me! You were supposed to be my mate!"

I scoffed. "You know it doesn't work that way. You can't know a wolf's nature before they grow into it."

"It doesn't matter. You were promised to me!"

"I promised myself to no one!"

"Our Alpha promised you to me. He knew that you were going to be nothing but another wolf! But you tricked him, tricked us all." He threw his hands up in anger and began pacing. "Suddenly you were a fucking Alpha! Shows how much the old ways are breaking down if a woman becomes an Alpha!"

As much as I didn't want to listen to this fucking trash bag piece of shit, being chained to the ceiling didn't give me much option.

"We don't choose our nature, asshole! It's why no one is mated until they come of age."

"And it's bullshit! We used to be paired off when we were pups, choosing our mates because we knew—*knew*—exactly what the wolf would become." He stepped closer and grabbed my bloody shirt. "Ronan promised you to me!"

I recoiled away from him but swung back just as quick. "*He* didn't own me," I hissed. "I was not his to give away."

"It doesn't matter. I have you now. I will take what I am owed—five years overdue."

"You can't mate with me against my will." I gave him a withering glance. "I'm stronger than you. An Alpha, unlike you. I'm not part of your pack anymore!"

He laughed and it sounded maniacal. "Neither am I! I was exiled. Kicked out. All because Ronan found out that I was still sending wolves after you. Because I wanted my promised mate!"

"There is so much wrong with you and what you're saying. How many wolves have you sent to their deaths? Your own brother too! Just to come after me?"

His lips curled into a savage smile as his hand traveled over my stomach toward my chest. I tried to move away but just swung back and forth, arms aflame with pain.

"I don't care how many wolves need to die to teach you a lesson. To make you sorry for ever thinking you could leave me." He shook his head, hand skipping past my chest to run fingertips up my throat to my chin. "You thought you could run away from the pack, and I wouldn't find you? And this scent." He leaned forward and made a show of sniffing me. "The scent of a human all over you. A mate scent. You tried to replace me with a human, of all things." He scoffed.

"Natalie," I gasped.

"You will lead your mate and the rest of your pack to me. Then we will destroy them, and if you live, I will make you mine. I swear it." He took my chin in his fingers and pulled my face to his. Dry, cracked lips pressed against my own and I struggled against him. His tongue probed into my mouth, and I fought to keep my teeth clenched until his grip on my chin moved to my throat and started to squeeze. Panicked, I opened for him, and that greasy appendage darted inside, and I clamped my teeth down on it.

He screamed and pulled away, leaving layers of tongue in my mouth as they scraped against my teeth.

"You bitch!" he shouted.

"That's right," I snarled, "I am a bitch. And I don't care what happens to me. The moment I get down from here, I am going to kill you." I stared him right in the eyes. "I swear it."

He shook his head and turned away, heading back into the shadows. "No, Wren. Your mate is going to come for you, and when she does, you will see why you have to be mine. Only mine."

He disappeared into the darkness as I swung back and forth on my chain. I felt Natalie getting closer and closer, a fierce determination suffusing our connection. I had to trust she wasn't coming alone. I had to trust that a human could survive in this world. Because if she died…

If she died, I didn't think I'd survive it.

CHAPTER THIRTY-SIX

Natalie

I flinched again as pain flared through the mate bond. Rory glanced over at me from the driver's seat with worry etching her face. She didn't say anything, and I was thankful. I didn't have any good answers for her. I was glad she was driving the clinic truck as I held a hand to my stomach, trying to send whatever strong feelings I could across the connection.

For the weeks after I'd left Terabend, the connection had felt like it was getting smaller, closing maybe. Like it had shrunk from the size of a massive pipeline to a thin plastic straw. Since I passed out in the gym, though, it had reopened with a vengeance, and I felt everything from Wren's side. Pain, fear, anger, despair, and most recently a sense of disgust that made me want to vomit. I tried to send her my support, my love, my anger at whatever had happened, but I couldn't say if it was doing any good.

Too many of my feelings for Wren were confused, erratic things. I missed her desperately, and I didn't want her to be hurt, but did I want her back? Did I even want to see her again after what she'd done? Sure, she apologized. It's what people did when they were wrong. But was I strong enough to forgive her? I wanted to be, but I couldn't just forget what had happened, what she had said. Maybe she wasn't talking about me being transgender, but damn it, she let me believe it for a month. That was a special kind of torture in and of itself.

I understood fear. I lived with it for far too long. My father wanted me to be like him—strong, unwavering, *male*. He'd worked with me and my sister from when we were little. He taught us survival skills, fighting, conditioning—everything he could. My mother went right along with him. Every time I stepped out of line even the smallest amount, he knew exactly what he had to do to push me back. And he was never afraid to do it. But I knew I wasn't like him, wasn't like them. I knew I was different. I wondered for so long why they wouldn't accept that I was different. It didn't mean I wasn't their child, or that I didn't want them in my life, or anything like that. I just wanted to be the person I felt that I was, not who they wanted me to be.

A broken leg, dislocated shoulder, fractured collarbone, and major concussion were what I got for being honest with them. I was in the hospital for a few weeks, and someone from the family was there at all times to make sure I didn't talk to the staff or authorities. Sixteen years old and I was being treated like I was a prisoner of war. Until the night when Uncle Denton fell asleep on his watch.

It was awkwardly easy to leave the hospital without rousing suspicion. The hard part was getting to the far side of the building with my broken leg and Denton's phone. After a single call to Misty and her family, they came and picked me up, and they promised that they wouldn't let my parents know where I was.

The tears had fallen for days, weeks after that. And through it all, Misty was there beside me. I shook my head. It was no wonder I felt like I owed her so much. When the hell had she changed? Was it because of me? Was the stress of looking after me and helping me too much, and it changed her? Was it my fault our relationship became so toxic?

I had to pull myself out of that deepening spiral of thoughts before I got lost. It was over. It was behind me. Wren was my present—more or less. Even if we decided together that we couldn't continue what we had, at the very least I couldn't just let her be taken from me. Not if there was something I could do about it. Maybe I didn't have the supernatural strength and speed of the women in the back seat. Maybe I didn't have the cunning and ferocity of Zeke and his family, who were following in several other vehicles. Even Rias was back there somewhere, willing to do what she could to help. I was just a human woman in love, armed with a silver knife taken from the assholes who tried to use me as bait in the first place.

"We're coming for you, Wren," I said under my breath. I pushed all of my feelings that came with those words down the connection at her and prayed that it would give her hope. We were coming for her. I would always come for her.

❖

I directed Rory off the highway about an hour south of Terabend. There was a barely paved road leading to an abandoned pulp mill. Cliché, I decided, as we drove past a broken chain link gate and entered a creepy gravel lot. Litter and debris from the building blew around in the wind kicked up by the truck. A hand from the back seat touched my shoulder.

"Is this the place?" Dr. Maru asked.

I nodded, knowing without a doubt that my mate was in that building. "I think it's safe to say she didn't just get lost or something."

Heather snorted. "I don't know, this is Wren we're talking about."

We shared a nervous chuckle—all except Gwen, whose eyes were focused on the building in front of us. "How are we doing this?"

"If we're dealing with the same assholes who attacked me and Meg back in Terabend, then we're going to be fighting wolf shifters. If it's something else, I have no idea," I said. "But I know I need to go in there and get her. I can't let whatever is happening to her continue." I sniffled and fought back a tear from the feelings Wren was letting slip between us. "She can't even call to her wolf. She's weak and so lonely."

Heather shuddered. "Let's go save her then."

We met up with Zeke and his people. The dozen of us congregated on the old asphalt of the parking lot. I glanced to Heather and Gwen, who were sniffing the air on the outskirts of our little huddle.

"It's a lot of them," Gwen said, "their scents are intermingled, like they've been together a long time."

Heather gave the werepanther a sharp nod. "Two dozen wolves, at least. Maybe a couple more. The scents are vaguely familiar but no one I know."

"Familiar?" I echoed, glancing at her. "Heather, what pack did you and Callum and Jason come from?"

"I thought you knew. We came from the Cardinal pack—where Wren grew up."

I stared at her for a long moment. Had Wren known? She hadn't told me anything about it. Was this more of her trying to protect me? I shook my head. Not something to worry about right now.

"What does that mean for us?" Zeke demanded.

"Not a lot," I said, "we still have to go through them to get to Wren. I just wanted to know who the hell is after her."

"Any friendlies in there?" he asked with bared teeth that were far too sharp to be human. "Or just Wren?"

I glanced to Heather, and she shook her head. "No friendlies but Wren. All lower wolves from the same pack. I can recognize their scents now that my wolf is free. I'm sure they're all expendable."

His smile widened savagely, mirrored by the six other ghouls standing with him. He turned and barked something that I couldn't understand, and the seven ghouls started charging toward the massive building, yelling and whooping in excitement. As they moved, they shed what human disguises they kept wrapped around their undead forms as their limbs elongated, mouths grew wide with sharp, pointed teeth, and eyes turned a terrifying red that glowed in the darkness. Their hungry screeches pierced my brain and paralyzed my limbs for a second before they had moved on and I could move again.

The rest of us glanced at each other. "Well, I was going to propose a stealthy infiltration," Dr. Maru muttered.

I shook my head. "What's done is done. Rias, cover Dr. Maru. Doc, do what you can to help the rest of us. I don't want to lose anybody." Dr. Maru nodded, relief on her face. "Gwen, Heather, find the asshole who's leading this pack and take him out if you can."

Heather hesitated. "Nat, I...I'm not sure how useful I can be."

I glanced at her. "Are you okay?"

"It's my wolf," she said softly. Gwen took several steps away to give us a modicum of privacy. "I don't...I can't control her that well yet. I'm worried I might hurt someone we like."

I put a hand on her shoulder. "I trust you to do what you can, Heather. Wren needs us right now. I think you can make this happen."

"What about you?" she asked softly. "I can't risk hurting my Lupa."

I blushed at her words. "I'm going to find Wren." I pulled out the silver knife, taking it in my right hand and flipping it a few times. "I trust you." Heather and Gwen cringed slightly at the sight of the blade.

The four of them headed for the building and left me alone with Rory.

"How can I help?"

"Stay with the truck," I told her. "Keep it running in case we need to make a quick getaway."

"What if someone comes out?"

"Hide, drive away, whatever you need to do to stay safe. Okay?"

She nodded and gave me a quick hug. "Go find our girl."

With everyone else settled, I closed my eyes and focused on our bond. I let it open up as wide as it could. Everything Wren was feeling bombarded me, and I fell to my knees with a cry of pain, of loneliness, of the knowledge that she was going to lose what she loved the most. Then something shifted, as if she felt what I'd done. It was like I could hear her, despite there being no words. She wanted me to run. To be safe.

To hell with that, I pushed back against her. Just because we were mates didn't give her the right to boss me around. I kept the knife ready and headed for the large front doors of the abandoned plant.

Most of the place was empty, dirt and dust and more garbage scattered across the floor. In some places things like desks or chairs were still around but were torn up and rusted with time. The front offices were small and the sounds inside were muffled. I went slowly, knowing that there could be a wolf around any corner that didn't want to either be my friend or sleep with me.

As if my thoughts could tell the future, I took a step forward and suddenly there was a tall, muscled beast of a man standing in front of me, staring down with golden eyes past a short muzzle that made room for his sharp teeth.

He snarled and lunged, forcing me back into the room as I leapt back. I swung the knife sideways and he pulled himself away from the glittering blade, golden eyes watching it like a hawk watches a fieldmouse. He sneered and came at me again. I ducked under his paw and drove the blade forward, scoring a thin slice across his massive thigh. He stumbled back with a pained howl, and I watched as the skin around the wound darkened. He swore and tore at his thigh, pulling away the damaged skin and fur with furious grunts. The infected skin sizzled on the floor, and I fought the urge not to throw up at the stench.

I started for the doorway he'd come through, but he was too quick. I barely made it two steps before he had fully shifted into a huge wolf form and stood between me and my destination, lips pulled back and snarling as saliva dripped to the ground. I brandished the knife in front of me again, watching him for any sign of the attack.

What the hell was I doing? Going toe-to-toe with a damned werewolf was not the best idea I'd ever had. But if the only way to Wren was through him, then that's where I'd go. The wolf lunged forward, and I rolled to the side, then brought the knife around. The blade cut through his side like a hot knife through butter, and he cried out and fell to the ground with a heaving whimper. I waited a second to make sure he wasn't going to get up again and then moved on. I had to ignore the idea that I might very well have just killed him.

The thought did cross my mind and I had to stop, dry heaving a little as I leaned against the wall. Maybe I wasn't cut out for this shit. It didn't matter. I knew how to fight and defend myself, thanks to my parents. And now I was going to use those skills for someone more important to me than they ever were.

The hallways were dark, lit only occasionally with what looked like old camping lanterns. I ignored most of the doors, most of them seeming like offices or meeting rooms or whatever else a place like this might've had. I followed the hall to a pair of heavy steel doors.

"Well, shit," I muttered, "this isn't ominous at all."

Wren was somewhere on the other side of those doors. Ominous or not, I had to go through.

I pushed through the doors, knife at the ready, then stopped as they slammed shut behind me. Heather hadn't been exaggerating how many different scents she could find. Hell, it seemed mostly like she'd lowballed the estimate. Fear stopped me from counting exactly how many pairs of eyes were staring at me now. The spell was broken as a voice rang out over the crowd.

"It's the mate! Take her alive!"

Then all hell broke loose.

As if waiting for an invitation, an army of ghouls, a werewolf, a werepanther, a vampire, and a witch emerged from the shadows or other doorways scattered around the room. The frenzy was intense, but there were still two shifters that charged at me, and I let the knife fly in a tight throw. The silver blade took the lead shifter in the chest, throwing him backward as a furry Heather tackled the other.

"Go!" she shouted. "Find Wren!"

I recovered my knife, ignoring the sickening squelch the knife made coming out, and dodged my way through the crowd as the supernatural free-for-all continued. I ducked under a leaping wolf and slashed the knife wildly, catching it across the hind leg. I kept moving forward, following the unerring connection of my mate.

I slipped out through a doorway at the far end of the large room. The next room wasn't as large and had a much lower ceiling, but the darkness made it difficult to see more than a few feet in front of me. I kept the knife in front of me, watching the darkness for any sign of movement.

Somewhere in the back of my head I was counting steps from the doorway. I had reached twenty-eight when I could make out a shape in the darkness. It wasn't more than a barely outlined blob, but my heart quickened as I took another step, then another.

"Wren!" The word fell from my mouth, and I dashed forward, heedless of any danger. My mate was dangling from the ceiling by her wrists, a glittering chain overlaid on her shoulders. Her eyes cracked open as I ran hands across her face, desperate to feel her under my fingers and know for sure that she was real. "Oh, Goddess, Wren!"

Her shirt was crusty with dried blood, and I lifted it away from her stomach to find bloody bandages tightly wrapped around her. I thought back to the dream, to the pain in my gut that made me pass out in the first place. This was the wound that had made her weak and vulnerable when they took her.

"Natalie…" Her voice was so soft I could barely hear her. "I'm sorry…"

I shook my head. "It's okay. It's okay, Wren. I'm here now. I'm not going to let you go. Never again."

She shook and her chains rattled above her. I lifted the silver chain off her shoulders and hurled it away into the darkness. Almost immediately, she seemed a little more aware, a little more awake.

"Natalie..." Her eyes met mine and relief flooded through me. "You need to go. Run. Please run."

"Not a fucking chance!" I hissed when I looked up at her wrists. "I'm not leaving without you."

She shook her head and her entire body swung back and forth. "It's not..." She was panting too hard to get the words out, and I felt her pain in my stomach. Whatever they'd stabbed her with had done the kind of damage a silver blade would've. She was recovering, but it was too slow. We needed to get out of there now.

"If you're going to try and talk, tell me how to get you down."

She huffed out a breath and I smirked. I placed my hands on her cheeks and stood on my toes to deliver a soft, chaste kiss to her cracked lips.

"I'm not going anywhere," I said. "Never again. I promise you. We're mates. We're meant to be together."

"My mate," she murmured.

Her eyes flickered over my shoulder. I readied the knife and prepared to spin. An instant too soon, pain blossomed through my stomach and nerveless fingers dropped the silver knife as I gasped for a desperate breath I didn't remember losing.

I looked down at a bloody clawed hand that clutched at the air between us. I followed the arm into my stomach and stared. That didn't make sense. When did I start growing a third arm? I almost laughed, wondering if I should talk to Dr. Maru about it. I met Wren's eyes again, and they were wide with panic as her mouth moved, but I didn't hear the words.

The arm disappeared as quickly as it appeared, and I was suddenly spun around like a top. I hit the ground hard, face down. Warmth covered my lower body while the rest of me started to go cold, like I'd just walked out into a northern Alberta blizzard. As my vision faded, I could swear I heard someone scream.

CHAPTER THIRTY-SEVEN

Wren

I watched her fall. I saw a partially shifted Craig behind her, saw his hand come out of her body like the alien from the movies. I cried out her name as she stared at it, confused. Dear Mother, she looked adorable when she was confused.

With a grunt, Craig pulled his arm back and Natalie spun around and collapsed. Her head hit the concrete floor with a sickening crack.

"Natalie!" I screamed again. I turned hard eyes to Craig, who was casually looking at his furred arm and the blood dripping from it.

"Such fragile things, humans are," he said. "A pity you had to involve her in all this. Humans have no place in our world."

"Fuck you!"

"Oh, there will be plenty of that. If you're good, you might even be allowed to enjoy it."

"I'm going to rip your fucking throat out!" My wolf howled inside me, mirroring everything I was feeling. I called to her, needing her strength, needing her to help me get out of this. But she was barely there, still weak from the silver. I was too weak. I couldn't save her. I couldn't save my mate. I needed to help her.

"Your mate is gone now," Craig sneered, "and you belong to me. As you always have."

"Never!" The word was followed with a sharp howl that sounded weird coming from a human throat. I didn't even know I could make a sound like that without shifting.

I don't remember how I broke free of the cuffs. One moment my arms were still above my head, the next I was lunging forward.

The scent of fear bloomed over him as he leapt back, barely avoiding my claws.

I drew on everything I could, all the power my wolf could give, and attacked. I caught him in the side, and his counterattack ripped open a gash in my right arm. I backed away, searching for an opening, then dodged away from his sudden lunge. My jaws snapped shut on empty air where his throat had been.

We circled each other, feinting and attacking in turn. He had the advantage of experience, but even with my wolf weakened he wouldn't hold out long against the strength of an Alpha. A strength he just didn't have. His wounds slowed him down, and I was only getting stronger as my wolf continued to awaken. His eyes said that he knew it too.

He charged abruptly and I threw myself back. I tripped on something soft and tumbled, eyes catching on Natalie's body, so still on the ground. That split second of inattention was his opening. He pounced on me, pushing aside my arms as I flailed at him.

"Fucking bitch!" he screamed. "You're mine! Ronan promised me!" I tried to wriggle out from under him as his fists came down like sledgehammers upon my head. I moved with the blows, trying to break loose, but he had the advantage, and my legs were still tangled around Nat's body.

My scrabbling fingers found purchase on something on the floor beside us. I struggled and got my fingers on something that burned.

Burned!

He reared back, bringing his fists together above his head. His shit-eating grin only grew wider with the murder in his eyes. I wrapped my hand around the burning metal, feeling the weakness begin. But it didn't matter. As his fists came down, I shoved the long silver blade into the bastard's side.

"Fuck you!" I screamed, and his answering scream almost burst my eardrums as he rolled away, scrabbling at the silver knife sticking out of him. I wiped my hand on the torn remnants of my shirt and rolled to my feet. Something clattered to the floor, and I spun in time to see Craig sprinting toward the far doors. I moved to go after him when I heard the barest gasp of breath.

"Nat!" I threw myself to my knees beside her. Her chest was barely moving, lifting her back up and down the tiniest inch. "Nat! Please! Don't leave me. I'm so sorry."

I lifted her, placing as much of her in my lap as I could. "It's all my fault," I cried. "I never meant for this to happen. I'm sorry, Nat! I'm so sorry!"

She was still in my arms. So still. So quiet. Tears tore themselves from my eyes, and I didn't bother to hide them. My mate. My fated one. And I'd driven her away. Lost her for too long, and now I was going to lose her forever.

"No!" There was something I could do. If only I could do it right.

Another pitiful gasp spasmed through her body, and my choice was made for me.

I'd read the chapter in the book. Okay, I'd skimmed over the first page in the hopes that maybe, someday, I'd be able to fix things with Natalie and maybe convince her to turn so I could have my mate. Either way, I knew, theoretically, how to turn a human into a wolf. Of course, I had no idea if I was prepared for it.

"Blood of my blood," I murmured and focused my intent on the well of magic inside me. The magic that let me shift, let me heal, let me forge a bond to my territory, and connected me to my pack members and my mate. "Blood of my blood, awaken a new wolf."

Again, like when I was in the woods with Heather and Callum, like when I freed Heather's wolf, the magic of the wolf within flooded the forefront of my brain. My wolf came rushing back and I felt my body begin to shift. The fur rippled over my skin, and my fingernails sharpened into claws. I felt my ears slide up to the top of my head and my fangs poke out of my mouth. I stayed partially shifted and followed the magic.

I lifted Natalie's arm and moved her sleeve up to reveal the flesh below her elbow. Before I could overthink it, I set my claw against the inside of her arm and sliced open her skin from wrist to elbow. She writhed slightly and I could feel her body getting colder by the second.

I lifted my claw and licked Natalie's blood from it. I swallowed the mouthful of her blood—and the taste was divine. My tongue caressed my claw—it was glorious. Beautiful. Addictive, even. But even as the thought of tearing my teeth into her crossed my mind, I released her and let her arm fall into my lap.

I turned the same claw on my own arm and mirrored the wound I'd given Natalie. "Blood of my blood," I intoned. "Awaken a new wolf." I pressed our wounds together. I had no idea how this was supposed to work, but apparently the magic did. I felt a piece of that magic leave me and slip through the connection in our blood, like a marble being sucked up by a vacuum.

It was done. My power was in her now.

As soon as I had that thought, Natalie's eyes flared open, and she gasped, her body flailing in my lap. I tried to soothe her, but she started convulsing, spittle flying from her mouth as I rolled her onto her back. I watched the wound in her stomach shrink and breathed a sigh of relief. It was okay. She was okay.

"Wren!"

Hikaru appeared beside us with Rias at her side. I only glanced at them for a second before Natalie convulsed again and slid clear out of my lap. Hikaru laid her hands on Natalie, and I growled at her.

"Enough! What happened here?"

"She was dying," I said through a mouth full of sharp teeth. I focused on shifting back to human and continued when my mouth could form words properly. "He tried to kill her. He—"

She shook her head. "You turned her?" I nodded quickly. Her eyes went wide with panic. "Come on, we need to go."

"What? Why?"

"She needs to be somewhere safe and familiar. Now!"

I wanted to argue. I wanted to sit here and wait until the magic did its work, and I could have my mate back. But she knew what she was talking about. She always did. I needed to trust her. Like I always had.

I lifted my mate in my arms and earned a flailing arm in the face for it. Heather appeared beside me, reaching to help, but my sharp bark stopped her in her tracks.

"Don't jostle her too much," Hikaru warned me. "We need to get her to the truck and back to Terabend."

I followed her lead, scared of the panic in her tone, knowing that we were in uncharted territory.

"Stay with me, Nat," I whispered to the shuddering form clutched in my arms. "Please. Stay with me."

❖

Another scream ripped through Hikaru's clinic, and I had to cover my ears to try to ignore the pain in the sound.

"Six hours!" I said. "It's been six hours and she's still screaming!"

"You think it's a quick process to rewrite someone's DNA? Their genetic structure?"

I shifted from foot to foot, unable to even look at the vampire. "It's fucking magic, isn't it? I don't know how long it takes."

"It takes as long as it takes!" Hikaru said. "And that's if it even works at all."

"What do you mean?"

"It's not perfect, Wren! Sometimes people's bodies can't take the transformation."

I shook my head. "Natalie will be fine. She has to be fine."

"I'm being honest, Wren."

"She's going to be okay. She needs to come back to me." I hated the whimper in my voice.

"There's no telling what's going to happen," Hikaru said, voice soft. "The transformation doesn't take, and she dies. Or she transforms and she lives as a shifter for the rest of her days."

"Is that it?"

She shook her head. "Wren, if this goes on too long, she will break down. Whether she shifts or not won't matter. She'll be a rabid animal, dangerous to anything and everything around her."

"No!" I shouted. "Not Natalie. That's not going to happen."

"You need to be prepared that it's a very real possibility, Wren!"

I shook my head again. "I need to go in there. I need to be with her."

"It's too dangerous."

"I don't care! I need to be with her. She needs me!"

I moved right past her. With her speed she could've stopped me, blocked me, hit me, whatever. But she didn't. I went through the door and shut it behind me. The dimly lit exam room looked the same as it always had. Save for the single figure hunched over in the far corner.

"Nat?"

She recoiled at the sound, and her dark and wild eyes stared at me across the room. "Go away!"

"Natalie, please. I'm here."

I took a step forward, but she shook and tried to back further into the corner.

"Get away from me! I don't want to hurt you!"

"Hurt me? You won't hurt me."

"I heard everything, Wren! Maru said I'd be rabid. A danger to everyone. I can't do that. I don't want to hurt anyone."

I took another step forward. "I won't let that happen, Nat. You know I won't."

She shivered again. "You'll take care of me?" I nodded as those dark eyes roamed over me. "You'll kill me?"

"That's not going to be necessary."

"Tell me you'll kill me, Wren!" she shouted. "I need to know! I need you to kill me if I don't make it through this!"

"Shut up!" I grabbed the exam table and wrenched it out of the floor. It slammed against the wall behind me. Nothing more was between us but air saturated in fear. "It's not going to happen! It's not!"

She opened her mouth to argue, but the words were engulfed in another scream as she convulsed again.

"Wren! Help me! Please!"

In a flash, I was by her side, arms wrapped tightly around her. I sighed into my mate, feeling her shiver and shudder, her body so hot it almost scalded my skin. Her fever was only getting worse. What was I supposed to do?

She arched her back against me, but the groan that slipped out was not one of pleasure.

"It hurts!" she whined. "I can't take it!"

"It'll be over soon. I promise, Nat. It'll be over soon."

She scratched at her skin, like she was trying to tear into it. "It's so hot! I can't...I can't stand it!" She pulled away from me. "Like something is under my skin! I can't get it out!"

I took her hands in mine. "It's okay. I can help you. I promise. I can get it out."

She shook her head. "No! Stay back! I won't hurt you!"

I pulled her in close, putting one hand behind her neck and the other on the small of her back. I gently skated my mouth over her cheek, tasting the sweat and tears and the decadence of her skin. Like a morning breeze after a rainstorm, like that first sip of cool water after a hard workout. She tasted like home. I cradled her in my arms and let my wolf rise to the forefront, initiating my shift once more.

"I'm here, Nat," I whispered. "I'm here. I love you."

She whimpered into my shoulder, mouth opening and closing in gasping cries. "Please! Wren, help me. Please, my Alpha. Help me."

And like that, I was reminded of a night barely more than a month ago. That night that I pushed her away. That night that I pulled the beautiful wolf out of another woman who couldn't shift. I knew what I had to do. My body, my brain, knew what I had to do. I pulled her tighter to me, wrapping myself around her, and whispered in her ear. "Come to me, my wolf. My mate."

She shivered and arched her back against me, throwing her head back in such a lovely position it sent slivers of heat down to my core. Her shoulders moved against me in violent contractions, almost pulling out of my grip, but I only held her tightly.

"Wren!" She cried out again and I pressed my lips to her collarbone, letting her feel the fangs in my mouth.

"Let her come, Natalie. Let her be free. I want to meet your wolf!"

She twisted and writhed as the sound of bones moving and grinding echoed through the small room. She threw her head back and screamed, but I could see the midnight black fur starting to sprout from her skin. Her stomach pulled from me, and I saw the mass of scar tissue from Craig's attack, and I knew that this had been the only way to save her. I had no other choice.

"I can't—" she gasped. "I can't do it!"

"Yes, you can!" I held her head steady and looked directly into her eyes. "Shift, Natalie! Show me your wolf!"

"It hurts!"

"You will not die here! My mate, my Lupa, you are mine and I will not lose you to this!" I cried. "Now *shift!*"

Her scream led into a howl as she slid from my arms and sprawled on the floor. I fell to my knees as she writhed and contorted, more fur rippling across her body as her bones broke and moved to create a different skeleton. A moment passed before the woman was gone and in her place was a small wolf with a midnight black pelt and exhausted gray eyes. On her stomach and her back were two patches of lighter gray fur—right where her scar would be. Her eyes focused on me, and I pushed myself through the rest of the shift, towering over her as she panted with her tongue sticking out.

Alpha? I heard her voice in my head.

I am here, Lupa. I moved to her side and curled up around her. *Welcome to your new life, my love.*

With an exhausted whine, the dark wolf laid her head on my legs, and I settled in around her. She was mine now. My Lupa. My fated mate.

I would never let her go again.

CHAPTER THIRTY-EIGHT

Natalie

Being a werewolf was pretty cool. The hearing and smelling took a while to get used to, though. Like the day I smelled some bad fish but couldn't figure out where it was coming from. Hint: someone left a raw fish carcass out in the woods about ten minutes from town. The wind just happened to be blowing the right way to make me fight to keep my lunch in my stomach.

Still, the strength was a bonus. It took three werewolves and a werepanther only two hours to move all my things from Rory's place in the city into Wren's cabin. Not including travel time, that is. As I headed outside after dropping off the last box, I glanced from the truck to the house and back again.

"I don't want to be a cliché," I said, "but does this make me a U-Haul lesbian?"

Wren, Heather, Gwen, Rory, Rias, and Hikaru all looked around at each other.

"Yup," Rory said.

"Yeah," was Gwen's answer.

"Definitely," Hikaru said, smirking.

The other girls all gave other signs of agreement and I sighed. "I know I can't get mad at most of you," I began, giving Heather a wink. "But, Heather, you should show more respect to your Lupa."

She lowered her eyes and glanced away, but couldn't hide the small smile that crossed her lips. "Sorry, Lupa."

We all had a good laugh and I looked around at this crowd of friends, new and old. A group of people who knew me better than I would ever have said people knew me before. I had brought myself to be honest with Wren that night after she took me into her home, and like water breaking through a dam, it made me want to be open and honest with others in my life. Heather had been next, and she had no problems with who I was. Neither did Gwen, or Rias, or Hikaru, or any of these wonderful women. Even Zeke and Vadi and some of the other supernatural folks in town knew what I used to call my secret. Every single one of them accepted me for who I was.

It was all so new to me. This love and acceptance—what I'd searched so long for but was always just out of reach. It was like I was in a dream.

"Ugh, I can't believe you're moving out here to live with all these wolves!" Gwen said. Wren gave her a withering look.

"She is a wolf now," Wren replied, "and she's a member of my pack. You'd do well to remember that."

"Oh, leave her alone," I told my Alpha. "She doesn't mean any harm. I've known her longer than I've known you."

Rory snorted. "That's not hard. It's been like two months."

Rias and Hikaru glanced at each other, grinning like maniacs.

"Yup," Rias began.

"Definitely a U-Haul lesbian," Hikaru finished.

I glared at them both. "If you guys are done, can you take the damned truck back to Zeke, please? I promised we wouldn't be too late with it tonight."

Rias waved. "I got this." She headed for the truck.

"My apartment's going to be empty without you there, you know," Rory said.

I brought my best friend in for a tight hug, trying to be mindful of my new strength and not crush the life out of her. "I know. I'm sorry. I can't be in the city right now."

Wren shot me a knowing look. I'd shifted a few times, with Wren as my chaperone, but it was still hard to come to terms with the wolf inside me. I didn't want to risk something happening in a big city. It must've been hard, having to do double duty of new-wolf babysitting between me and Heather. But she didn't complain.

"I get it, I do. But are you going to come back?"

Another glance to Wren. "I doubt it. Maybe temporarily. I mean, I still want to finish my schooling if I can. But I think I'm in Terabend to stay." Wren moved up beside me, taking my hand in hers. The warmth of her touch did more to ground and relax me than anything else I'd ever felt.

"Actually, Rory," Wren said softly as she beckoned to Hikaru, "we have a proposition for you."

Rory's eyes went wide. "For me?"

Hikaru nodded. "The strip mall where my clinic is has a couple of spaces for lease. We were wondering if you would like to open a veterinary practice here."

Rory's jaw dropped. "But…I mean…"

I smiled at her. "I know you inherited the one in the city from the old doc, but this'll give you a chance to start something of your own and be around your friends."

She gave a startled laugh. "But where would I—"

"You know your cabin is all fixed up," Heather added. She had been the one to replace the window and whatever else Wren tore up the last time we'd been there.

"But the money—"

"Nothing to worry about there," Hikaru cut her off. "There's nothing you can claim that we haven't thought of, Rory. You know who we are. You're part of this family. We want you here."

"And besides," Wren said, "if you open a practice here, then you'll have a beautiful assistant to help you."

I grinned at her. "So, what do you say?"

Rory glanced between all of us, even Gwen.

"Hey, don't look at me." Gwen sounded almost sullen. "I don't have a choice about going back."

Rory beamed at us. "Okay! I accept!"

The other girls crowded around Rory as I stepped away and turned to Gwen, who was standing like she was getting ready to bolt.

"I'm sorry," I said.

She shook her head. "It's fine."

I wrapped my arms around her tight, feeling her own shifter strength against me in a hug tighter than any I'd had from her in the past.

"Thank you," I whispered. "I wouldn't have her if it wasn't for you."

"I'm sure you—"

"No, Gwen. Don't do that. You helped. You didn't have to, but you did. That means a lot, to me and to Wren." I glanced at my mate, who was still busy talking animatedly with Rory. "I owe you. I owe you big time."

An uneasy look crossed her face. "The pride…"

I shook my head. "Not the pride. You. I owe you. So does Wren. If there's anything we can ever do for you, don't hesitate to call, okay?"

She nodded slowly. "Fine. Okay." She sighed, rubbing a hand across her face. "Now I need to figure out how to tell a bunch of feline shifters why I smell like wolf."

I winced. "Ouch. Make it an epic story. Throw in a ball of yarn or two. They'll eat that shit up."

"Har-har," she deadpanned.

"Don't be a stranger, okay?"

"Let me know when you come back to town," she said, "we can spar at the gym, just like old times."

I raised an eyebrow. "*Just* like old times?"

She smirked. "Maybe. Maybe not."

I gave her one last hug before waving her off. "Have a safe drive home," I told her. "And thank you again."

She gave me a warm smile and headed for her car, leaving without another good-bye. I watched her go until I felt Wren's arm around my shoulder.

"She okay?"

"Yeah, she just might get into a bit of a catfight at home."

Wren barked out a laugh. "I'm sure she'll dish it out just as well."

I pulled my mate closer to me as a breeze blew over the driveway. I didn't get cold per se. Not like I used to, but the wind did send a small shiver down my spine. Well, it was either the wind or it was the way Wren's fingers caressed the freshly made bite mark on my collarbone.

We were connected now. Forever and always, me and Wren.

Alpha and Lupa.

Fated mates.

About the Author

Elena (https://writerinawarehouse.wordpress.com) is a transwoman, parent, and wife to her amazing Goddess. She plays video games, reads books, and plays D&D on both sides of the DM screen. She lives in Edmonton, Alberta, with her wonderful spouse and child, alongside the pets who think they rule the house. Keep in touch through email at Writerprincess8@gmail.com or find her online on Twitter at @WriterElenaA or on her seldom-touched blog.

Books Available From Bold Strokes Books

Lucky in Lace by Melissa Brayden. Straitlaced stationery store owner Juliette Jennings's predictable life unravels when a sexy lingerie shop and its alluring owner move in next door. (978-1-63679-434-1)

Made for Her by Carsen Taite. Neal Walsh is a newly made member of the Mancuso crime family, but will her undeniable attraction to Anastasia Petrov, the wife of her boss's sworn enemy, be the ultimate test of her loyalty? (978-1-63679-265-1)

Off the Menu by Alaina Erdell. Reality TV sensation Restaurant Redo and its gorgeous host Erin Rasmussen will arrive to film in chef Taylor Mobley's kitchen. As the cameras roll, will they make the jump from enemies to lovers? (978-1-63679-295-8)

Pack of Her Own by Elena Abbott. When things heat up in a small town, steamy secrets are revealed between Alpha werewolf Wren Carne and her human mate, Natalie Donovan. (978-1-63679-370-2)

Return to McCall by Patricia Evans. Lily isn't looking for romance—not until she meets Alex, the gorgeous Cuban dance instructor at La Haven, a newly opened lesbian retreat. (978-1-63679-386-3)

So It Went Like This by C. Spencer. A candid and deeply personal exploration of fate, chosen family, and the vulnerability intrinsic in life's uncertainties. (978-1-63555-971-2)

Stolen Kiss by Spencer Greene. Anna and Louise share a stolen kiss, only to discover that Louise is dating Anna's brother. Surely, one kiss can't change everything…Can it? (978-1-63679-364-1)

The Fall Line by Kelly Wacker. When Jordan Burroughs arrives in the Deep South to paint a local endangered aquatic flower, she doesn't expect to become friends with a mischievous gin-drinking ghost who complicates her budding romance and leads her to an awful discovery and danger. (978-1-63679-205-7)

To Meet Again by Kadyan. When the stark reality of WW II separates cabaret singer Evelyn and Australian doctor Joan in Singapore, they must overcome all odds to find one another again. (978-1-63679-398-6)

Before She Was Mine by Emma L McGeown. When Dani and Lucy are thrust together to sort out their children's playground squabble, sparks fly, leaving both of them willing to risk it all for each other. (978-1-63679-315-3)

Chasing Cypress by Ana Hartnett Reichardt. Maggie Hyde wants to find a partner to settle down with and help her run the family farm, but instead she ends up chasing Cypress. Olivia Cypress. (978-1-63679-323-8)

Dark Truths by Sandra Barret. When Jade's ex-girlfriend and vampire maker barges back into her life, can Jade satisfy her ex's demands, keep Beth safe, and keep everyone's secrets…secret? (978-1-63679-369-6)

Desires Unleashed by Renee Roman. Kell Murphy and Taylor Simpson didn't go looking for love, but as they explore their desires unleashed, their hearts lead them on an unexpected journey. (978-1-63679-327-6)

Here For You by D. Jackson Leigh. A horse trainer must make a difficult business decision that could save her father's ranch from foreclosure but destroy her chance to win the heart of a feisty barrel racer vying for a spot in the National Rodeo Finals. (978-1-63679-299-6)

Maybe, Probably by Amanda Radley. Set against the backdrop of a viral pandemic, Gina and Eleanor are about to discover that loving another person is complicated when you're desperately searching for yourself. (978-1-63679-284-2)

The One by C.A. Popovich. Jody Acosta doesn't know what makes her more furious, that the wealthy Bergeron family refuses to be held accountable for her father's wrongful death, or that she can't ignore her knee-weakening attraction to Nicole Bergeron. (978-1-63679-318-4)

Tides of Love by Kimberly Cooper Griffin. Falling in love is the last thing on either of their minds, but when Mikayla and Gem meet, sparks of possibility begin to shine, revealing a future neither expected. (978-1-63679-319-1